The Hungry Tigress

If you have men who will exclude any of God's creatures from the shelter of compassion and pity, you will have men who will deal likewise with their fellow men.
—Francis of Assisi

A man...must sense that he lives in a world which in some respects is mysterious; that things happen and can be experienced which remain inexplicable; that not everything which happens can be anticipated. The unexpected and the incredible belong in this world. Only then is life whole.
—Carl Jung

What are human beings without the animals? If all the animals were gone humankind too would die from a great loneliness of spirit. For whatever happens to the animals soon happens to human beings. All things are connected.
—Chief Seattle

Cover art: Courtesy of Zen Center, Rochester, New York
Cover design: Lawrence Watson
Back cover photo: Sam Campanaro

The Hungry Tigress

Buddhist Legends and Jataka Tales

Revised and Expanded Edition
with Commentaries

Rafe Martin

Parallax Press
Berkeley, California

Parallax Press
P.O. Box 7355
Berkeley, California 94707

Printed in the United States of America

Library of Congress Cataloging-in-Publication Data

Martin, Rafe. 1946 -
  The hungry tigress.

  Revised and expanded edition of: The hungry tigress and
other traditional Asian tales.
  Includes bibliographical references (p.)
  1. Tripitaka. 2. Suttapitaka. 3. Khuddakanikaya.
  4. Jataka—Paraphrases, English. I. Title.
BQ1462.M38 1990   294.3'823   90-7993
  ISBN 0-938077-25-2

*Dedicated to the memories of
my mother, Sonia Martin,
and my mother-in-law, Matilda Feit*

Contents

Acknowledgments

To my wife Rose for her aid and support—at many levels (as well as for her considerable editorial skill and insight); to my son Jacob and daughter Ariya for their interest and good humored patience with this book's evolving life; and to the unfailing generosity of Philip Kapleau, Zen teacher and friend, this book is especially bound. Much thanks to them in, more than words.

Also thanks to Bodhin Kjolhede, Abbot of the Rochester Zen Center as well as to the members of the Zen Center and their children for giving me the opportunity to try out many of these stories over the years. (*To those children, one message: The Sleeping Sage sends his special thanks and regards.*)

Thanks, too, to the many friends and countless school teachers, parents, students, librarians, arts-in-education program directors, and adult fans of storytelling throughout the United States (and as far away as Japan) for helping me work on and explore so many different stories and different kinds of stories in the oldest way— not with pencil and paper, but with the eyes, faces, bodies, breath, and thoughts of a live audience. Their continued interest has allowed me to pursue, in the modern world, the ancient path of the storyteller.

Thanks in this regard are especially due to Karin Wieder, Director of Artists-in-Residence, Rochester, New York, and to Roy Ernst, Chairman of the Education Department of Education at the Eastman School of Music, and Director of the Aesthetic Education Institute. Without their support, some of these stories would certainly never have developed into versions capable of reaching contemporary audiences.

Thanks are also due Professor Jarold Ramsey of the University of Rochester, for giving me the opportunity to begin clarifying my understanding of the jatakas. In the process this book first began.

Barry Keesan, President of Logical Operations, made sure the entire draft of the manuscript was printed from computer disk on *very* short notice. It was much appreciated.

Finally, I would like to acknowledge my debt of gratitude to Arnie Kotler of Parallax Press for so enthusiastically giving me the opportunity to revise and expand the original edition of *The Hungry Tigress*. His editorial comments were to the point and much appreciated. Larry Barden, of Parallax Press, also gave invaluable help in bringing the book to its completion.

Foreword

Readers of Rafe Martin's original *Hungry Tigress* will find in this completely revised and expanded edition a cornucopia of new delights and edifications. Not only have all the stories been rewritten and some twenty new stories added, but the addition of a section of excellent commentaries on the individual stories makes this new book powerful, resonant, and uniquely valuable.

In the commentaries, the author not only reveals his deep understanding of Buddhism (from which the jataka tales emerged), but he makes arrestingly clear the ethical and social values lying at the heart of the stories themselves. The jatakas are not simply cautionary tales for children. In these new recountings and in the commentaries, we clearly see how these stories function within the traditional world of the storyteller as well as within the heart and mind of the Buddhist tradition. We see how these stories uphold, at all levels, the universally respected qualities of patience, courage, compassion, and self-sacrifice, the very virtues which seem to be in such short supply in our fear-dominated, greed-ridden society. And we come to understand the relevance of these stories for us today. Through their drama and humor, their compassion and insight, as well as through the vast, cosmic scale of their imagination, they speak with special urgency and clarity to us living in today's demythologized time.

Of course, to the casual reader many of the jatakas may seem mere superstition because the events in them seem contrary to reason. For example, how believable is it that the Buddha-to-be was a grown man before he saw for the first time a sick man, an aged man, and a corpse? Or that when the Buddha was born he took seven steps and, raising his right hand, cried: "Above the heavens and below the heavens, I am the most honored One"? But wait, here is Rafe Martin's answer:

"Myth and legend, it has been well said, reveal a truth too great to be limited by mere fact." And again: "Like cubism in painting, these stories distort ordinary reality enough to make their meaning, not their surfaces, come through all the more clearly."

These stories, like all powerful stories, should be felt and intuitively understood, not simply reasoned out. We can be grateful to the author for making this fine selection of Buddhist tales and legends so wonderfully and authentically accessible to a new generation of readers. This is, in short, not only a beautiful book but an important one. It remains one of the very few today to approach Buddhism in the traditional way—through story and from the depths of its mythic vision.

Roshi Philip Kapleau
April 8, 1990

Introduction

Buddhist jataka tales (tales of the Buddha's earlier births, often in animal-fable form), have had their effects on Western literature since relatively early times. There are suggestive and interesting parallels between Euripedes' *Hippolytus* and the jataka-legend *Kunala*. According to T.W. Rhys Davids, a nineteenth century translator of the jatakas, Chaucer's *The Pardoner's Tale*, and Shakespeare's *As You Like It* and *Merchant of Venice* all clearly reveal jataka-like story patterns, as do Aesop's *Fables* and *The Arabian Nights*. More recently, the work of Rudyard Kipling shows strong jataka affinities; "The King's Ankus," from *The Jungle Books*, is essentially a modern retelling of a jataka.

It is not hard to see how this merging of East and West could have occurred in the work of Kipling, who spent much of his childhood in India. The route of the jatakas to Chaucer and Shakespeare was quite a bit more circuitous. T.W. Rhys Davids believes the process probably began with Alexander's invasion of India (around 320 B.C.E.), when many jatakas were translated into Greek. Almost 1,500 years later, Crusaders returning from the Middle East brought with them Arabic retellings from the Greek. Jewish scholars of the early Middle Ages, taken with the idea of the animal-fable form and the compassion inherent in the tales, became skillful translators and adaptors of the stories. Translating from Arabic into Hebrew, Greek, and Latin, their initial translations eventually found their way into all the principal European languages. Although this is a greatly oversimplified description of the process, this seems to be the central route the stories took.

It was not until the latter part of the nineteenth century that stories clearly identifiable as jatakas became available in English. These translations, mostly from the Pali, owed their existence to the efforts of scholars of religion and folklore working outside of the Buddhist tradition. Their versions of the tales tended to be fairly dry renderings that often lacked the immediacy of a well-told story. Early in the twentieth century, more popular but simplistic versions were created from these translations specifically for children, giving the jatakas a reputation as quaint Aesop-like animal fables.

Alhough I am not a translator, I have tried in this collection of jatakas and Buddhist legends to share something of the life of these tales as I have come to understand it through years of both Zen practice and professional storytelling. I have tried to restore the tales to the 2,500-year-old Buddhist tradition out of which they emerged, so they could be known again in their original context. At the same time, I have sought to tell them in ways that emphasize their relevance for modern readers. This has been the approach of Buddhist storytellers and authors through the centuries.

I have also tried to restore something of the lively, direct, oral voice through which these tales originally spoke. Told stories must be told sparingly. They must demonstrate their meaning in action. Too much description, too much discourse, and the story slows like a stream wandering among weeds—and the audience is lost. Ornate description and long discourse are the earmarks of the written tale, meant for quiet reflection and concerned with inner states. But most of the stories in this collection were originally told, it is said, by the Buddha himself (Buddha is a Sanskrit term, a title meaning "Awakened One" or "Enlightened One"). Buddhist tradition holds that he told each "birth-tale" or "birthlet" as a way of setting some occurrence of interest to his monks in the context of its past-life actions and incidents. (Rebirth was generally accepted without question in India during the time of the Buddha.)

To Buddhists, jataka tales are accepted as stories of the Buddha's own earlier births as he evolved, over countless world cycles and lifetimes, towards full Enlightenment and Buddhahood. As such they form the backbone of the literary and artistic traditions of

Buddhist Asia. "[The Buddha's] words," writes Lama Govinda, "according to changing times may be interpreted in a variety of ways; his living example, however, speaks an eternal language, which will be understood at all times, as long as there are human beings."[1] As the fundamental expression of that "living example," the jatakas empower and dramatize some of the deepest values and beliefs of the culture. A compassionate reverence for all life, and a faith in the dynamic workings of cause and effect (*karma*) are two such implicit "values and beliefs" that extend through the jataka tradition.

The stories have been immensely popular, with a long history of being told, carved, drawn, sculpted and performed. Their artistic lineage goes back almost as far as the time of the Buddha himself. By the time of the Council of Vaisali, a gathering of the Buddhist community (*sangha*) some one hundred years after the Buddha's death (*Parinirvana*, meaning "an entry into *Nirvana*"), the jataka stories had been accepted as an authentic part of the canon. Carved and sculpted railings surrounding the relic shrines of Sanchi, Amaravati, and Bharut in India, dating from the third century B.C.E., clearly depict scenes from jataka tales.

Two major strands of jataka tales have come down to us today out of what was originally a much vaster oral tradition. The largest and oldest collection, the Pali *Jataka*, a collection of 547 jatakas and their verses, is arranged simply according to the number of verses in each tale. The verses are canonical, the tales being essentially commentaries on, or illustrations of, the verses. Each of the tales is preceded by a brief introductory story and followed by a brief identification of the characters, i.e., who they are now, in their "present" lives, as revealed by the historical Buddha. This written collection was put together in its final form (some say translated from a lost original) about 500 C.E. in Southeast Asia. However, as Ananda Coomaraswamy points out, while the final work is a literary creation, a formal, patterned structure that evolved over time, the stories preserved in it can be traced back as far as 300

B.C.E. The Pali jataka collection, as a finished work, then, is not that old. But the verses and stories contained in it have considerable antiquity.

The Pali jataka tales reveal that whether the Buddha, in his past lives, was born as human or animal, spirit or god, he strove for perfection of character and deeper wisdom. But, they also make it clear that while the Buddha was a person of extraordinary character and depth, he was a man and not a god, not to be seen as intrinsically more perfect than anyone else. He was a *bodhisattva*, a being en route to Full Enlightenment, or Buddha-hood.

Long ago—in an almost unimaginably distant past, the jatakas tell us—the Buddha was simply an ordinary man. However, growing aware of the unsatisfactory nature of unenlightened existence, he became determined to gain Enlightenment and deepen his Understanding and his Compassion to the utmost. After this, Buddhist tradition tells us, through countless lifetimes of existence at many levels of being—human, non-human, and superhuman—he continued to work towards this goal. In the end the keynote of the Pali *Jataka* is that the Buddha's attainment was the outcome of his own unceasing moral and spiritual efforts.

While many of the tales in the Pali *Jataka* fit this ideal, archetypal jataka model—i.e., tales of heroic action, wisdom, and compassion—there are also many other stories of truly ancient story-stock. Formed from fragments of epics and hero tales arising from deep in the collective Indian past, this material, already old by the time of the Buddha, was revised and reused by later Buddhist storytellers for their own purposes. Such transformations and reworkings (essentially a kind of thrifty recycling of still potent and viable story-stuff) are typical of oral traditions and reflect the essential vitality of these traditions around the world. There is a certain amount of narrow-minded, ascetic-monastic moralizing in the Pali *Jataka* too, which may have its roots both in earlier Hindu, yogic-ascetic traditions as well as in the experience of the monastic Buddhist writers who seem to have put the collection together. This grab-bag-like quality of the Pali *Jataka* prompted T.W. Rhys Davids to call it "the oldest, the most complete and the most important collection of folklore extant."[2]

His wife, Caroline A.F. Rhys Davids, also an outstanding Pali scholar, described the Pali jatakas and their traditional introduction (see note for "Dipankara and Sumedha") thus:

> [F]or all the...foolishness we find in [the jatakas], the oddities, the inconsistencies, the many distortions in ideals and in the quest of them, they are collectively the greatest epic, in literature, of the Ascent of Man, the greatest ballad-book on the theme that man willing the better becomes the better....[W]e are given the life history of the individual; not as a type...but as a human unit, with a long life history of his own...[3]

The other main grouping of jatakas is built up out of more thematic and literary Mahayana Sanskrit collections like the famous fourth century C.E. *Jatakamala* ("Garland of Jatakas") of Aryasura, a highly influential collection of thirty-four jatakas. It was these versions of the jatakas which were used as the basis for the beautiful sixth and seventh century paintings on the walls of the Ajanta caves in India. (Aryasura's own elegant recreations of the jatakas, may themselves have been based on texts very much like the Pali *Jataka*).

In such collections as Aryasura's, compassion and self-sacrifce come to the fore and the theme of Buddhism as a path of compassion emerges clearly. Tales from the Pali *Jataka*, which may do little more than reveal the workings of karma, are now retold so as to bring out the overwhelming goodness and eloquence of the Bodhisattva. Tales of deep compassion, which may be spread throughout the Pali *Jataka*, are drawn closely together in the Mahayana Sanskrit collections. One also enters a more refined and rarified world with an atmosphere of elegance, delight, and beauty. Polished philosophical passages are part of the pleasure of these works: "Earth with its forests, noble mountains and seas may perish a hundred times by fire, water and wind, as each

each eon comes to an end, but the great compassion of the Bodhisattva, never."[4] There is a surer literary sense. Dialogue tends to be richer, scenes more intimate, dramatic, and personal. More of the motivations and feelings of the characters are given imaginative expression and life. Descriptions of nature become lavish. There is a tenderness in these tales as well as a lofty religious sensibility. In the words of Wendy Doniger, mythologist and professor of the history of religions, the Pali jatakas tend to be "rather rough-hewn," whereas the *Jatakamala* "combines...the simple joys of rough peasant fare and the more epicurean (often even gourmand) pleasures of the cuisine of Sanskrit court poetry."[5]

In works like the *Jatakamala*, language itself is one of the heroes. Action, the life-blood of the folk tale, becomes hidden within discourse. Rhetorical action—the debate between good and evil, right and wrong—often takes center stage. The winning over of the mind through discourse and thinking about goodness is the real focus. Thus, each story opens and closes with a clear moral, rather than a quasi-historical context as in the Pali *Jataka*. "The pure in heart cannot succumb to the enticements of evil. Try, therefore, to make your hearts pure" is a typical opening and closing of a *Jatakamala* tale. The emphasis has shifted. No longer is it simply on what happened at one time in the historical Buddha's own path towards Enlightenment. Rather, it is on a way of living that is to be emulated by believers. The *Jatakamala* is a devotional work created to inspire. Says Aryasura in his prologue, "These praiseworthy exploits are like conspicuous signs pointing the way to perfection. As such may they soften even the hardest of hearts. And may these edifying tales give greater enjoyment than ever before."[6]

As beautiful as it is, the later *Jatakamala* does not supersede the Pali *Jataka*. Some of the most powerful, beautiful (in meaning if not in conscious artistry) and compassionate jatakas, such as "The Banyan Deer," are to be found in the Pali *Jataka* and not in the *Jatakamala*. And there they remain, told less artfully but more directly and simply, in the old folk-tale-like way. If they are rough-hewn, they are also sturdy. Filled with action rather than with discourse and thought, they clearly beg to be told, shared, and used, rather than quietly reflected upon. Viewed as a whole, however, the jataka tradition explores the meaning of life and death, and presents a remarkably coherent vision of the intrinsic unity of all living things.

Frank Waters, describing the beliefs of Native American peoples of the Southwestern United States, makes a statement that could be equally applied to of the Buddhist jatakas:

> It is an assurance which avoids the...terror that a soul exists only on earth in a human body for the short space of only one lifetime, and that it is irretrievably committed to the horrors of Hell or the celestial raptures of Heaven for all eternity on the basis of this short span. On the contrary, it reaffirms a belief in the ultimate evolution of every living thing, subhuman, human, and super-human.[7]

As literary forms, the jatakas raise the simple form of the animal fable to unexpected spiritual heights. And they give unique expression to a powerful impulse towards compassion. They have a storytelling genius to them too. The drama of the tales is immediate and gripping, and whether they were first told by the Buddha himself or whether they came into being later on through the efforts of various unknown Buddhist sages, teachers, and wandering storytellers, they remain true *tales*. That is, they ring true to the imagination, and open to us a world that is coherent, filled with life, energy, meaning, and wonder.

As the Great Vehicle of the Mahayana flourished, the tales of compassion in particular came to be seen as the "classic" jatakas, the ones that truly transmitted the essence of the tradition. It was these tales which most deeply affected the popular imagination. Interestingly, one of the most famous of all jatakas, "The Hungry Tigress," in which the Buddha, as a prince, offers his own body to a starving tigress, is one that does not appear in the Pali collection.

Tales like this which only appear in the later Sanskrit collections, and not in the Pali *Jataka*, must have been either original creations of Mahayana writers, storytellers, and teachers, or stories retained by Mahayana authors from even earlier jataka sources which had been lost to the Southeast Asian translators. In a non-historical (i.e. spiritual) sense it hardly matters which of these two scenarios is "true." Whatever their origins, such tales bring to life a vision and a set of values that are unmistakably Buddhist. As is often the case, through stories a tradition may both create and recreate itself. As Lama Govinda says:

> The bodhisattva ideal, in spite of its relatively late verbal formulation, is not some "invention" of the centuries after the Buddha's Parinirvana, but is one of the basic ideas of earlier Buddhism.[8]

The jataka stories as a whole have traditionally been seen as entertainment of the highest order. Not only do they bring delight, but they impart wisdom. The jatakas, as well as other Buddhist tales and legends, explore the range of the Buddha's teachings and make them dramatic and particular. They do what all narrative art does—they make their subjects *live*. Not philosophically, in the abstract, but intimately, in a way that transcends resistance and reservation. What before might have been distant and conceptual now pulses with life and meaning.

Giuseppi Tucci, a scholar of Buddhism, travelling in pre-Communist Buddhist Tibet, relates how the roughest sort of men, the muleteers and horse-traders of his caravan, would listen as jatakas were told around the campfires at night and weep unrestrainedly, like babies. Lama Govinda says:

> It was only when Buddhists again began to turn more consciously towards the figure of the Buddha, whose life and deeds were the most vital expression of his

teachings that Buddhism emerged from a number of quarreling sects as a world religion. In the cross-fire of conflicting views and opinions, what greater certainty could there be than to follow the example of the Buddha?....The exalted figure of the Buddha and the profound symbolism of his real as well as legendary life, in which his inner development is portrayed—and from which grew the immortal works of Buddhist art and literature—all this is of infinitely greater importance to humanity than all...philosophical systems and all...abstract classifications. Can there be a more profound demonstration of selflessness...of the Eightfold Path, of the Four Noble Truths, of the Law of Dependent Origination, enlightenment and liberation, than that of the Buddha's way, which encompassed all the heights and depths of the universe?

"Whatever be the highest perfection of the human mind, may I realize it for the benefit of all that lives!" This is the gist of the Bodhisattva vow.[9]

We live today in times that seem to grow more naturally Buddhistic every day. The universe as revealed by modern astrophysics transcends our ordinary, materialistic notions of a fixed creation, existing solidly in time and space, with a beginning and end. Chemistry, microbiology, and the behavioral sciences all confirm an essential kinship extending from the Earth itself through all living things, from the smallest bacteria to the largest blue whale. Our deepening awareness of the essential impermanence of even the most solid or stable seeming structures—mountains, seas, the atmosphere, the wheeling galaxies—has reached new poignancy. We know now that, ecologically, human life—indeed, all life as we know it—has a fragility to it which no past generations had glimpsed. In the ongoing effort to gain moral control over our economic drives and over those masterworks of impermanence—nuclear weapons—we must now struggle daily with our own spiritual responsibilities to the Earth and to all future generations, both human and non-human. The revolutionary thinking of Carl Jung and Albert Einstein, the thoughts and actions of peacemakers like Gandhi and Dr. Martin Luther King, the resurgence of interest in myth and mythic thinking popularized by Joseph Campbell, modern scientific thought and environmental concern—all work to align us naturally with the vision of the jatakas.

Cosmic dimensions in both time and space are natural to the jatakas, as is an evolutionary viewpoint in which we rediscover ourselves in the many interconnected life forms around us. (At the deepest level, these other life forms *are* us. At relative levels, we have been them; they are the bodies we have passed through to be who and what we are now.) In addition, the jatakas extol the importance of an active, non-dogmatic, nonviolent, and compassionate way of life.

These elements, which underlie so many of the Buddhist tales and legends, allow the tales to speak naturally to our modern imaginations. They are not stories whose structures have been outdated by scientific, social, psychological, or environmental thought. Indeed, one would have to look to contemporary science fiction for anything approaching the sheer scale of the jataka-imagination. The jataka tales give us a body of literature in which the role of the individual can be examined in relation to, not separated from, a backdrop which is as vast as the living universe itself. Or, as Huston Smith states in his introduction to *The Three Pillars of Zen*—

> [T]he extent to which Buddhist cosmology anticipated what contemporary science has empirically discovered...[is] impressive. Astronomical time and space, which irrevocably smashed the West's previous world view, slipped into the folds of Buddhist cosmology without a ripple. If we turn from macrocosm to microcosm we find the same uncanny prescience...
>
> "Very interesting," says the Buddhist, this being what his cosmology has taught him all along.[10]

The stories in this collection have been arranged to suggest something of the structure of the Buddhist cosmology, as revealed through the Buddha's legendary and historical life. Section One includes legendary material leading up to and including the Buddha's historical life.

In this section are the stories of the Buddha's leaving home, his Enlightenment, his teaching, and his death or Parinirvana, as well as tales set in the incalculably distant past. Section Two, the lengthiest by far, is comprised of tales which were purportedly told by the Buddha during his teaching career. These are the tales of the Buddha's past lives, or jatakas proper. The selection ranges widely through different emotions, styles, and eons of time. Section Three consists of tales set after the Buddha's historical life—first a group of traditional Buddhist stories which are not about the Buddha but grow out of his teachings ("Most Lovely Fugen," The Dog's Tooth," and "The Legend of Avalokitesvara"), and then several modern, original tales ("Stilson's Leap," "Digit," and "Kogi the Priest") which extend jataka-like patterns into our own time. Following the stories is a section of notes and commentaries, containing historical, literary, Buddhistic, and mythic background information for each tale.

The Commentaries are intrinsic to the vision of this book as a whole. Through them, the stories may again function fully, may live as they actually would have for their traditional audiences. In fact, this revised *Hungry Tigress* can be read from either direction—as a collection of stories that demonstrate the meanings revealed in the Commentaries or as a set of commentaries that reveal the stories' often-hidden function and depth.

The Commentaries are intended to fulfill two vital functions. First, they give the Buddhistic background to each of the stories. They explain technical terms and demonstrate principles which may help the reader grasp the full significance of each story. Second, through the Commentaries, the more generally mythic and symbolic significance of the stories are revealed. Stories which might seem totally implausible to modern readers and so be dismissed out of hand, can take on new relevance and meaning. In the jatakas, as the Commentaries make clear, surfaces may be distorted so that meanings can come to the fore. What the mind knows, not what the eye sees, is primary. This kind of vision is part of the traditional world out of which these stories arose and which, at one time, existed worldwide. The Commentaries are a doorway back into this way of seeing.

I should also mention that, as I am not a scholar of Buddhism, the Commentaries should not be seen as definitive scholarly pieces. Nonetheless, because they grow out of years of immersion in the Buddhist tradition, they have behind them the kind of validity that comes from both oral tradition and personal experience. I have not been exhaustive in my research. I have only tried to identify interesting sources for the versions presented as well as to share such information as I found to be of particular interest, meaning, and resonance. I encourage future scholars to take the work of definitive research farther.

In addition, as I am primarily a storyteller, my motivation in working on these stories was not so much to produce final, authoritative texts, but to recreate versions which might live authentically for readers and listeners today. In short, I was interested in keeping these good tales alive. In traditional cultures, of course, storytellers are not mere "memorizers," but creative participants in the ongoing life of the culture. It is traditional, then, for storytellers to comment meaningfully on the stories they tell, so that the tales may live more fully for those who have gathered to hear.

By necessity, the stories included in this collection reflect subjective criteria. The storyteller's job, after all, is to pass on those stories that have actually spoken to him or her, to share those stories that have been heard, not just with the ears, but with the heart. Because this is a storyteller's book, the principle guiding the selection of stories as well as the choice of information recorded in the Commentaries was the informal and natural one. As Ryokan, the famous nineteenth century Japanese Zen monk and poet, puts it:

> The wind brings
> Enough of fallen leaves
> To make a fire.[11]

As a storyteller, I hope that readers will find many of these stories suitable for reading and sharing aloud. Something unique happens when the human voice carries what are essentially oral tales. A kind of unrecognized life that printed words can only suggest comes to the fore. I hope then that others will be tempted to try such readings, even tellings, of these stories.

In the Commentaries, when applicable, each jataka is listed with its traditional number as it appears in the Cowell translation of the Pali. If it appears in the *Jatakamala*, that is also noted. In this way those interested may go to the original sources. For those who want to study further, a bibliography has been included.

A final word. The more I work with these stories, the more I think about, write, and tell them, the more their truth becomes apparent to me. Stories, of course, are always true—true to the imagination in which they live. For me, these stories are especially so. After working on these stories, I find myself observing flocks of pigeons wheeling between houses and thinking, as I watch, of the Buddha's lives as various birds. I observe our family dog and our cats in a new light. The Bodhisattvic presence, the jatakas suggest, is potentially everywhere. The ninth-century Japanese Buddhist pilgrim to China, Ennin, relates in his journals that when he arrived at Mount Wu-Tai, the mountain sacred to the Bodhisattva Manjusri, the Bodhisattva of Wisdom, he discovered that when resident monks or pilgrims to the mountain saw a lowly person, or even a donkey, none dared think a contemptuous thought. Rather they would spontaneously think, "Perhaps it is He!" and act accordingly.

Such positive transformation of our thoughts and lives is what traditional stories and legends are about. While among the oldest and the frailest of humanity's varied creations—they are, after all, only so many sounds on the air, so many squiggles on a page—they remain, even today, a most powerful tool for encouraging significant inner change.

Notes on *Introduction*

1. Lama Anagarika Govinda. *Foundations of Tibetan Mysticism,* p. 45.
2. T.W. Rhys Davids. *Buddhist Birth-Stories,* pp. iii-iv.
3. Caroline F.A. Rhys Davids. *Stories of the Buddha,* pp. xviii-xix.
4. Peter Khoroche, trans. *Once the Buddha was a Monkey: Aryasura's Jatakamala,* p. 166.
5. Wendy Doniger. Foreword to Koroche, *Op Cit.,* p. vii
6. *Ibid.,* p. 3.
7. Frank Waters. *Masked Gods: Navajo and Pueblo Ceremonialism,* p. 302.
8. Lama Anagarika Govinda. *A Living Buddhism for the West,* p. 12.
9. Lama Anagarika Govinda. *Foundations of Tibetan Mysticism,* p. 45.
10. Philip Kapleau. *The Three Pillars of Zen,* p. xii.
11. Robert Blyth, *Haiku,* Volume 4.

Section I:
Buddhist Legends

Beginnings

Once, many long ages ago, in a time beyond all reckoning, the Buddha was a king named Suprabhasa.

One day, King Suprabhasa told his elephant trainer to ready the great white elephant so that he might ride.

"My Lord," replied the trainer. "I cannot bring him. The great white elephant has broken his golden chains and gone back to the jungle. It is only temporary. He will return again. He has been well-trained."

The prince, angered, lost all self-control, shouted at the trainer, and dismissed him.

Next morning the trainer came before King Suprabhasa and announced, "Sire, the great white elephant has returned, my Lord, as I predicted. The training was good. We have conquered over his old, wild ways."

King Suprabhasa started. Those words touched his own fault. "Though I am a king," he realized, "holding great power over others, I have as yet failed to conquer what is closest—myself. I was not able to even control my own anger. This will not do."

"Tell me, trainer," he now asked, "are there any who have truly conquered themselves? For harder it must be, it seems to me, to conquer oneself than it is to control a powerful elephant when it seeks to have its way."

"My Lord," he answered the trainer, "there are the Conquerors, the Buddhas. Having triumphed over all greeds and desires, over all anger, hatred, and fear, they must surely be the noblest of all beings. Free from all egoistic delusions, they live in peace, seeing things as they really are."

At once, a great yearning arose in King Suprabhasa's heart, a yearning to conquer himself and also be free.

In this way Shakyamuni, the Buddha of our own age, many long ages ago, as an ordinary man of the world, first awoke to what was to be an ever-deepening longing for wisdom and truth.

Sumedha Meets Dipankara Buddha

Ages passed. And from the seed of that yearning, life after life, now in high station, now in low, now as god, now as human, now as a spirit, bird, or animal, the future Buddha worked towards the realization of his goal.

Then, four *asankheya kalpas* and a hundred thousand world cycles ago, a decisive moment was reached.

At that time the future Buddha was born into a wealthy Brahmin family in the city of Amaravati. He was named Sumedha.

He was blessed with all goodness—physical beauty, intelligence, friendliness, kindness, moral vigor.

His parents died when he was still a young man and, as the steward went through the list of all of Sumedha's inherited properties and wealth—noting so much from his mother, so much from his father, so much from his grandparents, so much from his great grandparents, and so on, back and back for seven generations—this young man, Sumedha, began to think: "My family has amassed wealth for seven generations. Yet neither my parents, nor my grandparents, nor any other of my ancestors were able to take any of it with them upon leaving this world. What is the point of amassing more? One day, I too will die. As there is a road that leads beyond the sufferings of this world, should I just remain idle? No, I will leave this sheltered life, become an ascetic, and find that Way."

And announcing his intention to the king, he gave away his money to the poor, and entered the forests.

The hermit Sumedha ate wild fruit and wore clothing of bark. His hair and beard grew long and matted. Striving energetically, whether standing, sitting, or lying down, in a short time he gained a profound insight into the True Nature of things, and a bright wisdom, never to be dimmed, arose in his mind. For many days he sat absorbed in the bliss of his newly won freedom and knowledge.

At this time the Buddha, Dipankara, surrounded by thousands of monks, nuns, and laypeople, was making his way to the city of Amaravati. Workmen were busy smoothing and leveling the road before the city in expectation of Dipankara Buddha's arrival.

The hermit Sumedha was roused from his trance. Seated cross-legged, he rose up into the air and flew over the forest, until he came to the road. Calling down to the workmen, he inquired, "What is the excitement? Why are you laboring in the midday heat? Why is the road being leveled and strewn with golden sands? Why these flowers and perfumes?"

"Venerable Sumedha!" replied the workmen, calling up to where the hermit sat hovering in the clear air. "Do you not know? The Buddha Dipankara is approaching the city. This evening he is to give public talks and reveal his Dharma!"

And Sumedha's heart leapt for joy! "A Buddha!" he thought. "Rare, indeed, is it to even hear the word, 'Buddha.' Rare beyond all comprehending is it to meet such a fully Realized One."

Descending from the air, he alighted beside the workmen and offered to assist them in leveling the road. Seeing that his powers were supernatural, the foreman assigned him a stretch of low, swampy ground to fill.

Then, with his heart pounding in expectation, his mind lit with joy, repeating to himself over and over "a Buddha! a Buddha!"—Sumedha began filling in the marshy ground with dry soil.

From up ahead, Sumedha heard drums and flutes and the murmuring of crowds. Looking up he saw bright banners swirling, saw flowers and jewels being tossed in the air. The Buddha Dipankara was approaching.

Sumedha saw six-hued rays of light extending outward from the Buddha Dipankara. He saw a great halo of golden light surrounding him, and ever-changing wreaths of light encircling him. Godly devas, tossing celestial flowers and strumming instruments of purest gold, flew overhead. Exquisite music filled the air.

Then these thoughts arose in Sumedha's mind: "Here is one who has attained all the super-knowledges, all wisdom. Here is one free from all greed, all anger, and ego-delusion, one in whom all goodness has been realized. I shall make an offering to the Buddha Dipankara for the sake of buddha-knowledge."

Loosening his long hair, Sumedha spread his bark-cloth cloak before him in the mud. Then he thought. "Like the Buddha Dipankara, I want to help all beings. I am determined. Despite difficulties and dangers, I will never turn back. I am resolved to attain what the Buddha Dipankara has attained, and benefit all beings."

Then Sumedha lay down upon his bark-cloth cape and spread his long hair making a passage for the Buddha Dipankara to walk over the mud.

The Buddha Dipankara arrived at the spot and, looking at Sumedha, thought, "This hermit lying here has formed the resolution to be a Buddha. Will he be successful?" Casting his mind far into the future with his prescient gaze, he saw that, four *asankheya kalpas* and one hundred thousand world cycles from that time, Sumedha would become a fully-realized, omniscient Buddha—an Awakened One—and that his name would be Gautama.

Standing there, surrounded by many thousands of people—monks, nuns, laymen, laywomen, and children—the Buddha Dipankara made this prophecy: "Four *asankheya kalpas* and one hundred thousand world cycles from now—far, far in the future—the hermit lying in the mud before us will fulfill his great vow. He will be a Buddha named Gautama. His birth will be in the city of Kapilavasthu. His mother's name will be Maya, his father's Suddhodhana. When he is grown he will see the four signs—old age, sickness, death, a monk—and he will leave the world. After great exertions he will receive, when he is near death on the banks of the Naranjana River, a life-saving meal of milk-rice. With strength renewed, he will make his way to the foot of a bo tree, seat himself there, and continuing his effort to the utmost, he will attain Supreme Buddhahood."

Lying in the mire Sumedha became delirious with joy, and thought to himself, "My deepest wish shall be attained! I shall be a Buddha!"

Then the Buddha Dipankara praised the Bodhisattva and encouraged him. He made an offering of flowers, saluted him, palm to palm, and accompanied by the thousands of monks, nuns, and lay followers—from all stations of life, beggar to king—he departed.

The Bodhisattva Sumedha arose, seated himself in the Lotus posture, and exclaimed, "The words of a Buddha cannot fail. They are certain. I shall, then, one day become a Buddha." Filled with joy and strengthened in purpose, he rose up into the clear air and returned to his retreat where he remained working hard towards his goal.

The Birth of the Buddha

Long ago, in India, Queen Maya, wife of the king, Suddhodhana, had a dream. She dreamed that a magnificent
six-tusked white elephant entered her room and touched
her right side with a lotus flower.

The king called for his wise men to interpret the
dream, and they all predicted that a son destined for
greatness would soon be born. "If he follows a worldly
path," they said, "he will become a great ruler, Emperor
of the World. If he recognizes the impermanence of life,
he will seek something higher. He will leave the palace
in quest of Enlightenment. Undergoing much hardship,
he will eventually attain the complete Understanding of
a Buddha and become a teacher to gods, beasts, and humankind."

The Queen was overjoyed, but King Suddhodhana was
troubled. He could not help but think of how he might
protect his son from hardship and danger so that the
boy might become the great man who would rule the
world.

One day, almost ten months later, Queen Maya set out
to visit her parents. On the way she passed a magnificent
park near the town of Lumbini, and she and her attendants stopped to rest there in a grove of sala trees.

Queen Maya stood beneath the largest and most ancient sala tree in the grove. Suddenly, many white flowers and golden-yellow lotus petals tumbled from the
skies. It was like a rain of flowers. From the earth rose
delicate fragrances of jasmine, roses, and sandalwood.
From the air itself sounded a music of bells, lutes, and
high, clear voices singing in a language of delight.

At that moment the child was born. Sky-walking
devas appeared at the mother's side and washed the
child in streams of heavenly dew. The baby Buddha took
seven steps, and at each step a lotus blossom sprang up
to support his feet. Raising one hand towards the heav-

ens, and pointing the other down towards the earth, he fearlessly sounded the Buddha's lion's roar—

"Above the heavens, below the heavens, I am the only One. In this life I shall become a Buddha!"

As Queen Maya gathered her long-awaited child into her arms, the magical infant lapsed from all signs of special consciousness or power. The Queen had heard, however, and she had seen. That day there could be no one happier than she.

Unless it was the Buddha himself. Though just a newborn child he already looked on each deva, man, woman, child, animal, flower, tree and stone with a parent's tender love. After countless ages of sustained effort he had at last come into life with the readiness to aid them all.

Leaving Home

Two-thousand, five-hundred years ago, he who was to be the Buddha was born as a prince in the foothills of the Himalayan mountains. Sages had prophesied that the child's merit, accumulated over countless lives, was now so great that he was destined to become either a world ruler, or an Awakened Buddha.

But one very old sage, Asita, prophesied that there could be no doubt. The child would be a Buddha. And he wept, for he saw that he himself would die before the child attained that goal.

King Suddhodhana, the child's father, being a king himself, wanted his son to be a great king. And he wanted to protect his child from pain and suffering. He named his child "Siddhartha," which means "He Whose Wishes Are Fulfilled," and, despite the death of the boy's mother, Maya, within days of the birth, strove to keep the boy's life happy and pleasant.

As a child, Siddhartha played in beautiful gardens. During the fierce heat of summer he roamed the cool halls of marble palaces. Anything he desired was his. Playmates, friends, and loving attendants surrounded him.

The King was happy. And the people were happy. Suddhodhana, the good king, had provided them with a worthy heir.

But Siddhartha, "He Whose Wishes Are Fulfilled," was himself not truly happy. He saw what his father and the others could no longer see: cobras hunting frogs in the garden pools; falcons dropping upon terrified pigeons and doves; dead deer slung on hunters' poles. He saw too the fleeting sadness of his companions and friends. In vain, he tried to recall the face of the mother he had never known.

As he grew, these impressions gathered within him, piling up like dry sticks a spark might ignite.

One day, though he was married and lived in luxury, with three different palaces—one each for the hot, cold, and rainy seasons—the thought struck him that he had never really seen the world of his subjects, of ordinary women and men. He went to his charioteer, Channa, and said, "Take me, Channa, into the towns. I want to see my people. I want to see how they live."

"Very good, Sire," answered Channa, the charioteer. "Let us go tomorrow. I will make the necessary arrangements."

And the prince was content.

Siddhartha's father, King Suddhodhana, and Siddhartha's foster-mother, Prajapatti, his maternal aunt, had long been dreading this moment—a sign of the prophecy's unfolding. Soon Siddhartha might see what his father, Suddhodhana, had worked so hard to keep from him—old age and sickness, change and death. And the king, his father, knew they would lose him should that happen.

The king, determined to keep Siddhartha from his high destiny, ordered the captain of his guards to go into the villages and see to it that the beggars, the aged, the sick, and the infirm were hidden from sight. "Strew the roads," he commanded, "with flowers and perfumes. Make sure that only those who are young, able-bodied, and handsome are on the streets."

These preparations were carried out just as the king had ordered. Yet King Suddhodhana's fear remained unrelieved.

The sun rose. The day broke. Siddhartha and Channa set off for the towns. The horses raced along the hard dirt road. Birds sang and soared among the trees. White clouds drifted overhead. A cool breeze blew and the mountains, rising behind them, glowed in the early light.

Soon they reached the nearest of the towns. Wreaths of bright flowers hung everywhere. Crowds of happy people cheered. Children laughed. Handsome couples strolled arm in arm. "So this is life," thought

Siddhartha. "Why, then, have I been sad and troubled? My people are happy."

But what was this? Suddenly a wrinkled and toothless old man, clothed in rags, bent and twisted with the burden of his years, tottered from the crowd. There he stood, leaning on a stick, blinking blindly and pitifully in the sunlight. Then, suddenly, he was gone!

The prince's horses laid back their ears and neighed in terror. Rearing up, they tried to back away. Siddhartha leapt from the chariot and grabbed their reins. "Channa!" he cried. "What was that? Was that a man, or some other kind of creature?"

"Noble Prince," replied Channa, for the gods had loosened his tongue, "that was indeed a man, even as you and I. But it was an old, old man, Sire."

"Tell me, Channa," the Prince asked, "do all, then, become like this? Do all grow 'old'?"

"Yes," sighed Channa, despite the king's order to keep this hidden, "they do. Smiling infants become men and women. Men and women then age. All creatures on this earth at last grow old, Noble Prince."

Shaken, the prince remounted his golden chariot. "Channa," he said, "let us turn the horses round and return. Though I am still young, black-haired, and in the full flush of my manhood, this is a bitter truth. Here is reason enough to spill an ocean of tears." Channa turned the horses and they rode back, dispirited, to the palace once again.

Then the king, Suddhodhana, had his men redouble their efforts. Once more the guards scoured the villages, cleared and prepared the streets.

That night Siddhartha tossed and turned feverishly in his bed. It was as if a blaze had begun burning within him.

But the next morning, the prince woke Channa when the sun rose, saying, "Whatever lies ahead must be faced. Let us face it bravely. Prepare the chariot and horses. We shall return to the towns. It is not yet over."

Once again the horses raced along the road. Once again the fine breezes blew.

Soon they entered another town where happy crowds cheered and smiled. Again, flowers and welcoming garlands flew through the air towards the handsome prince. Suddenly, from where no one knew, a sick man staggered forth. He was thin, sweaty, wild-eyed, and disheveled. He coughed horribly and almost fell. The happy people recoiled in alarm.

"What is that!" cried Siddhartha. "Channa! What has happened to that man—if man it is!"

"It is a man, my Prince, and he is sick," answered Channa. "He is feverish and tormented."

"Was he born like this?" asked the prince.

"No, Lord," Channa replied, but slowly, like a man being dragged to his doom, "he was in all likelihood born as sound as you or I."

"Can we all, then, become 'sick'?" asked the prince.

"Yes," admitted Channa, impelled again by the gods to speak the truth. "We can."

"Turn the horses round," exclaimed the prince in dismay. "With old age on one hand and sickness on the other, how can I wander on heedlessly? My blind faith in health and happy youth are gone. My love of festivity is over."

Once again, they travelled in silence back to the palace through the burning midday heat. As they passed through the crowds it seemed to the prince as if all those smiling people stood unawares at the edge of an abyss. It was to him as if they were pieces of paper about to be blown by unknown winds into a mountain of flames.

Cool night fell at last. But though the stars shone, sparkling overhead, what delight could the prince take in them? All night long he again lay tossing, feverishly consumed by thoughts of sickness and age. His wife, Yasodhara—his father, Suddhodhana—his mother, Prajapatti—Channa—friends—his great horse, Kanthaka—the crowds of his people—himself; he saw now that all were bound to the inexorable law of change.

That night, too, the King Suddhodhana tossed and turned. He had sent out all his companies of soldiers and given the strictest orders. No infirm, aged, ugly, or sick persons were to be allowed onto the streets. All through the night, his soldiers labored, going from house to house, so that the young prince would be sheltered from suffering's truth.

But when the sun rose over the mountains, hope awoke in the prince's heart. "Let what is to come, come," he thought. "Whatever it is, I shall meet it face-on and find a way through." Somehow he was certain that this was not yet the end of the road he was destined to travel.

So, once again, Siddhartha and Channa set off for the towns.

And once again, all seemed as before. Happy people gathered, tossing flowers. Children played. Doves and pigeons flew, wheeling in the sunlight. Yet, as they travelled on, the Prince's mind remained roused, alert. He was resolved to know the truth.

Suddenly, Siddhartha heard wailing cries. "Channa," he exclaimed, "What is that?"

"It is a funeral, Sire," said Channa with a shiver. "It marks a death."

Though Channa did not pull the reins, the horses stopped of their own accord. "Channa, that sleeping one there—why does he not move?" asked the prince with a sense of foreboding. "They cry loudly and it is midday. They lift him up onto a hard bed of wood, yet still he does not open his eyes. How can this be? But, what are they doing? There are flames all around him! His hair, his clothes are burning, on fire!"

"Calm yourself, my Lord," said Channa. "He does not feel the flames. He is dead."

"What?" cried the prince. "What do you mean, 'He is dead'?"

"His life is over, Lord," said Channa. "There will be no more movement or action or decision; no more sight or smell or taste or touch; no more hopes or dreams, no more laughter or tears for him. It is over. It is finished. His days are done. Friends and relatives may weep all they want. They will never see him again." These words of Channa's too were guided by the watchful gods. They knew the time had come. Siddhartha must set out and complete what he had begun so long ago.

"Channa," asked Siddhartha, *"does this happen to everyone?"*

Channa turned away. But the gods would have him speak the truth. "It does, my Lord. It happens to each, to all. After old age and sickness comes death."

"To all?" repeated the prince, staggering like a bull struck by the axe. "To Father, Mother, wife—to friends, oneself—to all?"

They turned away, then, riding back through the crowds as the flames and smoke rose still higher around the uncaring corpse. Again the smiling, garlanded crowds gathered but the prince hardly saw. In his mind, the crackling flames and billowing smoke persisted still.

"Old age and sickness await," said the prince. "And then at last comes death. No one knows when either sickness or death will strike. Yet, like the sure coming of old age, strike they must. So, is this, then, the end I have sought? Is there nothing more?"

"No, brave prince," said a steady voice. "It is not the end." There stood a homeless wanderer, a truth-seeker from the mountains, grasping a wooden staff and carrying a begging bowl. "This is where we begin. Walk on, young prince! The further you go into these mountains, the higher they get. You are in the foothills. Seek the heights, Siddhartha! There your wishes will indeed be fulfilled."

Then suddenly he was gone!

A messenger from the palace stood at the prince's side. "Your wife," he said, "Yasodhara, sends you greetings. She is well and shares with you her joy. This day she has borne you a son."

It was complete. Birth, old age, sickness, death—and the knowledge of a Path that led beyond them. "Old age approaches. Sickness and death may strike at any moment. Having been born I too am subject to these despoilers, as is my newborn son. Yet, there is a Path beyond such sorrow," he thought, "I shall take it. I shall find a way through this darkness. There is no time to lose."

Mounting his chariot, as if in a dream, the Prince Siddhartha—and Channa, his charioteer—rode back in silence to the palace once again. Words arose in the prince's mind, sounding over and over to the rhythm of the horse's hooves:

Now is the time to enter the mountains.
Now is the time to seek the great heights!

Like a flood, a river of hope and courage surged through the prince's heart. Standing firmly in the rocking chariot, he saw the mountains looming closer and closer, rising higher and higher as the horses sped on.

Enlightenment

At age twenty-nine, Siddhartha Gautama, the Prince of the Shakya Clan, saw for the first time an old man, then a sick man, then a dead man, and then, last of all, a solitary, wandering truth-seeker, and he was sorely troubled.

Late in the night he roused Channa, his charioteer, mounted Kanthaka, his splendid horse, and with Channa beside him rode to the river boundary of his father's kingdom. At the river's edge, in the faint, pre-dawn light, he severed his attachment to palace life, cutting off his long hair with a single stroke of his sword. He gave Kanthaka over into Channa's keeping. Then, crossing the river, he passed forever from his sheltered life of luxury and ease and disappeared, all alone, into the dark forests and lonely mountains.

He made his way to the hermitages of the two greatest religious teachers of his time, Arada Kalama and Udraka Ramaputra. He mastered their methods, first of the one, and then of the other, but still he found no true freedom from birth, old age, sickness, and death. So, declining requests from both these sages to remain and help lead their orders, he moved on, alone.

He went, then, to the most isolated of places—the deep forests, the graveyards, and the charnel grounds—and sat alone in the darkness of the night. Twigs snapped, leaves rustled. His heart pounded with dread. His hair stood straight up on end. One thought gripped his mind: "Run!" But he would not run. He sat on, facing and mastering the ancient terrors. Though his body sought to flee, he exerted his will against the terror and stayed silent and still. Gradually, his mind grew calm and fear passed. But still he found no release from what was conditioned, bound, and destined to wither and die.

Then he forced himself to undergo fearful austerities. He stood on one leg for hours, then days, then weeks at a time. The muscles cramped and shrivelled. The nails grew long, curled, and split. The sun burned down, birds nested in his hair, bugs bit and scurried over him but still he stood silent, unmoving. And still he had no true release.

So he built great fires and stood between them, baking himself dry through the burning midday heat. Then, climbing up into the peaks, he shivered exposed and naked as night's bitter cold fell on the mountains. But in this, too, he found no lasting freedom.

Then, gradually, he reduced his intake of food until, in the end, he was eating first a thousand, then a hundred, then ten, then, at last, just one single sesame seed a day. His flesh withered. His eyes sank deep into their sockets. His hair rotted and fell out. Every rib, each bony socket and joint, stood clearly exposed, like the wreck of a ship when the tide withdraws.

After six years of such effort, exhausted and at the point of death, he collapsed, more a skeleton held together by sinews, veins, and crusted dirt than a living man.

He had found no great truth and it seemed that he must die without attaining his goal. The bitterness of that moment, after six years of unrelenting but now, seemingly, wasted effort, was keener than any knife.

Suddenly, there flashed into his mind the memory of a festival of long ago on a day in his childhood. He had been seated quietly under a rose-apple tree watching his father, all the nobles, and the poor men alike, plowing the earth together. He remembered being aware of the earth breaking open in even, wave-like furrows; of the heat shimmering up off the freshly opened soil and shining on the sweat-slick brows and straining bodies of the men and oxen; of the sun continuously flashing off the gilded traces and horns of the oxen; of the senseless plodding rhythm of hooves and cowbells rolling in a solemn, sea-like way beneath the shriller shouts of the men and the whirring cries of the birds as they dove to peck at and devour the billowing hordes of insects, blind and glistening grubs, cut worms, and broken bodies of mice, which men, oxen, and plows had left in their wake.

The terribly obvious laboring, devouring, suffering, and dying which went on interminably beneath all the gay, surface tinselling of his own festival days had broken in upon him then and weighed heavily on his mind.

Seated alone, beneath the sweet-smelling rose-apple tree, reflecting deeply on the scene before him, he suddenly entered into a profound experience of oneness, of *samadhi.*

Now, at the brink of death and in the depths of despair, this memory returned to him, filling him with energy and sureness. If he had already glimpsed the Way, he reasoned, when still just a child, well-fed and clothed, then true seeking of the way did not consist in punishment of the body. He decided to take proper nourishment once again.

As if responding to this unspoken decision, Sujata, a maiden from a neighboring village, came before him and humbly offered a bowl of milk-rice.

He accepted this simple offering, and his five fellow-ascetic disciples, who had followed him through his six years of effort, became convinced that the ex-prince had abandoned his quest for Truth and resumed a worldly life, and they summarily left him.

Alone, he ate in silence. When he had finished, somehow he felt strong enough to stand, and leaning on his staff, he rose and made his way to the shore of the Naranjana River which flowed nearby. He bathed in the river, letting six years of matted filth, dirt, and sweat wash away at last.

Climbing up onto the shore, he announced, "If this is the day of my Supreme Enlightenment, may the bowl float upstream!" And he cast his empty offering bowl onto the rippling waters.

As the bowl touched the swirling surface of the river, it forged upstream, until it came at last to the whirlpool of Kala Nagaraja, the Black Snake King who dwells on the river bottom. There it whirled down down into the jewelled chambers of the Naga king's palace. It stopped against an endless row of identically-formed bowls. And hearing the little noise—*clink!*—the Black Naga King opened his eyes. Slowly he raised his great, hooded head and announced, "Only yesterday a Buddha arose. And, today, there shall be another Buddha! Awake! Rejoice!" Then, swaying in the shimmering light, he began to chant his ancient songs of assurance in the Bodhisattva's triumph and victory.

And the Bodhisattva, Siddhartha Gautama, strode like a roused lion towards the bo tree.

There, in the cool, soft light of the late afternoon, he met the poor grass-cutter, Sothiya. Awed, Sothiya offered the ragged stranger before him a gift of eight bundles of freshly cut grass to serve as a sitting cushion and mat.

Then the future Buddha, spreading all the sweet grass on the earth at the base of the tree, seated himself in the lotus posture. His resolve was deeply rooted, like a mountain. He announced, "Though only my skin, sinews and bones remain and my blood and flesh dry up and wither away, never from this seat will I stir until I have attained full Enlightenment."

And he pressed forward once again in his deep meditation.

Many fearsome and foul, as well as many seductive and pleasant visions arose before him. All the forces of life's clinging to states of joy, comfort, and ease came swaying gracefully to him in the form of three women, the three beautiful daughters of Mara the Tempter. They danced seductively before him, opening wide their arms to him and revealing the perfection of their bodies. They sang tenderly, calling him 'Great Hero', and 'Conqueror.' They offered him exquisite pleasure, unceasing comfort, endless rest, while all of life's terrors—fears of death and suffering, fears of hells, horrors, pain, ugliness, the unknown—mobbed him, shrieking of torment and deformity, of all manner of terrible and disgusting experience should he persist. Mara's army descended upon him, horse-headed, ten-eyed, tiger-faced, many-armed; with faces in their chests, with sharp yellow teeth, with blood-dripping mouths, with spiders for hands, hissing with adder's tongues, on they came— heaving stones, knives, spears; hurling flaming discs, mud, filth. Screaming madly, they whirled down upon him like a flock of hunger-maddened crows wildly striving to peck and tear some slight scraps of nourishment from a huge smooth stone.

But they could not.

The future Buddha sat on, viewing all these wild delusive displays evenly, surely, calmly, completely unmoved. It was as if he were watching the harmless antics of children at play. In an instant the hurled knives and spears turned into flowers; the mud and filth became incense and perfume. The beautiful women grew old. The armies became silent.

Then Mara the Tempter himself approached the future Buddha, and assuming the voice of Gautama's own innerness, the habit voice of his own thoughts, began to question the future Buddha with these words—

"*Are you sure you are the one?*

"*Sure you have this Buddha-Nature?*

"*Sure you are worthy of coming to Supreme Enlightenment today, right now?*

"*Think of it: Supreme Enlightenment!*

"*Supreme!*

"*Enlightenment!*"

But the Future Buddha only touched the earth lightly with his right hand, and asked the Earth to witness for him.

And the Earth replied with a hundred, a thousand, a hundred thousand thousand voices: the voices of furrows and graves; voices of youth and age, of man and woman and child; the unheeded cries of beasts; the quick, unknown silvery language of fish; the sweet twinings of plants and the warm, grey crumblings of stone. For all were one voice now thundering,

"*He is worthy!*

There is not one spot on this globe where he has not offered himself totally, selflessly, through countless, endless lifetimes to the attainment of Enlightenment, and to the welfare of all living beings!"

Mara's hosts dropped their weapons, and fled. His daughters prostrated and asked forgiveness. His great war elephant, "Mountain-Girded," crashed to the ground like a heap of stones. The flowers faded and the incense and perfume drifted away. Then all was gone.

Alone beneath the tree, the future Buddha only pressed on and on, deeper and deeper, without stopping anywhere, transcending all limitations, swallowing up the darkness with his own light until, with the dawn, his true Mind rose clear and radiant and obvious as the daybreak. And when he glanced at the morning star he found Enlightenment itself, crying out, "Wonder of wonders! Intrinsically all living beings are Buddhas, endowed with wisdom and virtue!"

He was thirty-five years of age and he had broken through to what others as yet had only half-dreamed. The Path had been re-opened. The Dharma was once again accessible to the efforts of humans and devas. In the steadily rising morning light, a Supreme Buddha now sat beneath the suddenly blossoming tree.

Angulimala the Robber

Long ago, in India, a child was born to a noble family that dwelt in the city of Sravasti, in the kingdom of Kosala. At the moment of his birth every weapon in the city, from the most elegant ivory-inlaid hunting spear to the crudest cold-hammered iron sword, glittered with a piercing light.

No one had ever seen such a thing. The king, disturbed, called in his wise men to explain this strange event. After studying the heavens they announced that the newborn child, having been born under the Constellation of the Robber, was himself destined to be a robber.

"Will he be a lone robber?" asked the king, "or the leader of a robber gang?"

"A lone robber, Sire."

Then the king announced, "We shall let the child live. His father is a faithful minister. What harm, after all, can one lone robber do?"

So it was decreed. And because of the King's words, the child was named Ahimsaka, meaning "the Harmless One."

As the years passed Ahimsaka grew to be a sensitive and intelligent child. When he was sixteen his father sent him to a noted Brahmin teacher to complete his education.

The teacher, impressed with the boy's kindness, intelligence, and willingness to learn, devoted special attention to Ahimsaka's education. But the other students grew jealous and began to plot against him.

Sometimes alone, sometimes in groups of two or three, they came before their teacher claiming to have seen Ahimsaka embracing the teacher's young wife.

At first the teacher laughed them out. But as his students continued to bring their tales of an intrigue, a seed of doubt was planted in his mind. Well-nurtured, the seed at last blossomed, and the teacher's love for the innocent boy turned to hatred. After much pondering, the teacher devised a plan that would send Ahimsaka to his death.

He called Ahimsaka to him and said, "My son, your spiritual training is almost completed. Only one more task remains. When it is finished your life of suffering will be over. Listen carefully. The task you must achieve is this—you must singlehandedly slay 1,000 men."

"What?" cried the astonished boy. "Kill a thousand men! Why, I couldn't kill one. No, not even a dog! Please, master, do not say such a thing, not even as a joke. You know that killing is the worst of all sins."

"This is no joke," replied the teacher. "I have pondered long and it is clear to me. Slay a thousand men, and your freedom is assured. Fail and you are lost. Come, Ahimsaka, my instruction has always brought you happiness, has it not? Don't be confused. Have courage. The race is almost won. Don't stumble or falter now! All shall be well. You shall see."

That night Ahimsaka paced his little room. "To kill is a grievous sin. That I know. My teacher has always praised kindness. He has always taught me well. Always his words have brought me benefit. Perhaps, then," he thought on, "there is some teaching here which I do not, cannot, as yet understand. Can I refuse his command? Yet how can I carry out such a horrible task? I cannot do this. Yet I must."

At last, against the deepest promptings of his own intuition and the warnings of his judgment and reason, Ahimsaka took up a sword, a spear, a bow, and a quiver of barbed arrows, and set out alone into the dark forest.

A curved, yellowed tooth of a moon slid above the clouds. Pale, ghostly mists coiled up from beneath the shadows of the trees. In the distance, a jackal mournfully howled. An owl hooted and Ahimsaka started with dread. For one last time he cast a lingering glance back towards the safety of the little compound of temples and huts he had come to call home. Then, forcing himself to move on, he let the darkness swallow him.

Soon, in horrible, silent, guilty despair he began to slay travellers on the road. Dropping them in the dust, singly and in pairs, he counted, "one, two..." as they fell. His once bright, quick mind turned grim and dark. His graceful, slender form grew lumpish and thick. His fists dangled at his sides like stones. He neither laughed nor spoke. He took no delight in the singing of the birds or the rustling of the green leaves. Prowling the forests like a beast with tangled locks, staring eyes, and blood-stained hands he drew his weapons and mechanically, without a thought, slew all whom he met.

In time Ahimsaka could not maintain his simple count. Numbers slithered madly through his mind without sequence or meaning, and gave him no peace.

So, he devised a simple way of keeping his count. Each time he killed, he cut a finger from his victim's hand and strung it on a greasy cord, the remnant of an earlier Brahmanic initiation, which still remained around his neck.

In time, a necklace of severed fingers dangled at his throat.

Then, throughout the land, the people whispered a new name, a name like the rattling of dry leaves in a hot wind. The name was Angulimala, "Grisly-Garland." This name the people themselves gave to that one who killed caravans of men, waylaid companies of soldiers, struck down the armed and unarmed alike however they might plead and weep. This was the name of the murderous robber who took a finger from every corpse.

Then the people hid themselves in their homes and stayed far from the forest roads, and such a great silence fell on the thoroughfares of the land it was as if famine or some blight stalked the kingdom and not a lone man.

And Angulimala, once Ahimsaka, counting his garland of fingers in dark simplicity, "one, two, three..." found that he neared his goal. Only one finger more was needed and his horrible task would be done.

A tremor of joy tore through his mind like a hound bounding through a thicket. For a moment his eyes grew clear. Gripping his heavy spear and his polished bow, he slung a quiver of rattling arrows over his shoulder, and set off to find his last victim and his own release.

Now, at this time, the Buddha was residing with his monks in a grove of trees not far from the city of Sravasti. As he sat beneath the trees, he heard a woman sobbing and wailing. He stood up and came to the road, and there he found the woman.

"What grieves you, mother?" asked the Buddha.

"Blessed One!" she sobbed, "It is my son, Ahimsaka, my gentle son. He is the robber, the one they call Angulimala. It is he and no other. I know it. I awoke in the night and my heart cried out beneath my breast and, suddenly," she moaned, "I knew. The king's army is searching. They will find him and slay him. But I shall find him first. I will bring him home. He shall return with me and beg for his pardon."

"I will bring him home for you," said the Buddha. "Be patient. Dry your eyes. The boy shall not die by the king's hand. I promise you he shall come safely home. Return now and do not grieve."

And the Buddha set off walking alone on the dusty road that led through the forest.

Soon the robber, Angulimala, lying in the shadows beneath the trees, saw a lone traveller approaching. Rising to his feet, he raised his spear and called, "Stop, traveller. Your destiny awaits!"

But the Buddha, without turning his head, only walked on. The robber Angulimala laughed. "Walk or run. Do your utmost, friend. These are your moments. Do with them as you will, for they are your last." Then, slinging on his sword and a quiver of arrows, taking up his bow and spear, he began to run after the Buddha.

But, strangely, no matter how fast or how far he ran he could not get within range for a spear or bow shot. The Buddha walked calmly while Angulimala, dripping sweat, his sides heaving, gasping for breath, ran and ran. Yet it was to no avail. He could not catch up.

At last Angulimala slowed, then stopped and stood, bent over, leaning on his spear and gasping for his breath. His lungs ached. Sweat burned his eyes. His glistening sides heaved like those of a dog winded from a long chase. As he raised his eyes, the road, trees, and hills seemed to ripple before him in waves. Spots of light danced in his mind.

Then the Buddha, still walking, turned back and said, "I have stopped, you have not."

"Oh monk," panted Angulimala, nearly in tears from both exertion and confusion, "Some great trickster you must be. For while you only walked, I ran and I could not catch you. Now you walk on, saying you have stopped—and you say I still go on, while I stand here. Come, I beg of you. What can you mean?"

"It means, 'Harmless One'," answered the Buddha, "that I have stopped harming others, while you most certainly have not."

For Angulimala, a veil was lifted. At that instant, he was Ahimsaka once more. Covering his face with his hands, he dropped into the dust, his weapons clattering around him, and cried out, bellowing with horror at the depth of his error and shame.

Then the Buddha asked if he would be willing to give up this life. And he who had been the boy Ahimsaka said, "Yes, I am most certainly willing to leave this life behind."

"Then rise," said the Buddha, "and follow."

But Angulimala said, "No, I cannot. Send for the king and his men. Tell them I shall not lift a finger against them. They must bind me and slay me for I cannot live with this knowledge of my deeds."

"Patience," said the Buddha. "Tie up your despair and your grief. There will always be time to surrender and die. But the time is short in which to struggle and live. Rise, I say, and follow."

So Angulimala rose. He followed, and became a monk.

As a monk, Angulimala discovered that he had power to help women in childbirth. Those exhausted by the difficulties of labor had only to be brought to him and their sufferings would cease instantly. Then, with the ease of water flowing from a pitcher, their children would be born. Even animals could be brought before him, and they too would quickly and painlessly deliver healthy young.

It was a great mystery. How could a man, who had slain so many without a thought of compassion, now have such compassion on those struggling to bring forth new life? Still, for the soothing and healing presence that he brought, the women praised and blessed him.

But Angulimala himself was neither soothed nor healed. Day and night, images of his own past cruelties arose in his mind. He saw tear-stained, bloodied, terrified faces. He saw hands raised protectively as if to ward off heavy blows. He felt dying fingers gripping his ankles in final, loosening supplication. He heard sighs, screams, and groans. In the muscles of his arm he knew again the heft of a sword, felt the shock of blade hitting bone. Voices screamed, "I have a wife. I have children. I have an aged mother! Spare me." Over and over he heard the cries of those who had wept for mercy and had yet been slain.

And as the hot tears gushed down his own cheeks, he cried out many times, "What have I done? How could I have been so blind? I have opened the gates of Hell!"

But always the Buddha counseled him, saying, "Patience, monk, patience."

One hot, dusty morning the monk, Angulimala, walked slowly through the city of Sravasti, the place of his birth, collecting alms for his meal. Though he had become a familiar figure, many still became silent or hurried away at his approach. Others turned their backs, or shut their doors. Now and then, a woman with a nursing child stepped quietly from the shelter of her doorway to place an offering of fruit or rice in his bowl. In silence, head down, Angulimala, with a bow to his donor, received the alms and walked on.

Then suddenly Angulimala staggered and fell. His begging bowl was knocked from his hands and shattered. His robes were torn from his shoulders as every stone flung at any mangy dog or crow, every whip or goad raised against horse or ox or other beast, every club, stick, dagger, knife, or sword lifted by any man against any other throughout that city as well as its surrounding forests and lands—all of these struck not their intended victims, but the monk, Angulimala, alone.

Bleeding, in great pain, with even the bones of his fingers broken, Angulimala gathered his robes to him and groped his way to the Buddha like a blind man.

Then the Buddha sat in the dust with the monk Angulimala and said, "This is the time for patience, monk. The time for great patience has come. Make the most of this moment for it brings the payment of all your debts. Your chance for final freedom has come."

Angulimala roused himself and raised up a great determination. Pushing his mind on and on, he allowed it to settle nowhere. He refused to give in to his agony or to seek refuge in hope, or grief, or fear. The awful and bloody memories came again, but now he let them go. Visions of his childhood, rippling laughter, running water, sunlight on flowers—a stream of sweet images— flowed through his mind. But he clung to nothing. Moment by moment he continued on, patiently enduring all. Suddenly, his pain vanished and his doubting, seeking mind lay shattered. For a timeless instant he knew the taste of Nirvana, the fruit of the Buddha's Path.

Flooded with a joy, like one cured of a long illness at last, he cried out:

"Lesser men subdue with swords, hooks, and sticks.
But, to my eternal relief, I have been subdued by the
  Buddha,
Who needs neither weapon nor whip."

And Ahimsaka, free at last, sighed once, twice, and peacefully died.

In the city of Sravasti, the treetops tossed in a sudden, cooling wind, and once again the weapons glittered, but now with a cleansing flame. The long wandering was over. The Harmless One had come home.

Nalagiri the Elephant

Nalagiri was an elephant, a great tusker. And he was a brute. Huge, violent, ill-tempered; as much like other elephants as an untamed stallion is like a child's pony.

Despite the danger, King Ajaatasatru liked the prestige that came from owning and riding Nalagiri. Also, it was said that rival kings hesitated to attack his kingdom, for fear that they might have to face Nalagiri in battle.

Devadatta, the Buddha's cousin, while a monk, remained proud, cruel, and selfish. Like Nalagiri he was undisciplined. In his quest for power, Devadatta knew no restraint, and had even made attempts—through courtesans, poison, and thugs—on the Buddha's life.

Somehow, all the efforts had failed.

Still Devadatta persisted, his mind twisting and turning, to find some final, foolproof plan. One day he hit upon a plan so simple yet so perfect that he wept for joy. "Nalagiri shall be my emissary!" Devadatta cried. "I shall get the monster drunk, madden him with noise and spears, and release him upon the Buddha's path. The perfect, unpunishable murder will commit itself!"

And off he hurried to the royal elephant stables of King Ajaatasatru. There Devadatta found a man raking the yard clean of soiled straw and elephant dung. "Friend," said Devadatta, "I seek a man who desires to rise in this world; a man willing to take hold of the golden chances that fortune offers."

"Speak on," said the man.

Devadatta smiled. "Friend," he said, "I have a problem. A cousin, mad with power, will not share the reins of his office. If you would help me, your task will be simple. Fill Nalagiri's trough with wine and let Nalagiri drink. Let the fire in the beast be soothed so that he may know peace. Let him be released from his bondage. Yes, at the right time let him know freedom. Release him

from his chains and he shall release me from my problem. Do you understand?"

"Are you not the Devadatta, cousin to the Buddha?"

Devadatta bowed. "At your service."

"It might prove expensive."

Devadatta smiled again. "Friend," he said, "kings wait
upon me. Women, gold, jewels—just name what you desire and you shall have it. Do not fear. Your fortune is
made. You shall shortly see the last of the land of elephant dung. Bring friends. I shall liberate them from
their difficulties too."

And so the plan was made.

The next night, in the early hours before dawn, six
men carried three large, clay jugs into Nalagiri's stall.
Nalagiri's ears fanned forward as he heard liquid
splashing into his trough. He lifted up his trunk and,
smelling the sweetness, walked forward, his chain
clanking. Then he drank. And it was sweet, as sweet as
flowers, as sweet as sugarcane.

Nalagiri's eyes grew soft, half-lidded, and became
flecked with gold. His trunk twirled this way and that.
His ears flapped. Slowly the great beast swayed, first to
one side, then to the other. He lifted a hind foot, then a
front. He gurgled as if singing to himself some long-for-
gotten, peaceful, elephant lullaby.

The stall-cleaner watched from the shadows of the
doorway. Slowly the darkness around him lightened. A
warmth touched his neck and a shadow stretched before
him as the sun crept over the palace wall. It was time.
The stall-cleaner picked up a spear and, signalling the
others to follow, crept forward towards where Nalagiri
swayed and gurgled in the darkness. All had drunk of
the palm wine and the air was sickly sweet with the
smell of it. Now they were set, crouched in place, directly
behind Nalagiri. Their eyes shone with greed and wine,
excitement and fear.

"Now!" shouted the stall-cleaner and they all yelled
loudly. Cymbals crashed. Drums thundered. Spears
jabbed. Nalagiri screamed a wild, mad cacophonous
scream trumpeting so loudly and so shrill that the walls

of the stable shook and the straw-dust billowed up in swirling, choking clouds.

Then Nalagiri whirled on his tormentors, straining with his trunk and tusks to reach and destroy them. The men, terrified, ran. But the chains held. Then the men, released from their fear, laughed and grew angry. One picked up a jagged stone and hurled it so that it struck with a great *thump!* on the bulging dome of Nalagiri's forehead. They laughed again. Nalagiri's eyes blazed with red fire. In his rage, he trumpeted madly and dug at the earth with his tusks. But again the men, made bold by the wine, and trusting in the strength of the chains, raced behind and jabbed the elephant with their spears. Again Nalagiri screamed and whirled. But the men raced behind him again. And again the cymbals crashed. Again the spear points pierced the tender folds of Nalagiri's skin.

"Enough!" shouted the stall-cleaner. "Unbar the gates! Release Nalagiri out onto the streets!" But it was too late. Nalagiri in his frenzy had a strength they had not bargained for.

With a scream Nalagiri hurled himself forward. The chains snapped. On he came, the broken chains whipping his ankles like goads, straight on at his tormentors he charged in his fury, and he caught them still inside the stable. He pounded them with his head and gored them with his tusks. He kneeled upon them, crushing them into the mud and dung and straw. He beat them into the earth with his tusks until only a bloody froth remained. He put his trunk into his own mouth and, in his madness, trumpeted loudly. Then Nalagiri, like some demon of unspeakable power, smashed down the still unbarred gates and stormed out into the early morning streets.

As the Buddha quietly walked through the streets of the city gathering offerings for his morning meal, he heard cries, screams. Crowds streamed past, racing through the streets. "Run, Master!" they yelled. "Run! Nalagiri is loose and he is furious!"

In a great splintering of beams and planks, nearby walls collapsed. There was a great roaring as masonry, stone and brick, came tumbling and crashing down. A black cloud of churning dust and smoke rose up. With a loud flapping of wings, flocks of screaming birds wheeled through the sky. Cattle were bellowing in terror. And above it all rose the wild trumpeting of Nalagiri raging in his madness.

The Buddha walked towards the sounds of destruction. At a safe distance behind him a large crowd of men, women, and children now gathered. Many gathered too on the rooftops and balconies to see what might happen when Nalagiri and the Buddha should meet.

Ananda, the Buddha's attendant and cousin, walked by his side. He had already decided that when the dreaded moment came he would throw himself before Nalagiri so that the Buddha himself might yet be saved.

As they approached the place of Nalagiri's rampage, a hush fell on the crowd. Those on the rooftops also grew silent. Now the only sound was that of Nalagiri in his rage.

The Buddha stopped. At the end of the street Nalagiri kicked at an already crumbling mud-brick wall. He lifted up a shattered bed and flung it into the air. Broken carts, pots, tables, and chairs littered the ground. The body of a bull, its neck broken, lay crumpled against a half-demolished house.

"Come Nalagiri. Come friend," called the Buddha.

Nalagiri spun to face this new threat. He lifted his trunk, sniffing the dust-laden air. Then, trumpeting wildly, he charged.

The crowds, screaming, scattered wildly. Even the monks broke ranks and fled, their orange robes fluttering like great, panicked butterflies around them. But the Buddha stood firm, as Ananda, struggling mightily with his rising fear, remained by his side.

Nalagiri, like a great black cloud, his tusks gleaming like lightning, hurtled toward them. The Buddha smiled, and, advising Ananda to remain where he was, stepped forward and said, "Come then, Nalagiri. Since you seek you shall find." And he extended an infinite tenderness towards Nalagiri, lost and alone in his madness.

Like a shadow of the wind racing along the bending grass blades; like a white, glimmering wave spreading along the shore; like a faint whirring and whirling in the sunlight; like the curling of heated air over the paved roads, something raced towards Nalagiri and broke at last against the rock of his brow.

Nalagiri staggered, slowed. His ears fanned back and forth. His trunk lifted this way and that, sniffing, searching the wind. He stepped uncertainly—now this way, now that—like one lost or confused. The fire in his eyes softened. Tears hung from the long lashes and rolled down the thick gray-black wrinkled hide.

"Come Nalagiri, come friend," repeated the Buddha in a voice sweet as honey.

And Nalagiri, trunk extended, eyes half-closed, stumbled blindly forward; came forward like a lost child that hears its mother calling, like a calf seeking the teat.

The Buddha reached forward his hand and gently touched the curled, thick-skinned, bristly trunk-tip.

Every hair on Nalagiri's body stood erect. His eyes opened wide, rolled upward. His knees buckled and slowly, like a great mountain sinking into the sea, like a mountain of sand washing slowly away in the tide, Nalagiri sank down before the Buddha, sighed once, and rested his great tusked head upon the earth.

"Suffering, friend Nalagiri," said the Buddha, stroking lightly the great dome of Nalagiri's forehead, "is the condition of all life. But there is a Path that leads beyond it. Walk on, friend, with no thoughts of harm towards any living thing. Then shall the darkness lift. Rise now, Nalagiri, and be at peace."

Then Nalagiri arose, and flinging his trunk back up upon his head, trumpeted the royal salute. After that he stood calmly, quietly swinging his trunk and tail, until his frightened mahout came forward and led him back to the palace stables.

Then the people cheered, tossing scarves, coins, and flowers into the air. Musicians beat drums and loudly played flutes and pipes. The king himself rushed down from a palace balcony and exclaimed, "Today we have seen such a miracle as never before. The Buddha, without weapons or force, has stopped Nalagiri in his rampage. He has pacified the heart of that great beast. So let us celebrate! Whoever has suffered losses this day, even so little as the smallest grain of rice, let them come forward and they shall have compensation from my own hands. Tonight, O World-Honored One, dine with me at the palace. Speak, and tonight I shall listen! This very day a flower of faith has opened in my heart!"

In a nearby alley, one lone angry face brooded from the shadows. It was Devadatta. For an instant, the walls of his pride had fallen, and he too had gazed with wonder upon the unlikely scene. In that instant a sudden, wild impulse had arisen in his heart, an impulse to rush forward and, with Nalagiri, also find peace. But no, he would not give in to it. Wrapping his robes even more tightly around him he withdrew further yet into the shadows.

The Buddha saw that slight movement and sorrowed. Yet at the same time he saw, too, that distant day, ages hence, when Devadatta himself would step forever from all darkness. After countless kalpas in the deepest hells he would rise, restored to himself at last, and be a Buddha.

So, with the faithful Ananda by his side and amidst the great joyful noise of the people, the Buddha set off through the city towards the palace of his host, the king.

Kisa Gotami

Once, a young woman named Kisa Gotami married into a wealthy family, but it was not until she had had a child, a son, that she was fully accepted by her in-laws. Kisa Gotami doted on the child, loving to distraction its every perfect bone, its dark eyes, its tiny toes, its smiles and sighs.

When Kisa Gotami's child grew sick, and then, despite all efforts, died, she became crazed. She would let no one take the child from her. In her unbalanced mind she clung to one thought: the Buddha, the Teacher, the Great Physician, could save her from this nightmare and restore her child.

With the child on her hip, she left her husband's home and set off to find the Buddha. She arrived at the assembly and approached the Buddha to make her request. "World Honored One," she begged, "please restore my child."

The Buddha said this to the heart-broken woman, Kisa Gotami. "I will do so under one condition. You must bring to me one tiny mustard seed from a house in which no one has died. Then I shall bring your child to life again."

Kisa Gotami ran off in joy. Entering the town she knocked on the first door. "Have you," she breathlessly asked, "any mustard seed? It is for my child."

The woman of the house said, "Yes, my dear, I can give you some mustard seed."

"I need only one," said Kisa Gotami

"One seed?" asked the woman, surprised.

"Yes, one."

"I can give you one mustard seed."

Kisa Gotami's heart leaped. Soon her child would live, would smile and sigh and laugh and cling to her with tiny perfect hands. "Excuse me, but no one has died in this house, have they?" asked Kisa Gotami.

"My dear," answered the woman at the door, "my father died only last week."

"Oh," said Kisa Gotami, "I must find my seed elsewhere."

Again she knocked, and again she requested a mustard seed, and again a mustard seed was offered. Who did not have one tiny mustard seed to spare for a distraught woman and her child?

"Excuse me," said Kisa Gotami. "You have not had a death here recently?"

"My dear, my husband passed away a month ago."

"I must search elsewhere," said Kisa Gotami.

To house after house she went. Household after household freely offered her the mustard seed she required. But from house after house Kisa Gotami turned away with a sinking heart. In each house the story was the same. "My mother has died, my aunt, my mother-in-law, my wife, my daughter, my brother, my uncle, my father, my nephew, my cousin, my father-in-law, my son." On and on, like an endless lament rising from every household. There was not a single household in the city, from the palace of the king to the beggars' hovels, in which such a magical mustard seed could be found, a mustard seed from a household in which no one had died.

Kisa Gotami found herself walking the streets of the city with her dead baby on her hip. She had come back to herself. Her eyes were clear, her mind alert. The sorrow she now bore was no longer her sorrow alone. It was the sorrow of all. All that is born, she now knew, dies. All that comes into being must, sooner or later, exit again from being. There is no household that death spares. This was the hard, simple truth. She knew it now.

She took up her dead child in her arms and kissed it gently. She kissed the perfect forehead, the curling fingers, the tiny toes. She brought her baby home, wrapped a tiny mustard seed in its funeral garments and, at last, said her farewell. When the funeral was completed she left that house, and returned to the Buddha.

"Well, Kisa Gotami," asked the Buddha, "was your quest successful? Did you, my sister, find the mustard seed that brings life from death?"

"World Honored One," she answered, "the mustard seed that I could find I have already left with my own beloved child. All that is born dies. Every child. Every mother. Every king. Every man. Every woman. Every cow, dog, tree, and star. All go the same route. I have found the mustard seed. Now I make of you one request. Accept me in the Order. I was dead. I have come to learn how to live."

Kisa Gotami was received by the Buddha into the Order and, working hard, gained Liberation.

Parinirvana

In his eightieth year, the Buddha became ill and admitted to Ananda that the time of his departure was near. His body, he said, was like a worn out cart that could only be kept going with difficulty. Only in meditation, he added, when all sense of the body had been transcended, did he know any ease.

The Buddha then addressed his monks saying, "Brothers, all component things grow old. Work out your salvation with diligence. Time waits for no one. In three months' time the Tathagata, One-Who-Has-Thus-Come, will enter Nirvana!"

Hearing this, tears ran from Ananda's eyes like sap from a broken tree.

Then the Buddha, accompanied by many monks and with Ananda by his side, walked to Pava, stopping at the mango grove of the smith, Cunda. The smith received instruction from the Teacher; then, his heart gladdened, he fed the assembly a lavish meal.

During that meal, the Buddha ate some mushrooms. Immediately he told Ananda to set the dish aside and let no one else eat of it, for the mushrooms were spoiled. Shortly after this he was struck with such pain that he could hardly stand. When the pain had abated, he and Ananda set off for Kusinara.

The Buddha was quite weak now, and they walked slowly, taking their time to complete the journey, resting by the riverbanks and beneath the trees as they went. During that journey the Buddha counseled Ananda that no one was to blame Cunda the smith, nor was the smith himself to feel any blame, for serving the meal. "Two meals are supremely precious to all Buddhas," he said. "One is received just before the One-Who-Has-Thus-Come attains to perfect Enlightenment and the second is the last meal, the one received just prior to a Buddha's entrance into Nirvana. Therefore," he added, "everyone

should know that, with this final meal, Cunda the smith
has established a very good karma, beneficial to himself
and to others. There is no reason at all for him to
grieve."

At last they arrived at the sala tree grove of the
Mallas at Kusinara, on the far shore of the Hiranyavati
River. It was almost three months to the day from the
time of the Buddha's initial pronouncement of his going
forth into Nirvana. Then the Buddha turned to Ananda
and said, "Ananda, please set up a couch for me between
the twin sala trees, with my head lying to the North. I
must lie down now. I can go no further."

Weeping, Ananda did as the Buddha requested, spreading and folding a cloth over the great stone couch that
lay between the trees. The Buddha then reclined on his
right side upon this couch, and ever mindful, alert, and
self-possessed, rested beneath the trees.

Though it was out of season, the twin sala trees flow-
ered, and blossoms rained down from the branches and
from the sky. Unearthly music sounded. Ananda was astonished by these miracles, but the Buddha said, "It is
not thus that the World Honored One is truly revered.
Those who do good, who uphold the practices and precepts of good character, who fulfill their duties in life,
both great and small; those who gain an entry into the
Dharma and discover that they and all beings are intrinsically Buddhas, it is such as these who, whether
monks or nuns, laymen or laywomen, of this faith or
any other, truly revere the Tathagata. Now know,
Ananda, this very night the Tathagata will enter
Nirvana. Then there will be no more limited return, no
further error or suffering."

The birds grew very quiet and uttered no sound, sitting along the branches as if in trance, their bodies relaxed. Monks and nuns, advanced disciples and begin-
ners, their faces covered with tears, gathered in the grove
as the light of the afternoon deepened and gathered.

"Go Ananda," said the Blessed One, "and tell the
Mallas that the time has come. They will be stricken
with grief if they are not permitted to attend me before

my Nirvana." Ananda, faint with grief himself, obeyed the order.

The Mallas, their eyes streaming with tears, soon arrived. Ananda presented them to the reclining Buddha, as family by family paid homage to the Teacher. Then, anguish in their minds, they stood weeping among the trees of their sala grove.

A lone, wandering truth-seeker named Subhadda, troubled with doubts, arrived hoping to see the Buddha while time remained. But Ananda refused him an interview, saying, "The Exalted One is growing weaker, friend. The hour is late. Do not trouble him now." But the Buddha overheard this, and asked that the wanderer Subhadda be admitted to him. Subhadda questioned the Buddha, and with the Buddha's replies his doubts were resolved. He was admitted into the Order, the last disciple to be personally accepted by the Buddha.

Then the World Honored One, seeing the Mallas still so caught in the coils of their distress, called them to him and said: "In this hour of joy, there is no need to grieve. Your despair is inappropriate and you should regain your composure! The goal, so hard to win, which for so many eons I have wished for, longed for, and worked hard for, is now at hand. When that is won there is no earth, water, fire, wind, or air present, but unchanging bliss, beyond all objects of the senses, a peace which none can ever take away. The highest thing alone there is. When you hear of that and know that no becoming mars it and that nothing there can ever pass away—how then can there still be any room in your minds for grief? At Bodh Gaya, when I won Enlightenment, I got rid of the causes of becoming which are really nothing but a gang of harmful vipers. Now the hour nears when I also will get rid of this body, the crystallization of my own thoughts and deeds arising from an endless past. Now that at last the frightful dangers of becoming are about to become extinct, now that they are to be blown out, as a candle's flame is blown out by the wind, now that at last I emerge from the vast and endless suffering—is this really the time for you to grieve?"

The oldest of the Mallas alone found the strength to respond. "You all weep, but why? We should look upon the Awakened One as a man who has escaped from the danger of a house on fire! The gods see it like that; so should we too. Yet the cause of our grief remains. This mighty man, the Tathagata, once he has won Nirvana, will pass beyond our knowledge and sight. When those who travel in the wilderness lose their guide, they fall into distress. That is how we feel. People who walk away from a gold mine with no riches themselves are to be pitied. Likewise those who have seen the great Teacher in his actual person ought to have gained some spiritual achievement of their own! O World Honored One, this is why we weep!" They all folded their hands, palm to palm and stood like children before their father. The old man had spoken to the point.

Then the Buddha, aiming at their welfare, addressed them a final time. "Salvation cannot come from the mere sight of me. It demands strenuous efforts in actual spiritual practice. But if someone has truly seen my Dharma, then he is released from the net of suffering, even though he has never seen me at all. Similarly, the mere sight of a physician cures no illness. One must actually take the medicine to be well. The mere sight of me enables no one to conquer suffering; each person has to meditate for himself or herself to discover the truth of the experience I have communicated. If disciplined, a man or woman may live as far away from me as can be. If he or she only sees my Dharma then that person truly sees me as well. But if a person should neglect to strive in concentrated calm for higher things, then, though he or she may live quite near to me, it will be as if they are far away. So work hard for truth's sake. Do good deeds and strive resolutely for mindfulness. Be vigilant! Remember life is continually shaken by many kinds of suffering even as the flame of a lamp is shaken by the wind."

In this way the Sage, the Best of All Who Live, encouraged and fortified the Mallas. But still their tears continued to flow, and as they went back to Kusinara each one felt helpless and alone, as if crossing a swollen river on a dark and stormy night.

Then the Buddha turned to his disciples and said to them: "Everything comes to an end, though it may last for an eon. The hour of parting is bound to come. Now I have done all I could do, both for myself and for others; to stay here from now on would be without purpose. I have disciplined, in Heaven and on Earth, all those I could discipline. I have trained them and motivated them and have set them in the stream that leads to liberation. Hereafter, my Dharma shall abide for generations and generations among living beings. Recognize the True Nature of the living world, and do not be anxious. Separation cannot be avoided. All that lives is subject to this law—yet strive from this day onwards that it shall be no more! When the light of Wisdom has dispelled the darkness of Ignorance, when all existence has been seen as without abiding substance, peace ensues when life draws to an end, a peace which seems to cure a long sickness at last. Everything, whether stationary or movable, is bound to perish in the end. Be mindful and vigilant! The time for my entry into Nirvana has arrived! These are my last words!"

As the Buddha entered Nirvana, the Earth quivered like a ship at sea struck by a storm, and firebrands fell from the sky. Rivers boiled. The heavens were lit by fire that burned without fuel or smoke. Thunderbolts crashed, winds raged. The moon's light waned and, in spite of a cloudless sky, darkness spread everywhere. Beautiful flowers grew out of season on the sala trees above the Buddha's couch, and the trees bent down over him and showered his golden body with blossoms.

The mighty five-headed Nagas, the great serpents, stood motionless in the sky, their eyes red with grief, their hoods closed as, with deep devotion, they gazed on the body of the Sage. The Gods of the Pure Abode remained composed, deep in their non-attachment to the things of this world. The kings of the Gandharavas and Nagas as well as the yakshas and devas who rejoice in the Dharma all appeared in the sky, mourning and absorbed in the utmost grief.

The world, when the great Sage had passed beyond, became like a mountain whose peak had been shattered by a thunderbolt; it became like the sky without the moon, like a pond whose lotuses have been withered by the frost.

Those who had not yet gotten rid of their passions shed bitter tears. Most of the monks lost their composure and gave way to their grief. Only those who had completed their training were not shaken to their depths. For, like the Buddha himself, they well understood that it is in the nature of all created things to pass away.

On the seventh day after the passing into Nirvana, the body of the Buddha was borne in state to the shrine of the Mallas, where it was set upon a perfumed pyre and consigned to the flames. The bones that remained were honored for another seven days. Then, at last, these relics of the Great Teacher were divided into eight portions and distributed equally among those families and territories among whom the Buddha had most often taught and travelled.

Section II:
Jataka Tales

Give It All You've Got

In a certain lifetime, long ago, the Buddha was a merchant and a traveller. He gained much experience of life, survived many hardships, and learned much about the ways of differing peoples. He became wise and gathered some wealth.

At one time, when he was already a grey-bearded and dignified man, he was bringing a caravan of goods across a sandy desert. He had almost one hundred ox-drawn carts filled with cloth, spices, and grain. Many men were in his employ at that time, and he hired, in addition, a desert pilot to guide them safely through the vast wasteland.

A desert pilot is a man who knows the land and knows the stars. Like a pilot at sea, he navigates by starlight, and so can lead a caravan safely across the most featureless desert terrain.

Because of the terrible heat, the caravan rested during the day under awnings, men and oxen both. Then at night, in the coolness after the sun had gone down, the men would hitch up the oxen and set off again under the stars. In this way they travelled safely some six days across the sands. They had water and wood and food enough for yet another day or so of travelling, and the men and oxen were tired.

That night the pilot, seated in the lead wagon, announced that by morning they would be beyond the desert. Wood, water, food—all would again be plentiful. So they unloaded the remaining water jars, the sacks of rice, and the wood they carried for building cooking fires and, with their loads lightened, set off on the final trek.

The pilot had been up, on constant watch for six nights. The excessive heat and glaring light of the day had made sleep difficult. Now, as they neared their destination, he dozed off. The wagons rolled on. The oxen marched steadily through the darkness. The stars glittered overhead in the clear desert air. Men laughed and joked.

Just before dawn the pilot awoke with a start. He glanced at the stars and cried out in alarm. Rather than going straight and true on their course they had been veering in a great half-circle through the night. They were no nearer the desert's ending than they had been at the sun's going down! Men and oxen were already quite thirsty. In an hour the sun would rise like a great ball of fire. The desert would become hot as a blast-furnace. Soon they would all be consumed by thirst. Their water had been left behind. "Halt!" cried the pilot. "Stop the wagons! Stop!"

The open, cloth shelter was erected and all huddled beneath the protection it offered from the searing rays of the desert sun.

The merchant leader of the caravan was no newcomer to danger. He stepped out from the shade of the shelter and began to walk along the dunes.

Soon he spied what he had been searching for. A few pale tufts of grass rising from the sand.

"Bring shovels!" he called, "and quickly!" His men hurried forward, shovels and picks in hand. "Dig," he said, "where this grass grows. Dig, for our lives depend upon it."

Down they dug into the sands, deeper and deeper. The exertion in that heat was terrible. Men gasped and fainted. Many times they thought to just give up and wait for death. But the merchant stood firmly by them. "Dig," he said. "I know it is hard, but where grass grows there is water. Just trust me and do your best." So, on they dug.

At last they had a narrow well-pit extending some fifteen feet straight down. At the very bottom of the shaft the sand was cool and carried some moisture in it. So, parched and exhausted as they were, they had hope and took turns going down to the well bottom and digging on with a will. Soon, it seemed they would have cool water.

But, alas, their efforts were doomed to fail. After another foot or two of digging they hit a great stone running across their way. There was no way to dig around it. The narrow shaft, already sliding with sand, would collapse if the base were widened any further. In despair they all lay exposed on the hot sands and wept.

"Don't give up yet," said the grizzled merchant. "Tie a rope around me and lower me down into the well."

As they lowered him down loose, shifting sand slid and hissed ominously down around him. He knelt upon the stone and put his ear to it. He could hear, like a distant hum, the movement of water beneath the stone. "Up!" he called. "Draw me up."

The tunnel was treacherous. With every pull he had to keep from brushing the well-sides and causing the whole shaft to collapse. He came out covered with sand; grim, but smiling.

"The water is just below the stone," said the wise merchant. "Get a sledge hammer and bring to me the strongest and most well-rested man among you."

A sledge hammer was brought and a large-framed, big-boned youth was led before the merchant.

"Son," said the merchant, "it's up to you. The stone at the well-bottom must be broken. The water is flowing just below that stone. Rouse your every confidence. You are the strongest among us. Our lives depend on your determination. Take this hammer and break that stone."

The youth was lowered carefully down into the hole and landed safely upon the stone. There was hardly room for him to swing the hammer, but he lifted it up and hit the stone a great blow. The stone didn't budge. He tried again. And again. It was nerve-wracking work. The water was definitely just below. He could feel the whole stone humming with the force of its flow. But if one careless swing were to hit the tunnel wall the whole shaft might cave in upon him. He wiped his brow, again carefully lifted up the hammer and again brought it down with a great jarring blow. Again and again he swung. Still the stone would not break.

The youth could not go on. The constant threat of the tunnel's collapse, his own thirst and weakness, the solidity of that unyielding stone, the hissing of the sands sliding down the shaft, all conspired to sap his deepest reserves of strength.

"Pull me up!" he cried. "Get me out! It is hopeless."

The merchant stuck his head down into the dry well shaft. "Son, it's difficult, but not hopeless. You can do it. The stone will break. Don't give up. If there was ever a time to exert your strength to the limit this is it. Give it one more shot and give it all you've got!"

Heartened, the youth lifted up the hammer one more time and swung it with his whole heart and strength. The rock cracked, split, and a geyser of cool water shot up.

Quickly, they hoisted him out of the well as the water surged up, bubbling and dancing from the hole.

The merchant's fortitude and the youth's strength had saved them.

After drinking their fill and filling their vessels they tended to the oxen, then made their way safely out of the desert.

In that desert the well bubbles still. Even today, travellers in the wasteland praise the men who left this bounty for them.

The Brave Lion
and the Foolish Rabbit

Once a foolish little rabbit was resting peacefully in the shade beneath a mango tree. He wasn't wide awake, and he wasn't completely asleep. He just lay there drifting between waking and sleeping. As he lay there, a foolish thought crossed his mind. "What if the earth broke up?" He sat up now, wide awake. "What if the earth broke up today?!"

Suddenly, he heard a loud *CRASH!* right behind him. And, without turning to see what it was, he jumped up and ran off crying, "The earth is breaking up! The earth's breaking up! Run! Run!"

As he ran, he passed a second little rabbit. "Say, friend," called out this second rabbit, "what's the hurry? Why are you running?"

But the first rabbit was too scared. He wouldn't stop. He wouldn't tell his friend what it was that was bothering him. He just turned, looked over his shoulder and shouted out, "The earth is breaking up! The earth is breaking up! Run! Run!"

"The earth's breaking up?! The earth's breaking up?!" cried the second rabbit. "Why, then, wait for me!" And off he ran too.

Pretty soon they passed a third rabbit. "What's happening?" called the third rabbit. "Why are you both running?"

But those two rabbits were too scared. They wouldn't stop. They just looked over their shoulders as they ran past and shouted out loudly, "Run! Run! The earth's breaking up!"

And that third rabbit said, "The earth's breaking up!! Well, wait for me!"

So now there were three rabbits running along. Pretty soon there were four rabbits, then five rabbits, then ten rabbits, twenty rabbits, thirty rabbits, forty rabbits, fifty rabbits, one hundred rabbits all running along.

And they all ran past a big, sleepy bear. The bear rubbed his sleepy eyes and said, "Wha-at's hap-pen-ing? Why are you all run-ning?"

But the rabbits were too scared to stop. They just shouted over their shoulders, "The earth's breaking up! Run! Run!"

"The earth's break-ing up?" repeated the bear in shock, "The earth's break-ing up?! Why, why, why if the earth's break-ing up, I'd better get go-ing too!"

And off he ran, crying out in his slow, sturdy bear's voice, "The earth's break-ing up! The earth's break-ing up! Run! Run!"

Soon he passed another bear. And that bear called, "What's going on? Why are you running?" But that first bear was too scared. He just looked over his shoulder as he ran past, and shouted, "Run! Run! The earth's break-ing up!"

And that second bear said, "The earth's break-ing up? The earth's break-ing up?! Why, why if the earth's breaking up, wait for me!" So now there were two bears running along.

Pretty soon they passed a third bear. He was sitting on the ground chewing on a piece of dripping honeycomb and batting at the bees buzzing all around him. "Hey," he called out. "Where are you going? Why are you running? Stop and tell me!"

But those two bears were too scared to stop. They wouldn't even stop for some of that sweet honeycomb. They just turned, looked over their shoulders, and shouted out, "The earth's breaking up! Run! Run!" And they kept on running.

"What?! What's that you say?" exclaimed the third bear rising to his feet. "The earth's breaking up? The earth's breaking up. Well wait for me!" And pushing all of the remaining honeycomb into his mouth he scrambled off leaving the bees buzzing angrily in the empty air.

Now there were three bears running along. Pretty soon there were four bears, then five bears, then ten bears, twenty bears, thirty bears, forty bears, fifty bears, one hundred frightened bears all running along. Oh what a howling and growling; what a din they made!

And they all ran past an elephant. The elephant stood dozing under a great shade tree. His huge ears fanned slowly back and forth. His tail swished behind him, this way and that, sweeping off the droning flies. Suddenly his ears swung forward and stopped. His eyes opened wide. One hundred screaming rabbits and one hundred moaning bears burst through the bushes and rushed past him. "What's going on?" trumpeted the elephant. "Why are you all running?" he demanded. "Stop and tell me!"

But those animals were too scared. They wouldn't stop. They just turned, looked over their shoulders, and shouted out, "The earth's breaking up! The earth's breaking up! Run! Run!" And they were gone!

The elephant was wide awake now! "The earth's breaking up?" he exclaimed. "The earth's breaking up?! Why, I'm the biggest and heaviest of all creatures. If the earth's breaking up I'll be the first one to fall in!" And trumpeting in terror, he too charged off, his tail pointed straight out behind him, running madly after the others.

Soon they ran past a second elephant. Then another and another. Soon there were five trumpeting elephants stampeding along behind the rabbits and the bears. Then ten elephants, twenty elephants, thirty elephants, forty elephants, fifty elephants, one hundred elephants all trumpeting loudly in their fear and charging along as fast as they could. On they went, tearing up trees and bushes, tossing boulders, pounding the earth with their great feet, raising up a great cloud of dust, and a great, wild trumpeting cry.

They all passed a snake sunning itself on a warm rock ledge. "Ssssay," hissed the snake, anxiously lifting his smooth, scaled head. "What'ssss happening? Why are you all running? The earth issss ssshaking sssso. Issss it an earthquake?"

"The earth's breaking up!" trumpeted the elephants with their snake-like trunks. "Run! Run!"

"The earth'ssss breaking up?" hissed the snake. The earth'ssss breaking up? Why, if the earthssss breaking up, it issss the end! I'd better get ssssliding!" And off he went, sliding over boulders, under bushes, around trees. Soon they passed another snake.

"Ssssay," hissed that snake. "Whatssss the hurry? Whatssss happening?"

"The earth'ssss breaking up!" called the first snake. "Sssslither! Sssslide!" And, without pausing an instant or diverting the set of his ruby eyes, he flowed quickly on over stones and stumps, following the great crowd of animals running ahead, and was gone!

"The earth'ssss breaking up!" repeated that second snake, shocked. And then off he slid as well.

Soon they passed another snake. And another. Then there were four, five, ten, twenty, thirty, forty, fifty, one hundred snakes all sliding along. One hundred elephants charging straight ahead, one hundred bears barrelling through the bushes, one hundred rabbits leaping leaping leaping. And all of them were so scared they were shouting loudly, at the tops of their lungs, "Help! help! The earth's breaking up! Run! Run!" Soon the buffalo had joined in this great flight of the beasts, as did the rhinoceros, the boars, and the deer. Now a great host of beasts was charging through the jungle.

Up on top of a mountain overlooking this jungle was a brave lion, asleep. The lion, the Buddha in an earlier birth, heard all those screams and cries. Opening his golden eyes, he looked out over the jungles and saw all those animals running madly in great terror. But he couldn't see why they were running. As he watched he saw that unless someone stopped them quickly they would run over the edge of a cliff and die.

"Someone should help those frightened animals," said the lion to himself. "Why," he said, "I'll help."

Rising to his feet he shook his heavy mane. Rousing all his great lion's strength he *leaped* out over the jungle, his golden mane streaming behind him, and landed in front of all those terrified animals.

"*ARRRRAAAUGHHHHRROARRRRR!*" roared the lion, stopping the flight of the maddened beasts. "Why are you all running?"

"Because the earth's breaking up! The earth's breaking up!" cried the frightened animals. "Let us go, mighty lion, before we are all killed!"

"The earth's not breaking up. Look," said the lion, "here's the earth, right under your feet. It's as solid as it's ever been," and he tapped the earth with his paw to prove it. "Who told you that the earth was breaking up?"

The deer said "boars;" the boars, "rhinoceros;" the rhinoceros, "buffalo;" the buffalo, "snakes." "It wassss the elephantssss" hissed the snakes. "Bears!" trumpeted the elephants. "Uh, rab-bits," said the bears. "Him, him, him, him, him, him, him, him, him, him!" said the rabbits, pointing down the whole long line of rabbits until they came to the foolish little rabbit. "He told us," they all said.

"Well, little rabbit," asked the lion gently, "where did you see the earth breaking up?

"I heard it," said the little rabbit. "Back there." And he pointed back into the forest. "Under a great mango tree."

"You heard it?" repeated the lion, "and under a mango tree?" *Why*, he thought to himself, *this little rabbit must have heard a ripe fruit falling from the tree and hitting the earth. I must show these animals they have nothing to fear.*

"Come little rabbit," said the lion, "get up on my back. Let's go back to the tree together and see what it was that really scared you."

"Oh no," said the little rabbit, still shaking with fear. "I couldn't do that. It's much too dangerous."

"Do not worry," said the lion gently. "There is nothing to fear. But as you alone can guide me to your tree, you must come with me." Then, placing the frightened rabbit on his back, he set off in great lion leaps back along the trail they had originally travelled.

Soon they reached the tree. The lion stalked around the tree. He sniffed the earth. Then he picked up something with his paw and he laughed.

There, sure enough, was the mango, a ripe mango that had fallen from the tree.

"Here's your earth breaking up, little rabbit," said the lion. "You heard this ripened fruit fall from the tree and you thought it was the earth breaking up!" And he handed the mango to the rabbit. "Now let us return and tell the others."

Then, once again, with the great speed of a lion, he raced back along the trail to where the others waited.

"Friends," said the lion, when they had returned, "I have been to the rabbit's tree myself and can tell you that it was only a ripe fruit falling from the tree that led to your mad flight. The thud of a falling mango, this was your 'earth breaking up.' Remember this next time something frightens you. Take a good look at it for yourselves, and do not be afraid. Maybe you'll discover that, like this falling mango, it is nothing that can really hurt you."

Then the animals returned happily to their homes.

The lion leaped back up onto his mountaintop, lay down, and calmly surveyed the now peaceful jungle below.

The little rabbit, still holding his mango, hopped back to his tree, lay down under the tree, and took a big bite of the mango. Ummm, but it was sweet!

The Quail and the Falcon

Once the Buddha was a little quail. One day, he decided he'd had enough of pecking out his living on the hard, sun-baked earth.

"I'll make my way into greener fields," he said. "I need a change."

Flapping his wings, he rose up and flew off over the dry plains without a regret. Soon he was flying over entirely new terrain. Green grass waved in the sunlight. Streams rippled and ran below. The little quail was beside himself with delight. "This is it," he said to himself. "Paradise!" And down he spiralled towards his new home.

But he was not alone. A great falcon, flying high above, saw the little quail and, folding his wings, dove down upon him. In less than a minute the little quail had been plucked from the sky and, in shock, found himself in the falcon's grasp.

"I'm lost! What chance do I have?!" thought the little quail in despair. But before sinking down into a final flutter of panic, he said to himself, "He is a fierce falcon, and I'm just a little quail. Still, if I just keep my wits about me, I may even the odds yet."

And, instead of weeping and crying, he now shouted loudly, "Unfair! Unfair!"

"What?" said the falcon, surprised. "Why, little bird, whatever can you mean?"

"Just that you caught me at a disadvantage, that's all!" exclaimed the little quail. "You caught me far from my home. But on my own home ground you never could have caught me. There you'd find it impossible to turn me into a meal!"

The falcon found this hard to believe. Yet he was intrigued. No quail had ever said such things to him before. The others had wept or screamed, had fainted away or pleaded for their lives. And in the end, he had eaten them all. This was a new twist. "Little bird," he said, bending his great sharp beak and fierce yellow eyes down towards the quail, "whatever do you mean?"

"I mean that on my home ground I'm free. Just try and get me there. Big as you are, you'd be no match for me there!"

"Surely you jest," said the falcon, bringing the razor-like edge of his beak even closer.

The little quail closed his eyes, took a deep breath, and said, "Why should I jest? If I'm wrong you'll eat me. I'll be your supper anyway. What's the matter?" he added bravely, opening his eyes once more, "don't you think you can bring it off?"

"Come," said the falcon, irritated despite himself, "show me your home ground, you foolish little braggart, and that," he added with a meaningful squeeze of his claws, "will be that!"

When the little quail felt the falcon's claws closing tighter around him, he almost gave up all hope. But then, catching his breath, he yelled, "Just fly on, fly on. We're almost there." And sure enough, in another minute his own old dry, dusty patch was directly below. A wave of relief and joy flooded the little quail's heart and yelling even louder now he called out, "There it is! Down below!"

"What?" said the falcon, peering down, "that sun-baked field? Surely, you can't have grown into such a great, big, powerful bird like yourself down there?" And he laughed.

"Well," said the quail, "just set me down in the middle of my field and we'll soon see who's strongest!"

"All right," said the falcon, "I will."

And swooping down he set the little quail free in the center of the field. The earth was dry and sun-baked, the grasses yellow and stiff. But the little quail hopped up and down with excitement. "This is it. Home sweet home! Watch out now! Just try and get me!"

"Be right back," smiled the falcon, and with a great flapping of his wings, he soared up and up and up, higher and higher and higher. At last he was so high up that he looked like a tiny dot, almost lost against the bright sky and sun. At the top of his climb, the falcon suddenly turned, folded his wings in against his body, and dropped, sharp beak first, straight down, like a living stone, toward the little quail who sat exposed and alone in the center of the field. Down, down, down he fell, faster and faster and faster.

The defenseless quail crouched down low against the hard, sun-baked earth and watched the falcon growing larger and larger above him. First the falcon seemed to be only a speck, then a dot, then a pebble, then, at last, a great, fierce, yellow-eyed bird, talons outstretched, dropping like a lightning bolt, directly upon him. The time had come.

With a sudden motion the little quail hopped up and leapt aside. And the falcon, wide-eyed, tearing down at top speed, had no chance to swerve aside. *CRASH!* He hurtled into the rock-hard earth and instantly died.

Then the little quail flapped his wings, whistled, and danced for joy. His home ground had, indeed, saved him.

The Steadfast Parrot

Once there was a parrot. His feathers were beautiful, with rich colors of green, red, and yellow. His eyes were shiny and black, his beak a pale yellow. Altogether, he was a most handsome bird.

This parrot lived in a fig tree. And oh, how he loved that tree! He loved the way its leaves shaded him from the harsh, glaring light of the midday sun. He loved the cool shade it cast over him. He loved its endless whisperings, its creakings and rustlings. He loved the way its branches rose and fell, swaying with every breeze. He loved the feel of the cool, smooth bark beneath his toes. He loved the sweet fruit it so freely gave him.

Every evening as he settled on the branches of his tree-home, he would say, "How happy I am. How content, peaceful, and free. I owe my tree so very much. I'll never abandon it for another refuge." And closing his eyes he would listen with delight to the soft music of the tree's fluttering leaves.

Shakra, King of the Gods, heard the parrot's words and decided to test him. He withered the tree and dried it until the leaves blackened and died. Dust now lay on the branches where sweet dews once gathered.

But the parrot would not leave. He sat on the dead branches. Slowly lifting his claws, he climbed from branch to branch, circling the tree to keep from the glaring sunlight which beat upon him. In his mind's eye he could see it, covered not with dust, but with green leaves, all swaying and rustling in the breeze. "Should friends part just because bitter fortune has struck?" said the parrot to himself. "Days pass and fortunes change.

"My words were sincere and true
And my tree I'll not leave you."

And he would not leave. Though days passed the parrot remained steadfast and content. Perched on the dead branches among the dry, rattling leaves, he watched the sun rise and he watched it set. But he did not abandon his tree-home.

Shakra, watching, smiled—and a golden breeze blew. New buds formed, green leaves unfolded, fruits swelled, and the dust, whirling, blew away. Amazed, the parrot sat sheltered once again among the green, leafy branches of his beloved tree.

"Little bird," said the King of the Gods, "the whole universe is brought to life by a steadfast and faithful heart. Even the lofty gods smile when meeting one who has attained such unwavering contentment. While outwardly you may only be a little bird, inwardly you bear the gift of life.

"Live contented with your tree
And may all beings so contented be."

And, laughing, the great god Shakra rose up into the bluest of blue skies.

The steadfast little parrot, once again sipping the sweet dews, rubbed his beak against the cool, smooth bark. Oh, how contented he was!

Prince Five-Weapons

Once, long ago, the Buddha was born as a prince. When the boy was sixteen years of age, his father, the king, said to him. "My son, you are almost grown. Soon you shall be old enough to help me rule the kingdom. The time has come for you to journey to the city of Takkasila, where the greatest weapons-masters live. Learn to master the five weapons, then return and help me rule. Now," he added, "are you ready for this journey?"

"Of course, Father!" said the boy. And the next morning, just as the sun was rising and the birds were beginning to sing, he set off on the roads. He walked and walked. He climbed high mountains, crossed swift rivers, and went through dark forests. At last he arrived at the city of Takkasila, the city famed for its weapons-masters. And there, under the direction of a wise weapons-master, he began to train in the use of the five weapons.

Each day, just as the sun was rising, out he would go into the practice yard to shoot arrow after arrow from his sturdy bow. When his arrows were all gone he'd lift his spear and hurl it. Then, drawing his sword, he'd slash and lunge and parry. Finally, he'd raise a great club and smash and pound with it. By the time the sun was setting, the boy, exhausted, collapsed onto his little bed to sleep until the sun rose again.

And when the sun rose, once more out the young prince would go, and all would begin as before—shooting and throwing and slashing and smashing. Gradually, the prince became stronger and faster. His eyes grew keener, his aim surer. Days turned into weeks. Weeks became months. Months were soon a year. Still the young prince practiced on.

Then, one day, when a year had passed, the old weapons-master called the boy to him and said, "Young prince, you are disciplined and accomplished. The time has come for you to return and help your father rule his kingdom. I give you a new name. You shall be called Prince Five-Weapons. Use your powers for good and luck will go with you."

The prince thanked his old teacher, lifted up his weapons and set off on the roads, back to his father's kingdom. He walked and walked. He climbed high mountains, crossed swift rivers, and went through dark forests.

Now, just where the road narrowed to enter a dark forest, the prince came upon a barricade of logs lying across his path. Armed soldiers stood at this barricade and they called out, "Stop, young prince! Do not go down this path!"

"And why not?" asked Prince Five-Weapons.

"Because," said the soldiers, "a monster named Sticky-Hair lives down this road, and he is heartless. He grabs people and gobbles them up. If you value your life, take some other path."

"What?" exclaimed the prince, "Shall I turn and run when danger threatens? I've made up my mind to be of some good in this world. I've spent a year learning to use the five weapons. I'll go down this path and make it safe for others to travel on."

So the prince went around the logs and set off down the forest path. As he walked deeper into the forest, the trees grew taller on either side of the road, so that their arching branches blocked the sun. The bushes, too, grew more wild and tangled, so that with every step his path became darker and darker.

Was the prince afraid? No, of course not. Not at all. He just walked straight ahead, down the forest path.

Soon the prince heard rustlings and creakings from the bushes on either side of the path. *Flap, flap, flap!* A glossy black crow flew across the path before him. *Whooo! Whooo! Whooo!* An owl hooted from the tangled gloom above. Suddenly, with a great crash, the tops of the tallest trees came splintering to the ground. And there, peering down, one hundred feet tall, was the Monster Sticky-Hair!

The monster's eyes were as big as doors, and his nostrils like boulders. His hands were the size of horse-drawn carts, and his fingernails long as broom sticks. His yellow, crooked teeth had holes in them so big that birds flew in and out, and even nested in them. He was horrible. He was immense. And he was covered with sticky, sticky hair.

Was the prince afraid? No, he was not afraid! He was not afraid at all! He put an arrow to his bow, drew the bow-string back, and said, "One more step, you Monster Sticky-Hair, and I'll send this arrow through your heart. For I am Prince Five-Weapons, and I've come into this dark forest to make you change your evil ways or to strike you dead."

But the Monster Sticky-Hair just laughed loudly, in a booming voice, "*HA HA HA HA HA HA!*" and strode forward, trees crashing down around him as he came.

The prince let his arrow fly. *Woooooooosh!* Straight as a falcon it flew, straight to the monster's heart and *thuuuuuup!* it struck! But what was this? The arrow hadn't hurt him at all. It just stuck to the Monster's sticky, sticky hair!

So the prince put another arrow to his bow and shot it, and another and another. Fifty arrows in all he shot, straight and true at the Monster's heart. *Thuuup, thuuup, thuuup, thuuup, thuuup!* They all struck! But what was this? Not one had hurt the Monster at all! They all just hung there, stuck to the sticky hair. The Monster laughed and shook himself like a wet dog. The arrows rattled together and flew off in every direction. And on the Monster came.

Was the prince afraid? No, he was not afraid! He was not afraid at all! He lifted up his spear and hurled it straight at the Monster's heart. *Thuuuuuuump!* It struck! But what was this? It too just stuck there, dangling from the sticky, sticky hair. And on the Monster came, closer and closer.

Was Prince Five-Weapons afraid now? No, absolutely not! He simply drew his shining sword, swung it once, twice, three times and *slaaaassssh*, struck the Monster's gigantic leg. But what was this? Why, the sword, too, just stuck to the sticky, sticky hair!

Now the Monster was looming right over the prince, ready to grab him and gobble him up. Did the prince turn away? Did he run? No! He simply lifted up his club, made of ironwood and knotted like a great fist, and brought it down, *Crash!* on the Monster's foot. But what was this? The club as well stuck to the sticky, sticky hair. It hadn't hurt the monster at all.

Now the monster was right over him, bending down to grab the prince and gobble him up. But was the prince afraid? No, he was not afraid! He was not afraid at all! He said to himself, "When I came into this forest I didn't just trust in my weapons. I trusted in myself. If I have to I'll beat this monster to dust with my fists."

And drawing back with his right fist he swung at the monster with all his strength. *Bop!* But what was this? His right fist was stuck to the sticky hair! "Oho," said the prince. "So that's how it is! Well, my left fist is by far the stronger. This is the end for you, Sticky-Hair!" Then the prince drew back with his left fist and *bop!* once again struck the Monster with all his might. But what was this? His left fist too was stuck to the sticky hair!

Then the prince said, "My right leg is stronger than my fists. Prepare to meet your doom, you Monster Sticky-Hair!" And drawing back with his right leg, *Whaap!* He kicked that Monster as hard as he could. But what was this? Why, the prince's right leg was stuck to the sticky hair!

"Well," said the prince, "my left leg is even stronger than my right. One kick, and I can shatter boulders. It's the end for you, Monster Sticky-Hair!" And, drawing back with his left leg, *Whaack!* He kicked that Monster a terrible and a mighty blow. But, what was this? The Prince's left leg just stuck to the Monster's sticky hair.

Then the prince said to himself. "The time has come for me to use my head." And, drawing back his head, he struck the Monster a terrible blow—*Crash!* But, what was this? Why, the prince's head, too, just stuck to the Monster's sticky, sticky hair. The prince was stuck head, hands, and feet. He couldn't move this way. He couldn't move that way. He couldn't move at all!

But, was he afraid? *NO!* He was not afraid. He was not afraid at all!

And the Monster could tell. He could sense no quiver of fear in the prince at all. And now he began to get nervous himself. He hesitated. "I don't like this," said the monster to himself. "Everyone else, as soon as they see me, they turn and run. But this prince came straight on, like a lion, like a hero. He didn't turn. He didn't run. And now that I've got him completely stuck, he's still fearless. Something is not right. He must have a secret weapon protecting him. Yes, that must be it. Even though he's completely stuck—head, hands, and feet—he might still be dangerous. I'd better look into this before I do something rash. I could get hurt."

And bending down towards the prince, the Monster said, "Ahem, Prince?"

"Yes?" said the prince.

"Do you have some kind of secret, er, weapon about you?"

"Yes!" said the prince.

"I thought so," lamented the Monster. "What is it?"

"I have a sword of Truth within me," said the prince, "and if you try to eat me, it will cut you open so that I may leap out, completely free. Why should I fear? You can never hold me."

"I believe you!" exclaimed the Monster. "Don't hurt me. I knew I could never eat you up. No, I could never have digested the tiniest piece of a hero like you—not even a piece as big as a bean. I'll let you go!" And bending down, the Monster pulled Prince Five-Weapons from his sticky hair and set him free, saying, "I set you free like the moon when it comes out at last from behind the clouds."

But the prince, collecting his weapons said, "I don't set you free, you Monster! Don't you know that you've become a miserable monster just because you've treated others so unkindly? If you treated others better you'd become happier. Someday, you'd be a real human being, and a whole new world would open to you."

"It's true," said the Monster, "I have been pretty miserable. Well, I'll do it! I will treat others with kindness. I'll protect travellers from lions and tigers, from robbers and other dangers. I won't gobble them up ever again. From now on, I'll help."

"See that you do," said the prince, "or I'll be be back to check up on you." And, shouldering his weapons, he once again set off down the path. After a time he came again to his father's kingdom, and did indeed help his father rule. Years later, the prince became king and was known as "King Five-Weapons, The Opener of the Ways."

As for the Monster, he did just as the prince had told him to do. He was kinder. He helped travellers who went down that forest path, and he protected them from dangers. With his long-clawed hands he pushed apart the tangled tree branches so that bright sunlight could stream down into the dark forest. Flowers began to grow there and, in time, it became quite beautiful.

The Monster became happier. Happier and happier. Thousands of years went by. Life after life. He was born as many different kinds of creatures—tiger, lion, bear, wolf, horse, elephant, monkey, human being. Recently, he was again born as a human being, and lives happily right here in our own city.

The Wise Quail

Once, the Buddha was a wise quail, the leader of a flock. One day, a hunter came into the forest. Imitating the quails' own calls, he began to trap unwary birds.

The wise quail noticed that something was amiss. Calling his flock together, he announced, "My fellow quail, I am afraid that there is a hunter in our forest. Many of our brothers and sisters are missing. We must be alert. Danger is all around us. Still, if we work together we can stay free. Please listen to my plan. If you should hear a whistling call—*twe whee! twe whee! twe whee!*—as if a brother or sister were calling, be very watchful! If you follow that call, you may find darkness descending upon you. Your wings may be pinned so that you cannot fly, and the fear of death may grip your heart. If these things happen, just understand that you have been trapped by the hunter's net and *do not give up!* Remember, if you work together you can be free.

"Now, this is my plan. You must stick your heads out through webs of the net and, then, you must all flap your wings together. As a group, though you are still bound in the net, you will rise up into the air. Fly to a bush. Let the net drape on the branches of the bush so you can each drop to the ground, and fly away from under the net, this way and that, to freedom. Do you understand? Can you do this?"

"We do understand," answered all the quail as one, "and we will do it! We will work together and be free."

Hearing this, the wise quail was content.

The very next day a group of quail were pecking on the ground when they heard a long whistling call. *Twe whee! twe whee! twe whee!* It was the cry of a quail in distress! Off they rushed.

Suddenly darkness descended on them and their wings were pinned. They had indeed been trapped by the hunter's net. But, remembering the wise quail's words, they did not panic. Sticking their heads out through the webs of the net they flapped their wings together, harder and harder and slowly, slowly, with the net still draped upon them, they rose, as a group, through the air. They flew to a bush. They dropped down through the bush, leaving the net hung on the outer branches, then flew away, each in their own direction, this way and that, to freedom. The plan had worked! They were safe! They had escaped from the jaws of death. And, oh, they were happy!

But the hunter was not happy. He could not understand how the quail had escaped him. And this happened not just once, but many times. At last, the hunter realized the truth. "Why," he said, amazed, "those quail are cooperating! They are working together! But it can't last. They are only birds, featherbrains after all. Sooner or later they will argue. And when they do, I shall have them." And so, he was patient.

Now, the wise quail had had the same thought. Sooner or later the birds of his flock would begin to argue, and when that happened they would be lost. So he decided to take them deeper into the forest, far from their present danger.

That very day something happened to confirm the wise quail's thought.

A quail was pecking on the ground for seeds when another bird of the flock, descending rapidly, accidentally struck it with its wing-tip. "Hey! Watch it, stupid!" called the first quail, in anger.

"Stupid is it?" responded the newly-landed quail, flustered because he had been careless, "Why are you so high and mighty? You were too dumb to move out of my way! Yes, you were too dumb—you dumb cluck!"

"Dumb cluck is it?" cried the first quail, "Dumb cluck? Why, talking of dumb, it's clear that you can't even land without slapping someone in the face! If that isn't 'dumb,' I don't know what is! Who taught you to fly anyway—the naked-winged bats?"

"Bats is it?" yelled the second quail, enraged, "Bats? Why, I'll give you a bat, you feathered ninny!" And with a loud chirruping whistle he hurled himself straight at the other quail.

Chasing furiously after one another, loudly hurling insults and threats back and forth, they flew, twisting and turning, between the great, silent trees of the grove. An argument had started and, as is the way of arguments, no end was in sight.

The wise quail was nearby and he heard it all. At once he knew that danger was again upon them. If they could not work together the hunter was sure to have them.

So again he called his flock together and said, "My dear brother and sister quail. The hunter is here. Let us go elsewhere, deeper into the forest and there, in seclusion, discipline ourselves, practicing our skills in working together. In this way we shall become truly free from the danger."

Many of the birds said, "Though we love our present home, we shall go with you, Wise Quail. The danger is great and we wish to find safety."

But others said, "Why go from this pleasant spot? You yourself, Wise Quail, have taught us all we need to know in order to be free. We know what to do. We just have to stick our heads out, flap our wings together, and fly away. Any dumb cluck can do it! We're going to stay."

So some of the birds flew off with the wise quail, while the others stayed.

A few days later, while some of those who stayed were scratching around for their dinner, they heard a whistling call. *Twe whee! twe whee! twe whee!* They ran to answer the call when suddenly, darkness descended upon them. Fear gripped their hearts. They were trapped in the hunter's net! But, remembering the wise quail's teaching, they stuck their heads through the net, and one bird said, "On the count of three we all flap. Ready? One two, thr—"

"Hey!" called another bird, "Who made you boss? Who said you could give the orders?"

"I'm the hardest worker and the strongest," said the first bird. "When I flap my wings, the dust rises from the earth and whirls up in clouds. Without me you'd never get this net off the ground. So I give the orders, see?"

"No, I don't see!" shouted another bird. "What you've just described is nothing. Why, when I flap my wings, all the leaves move on the trees, the branches bend and even the trunks sway. That's how strong I am. So if anyone should be giving orders around here it's me!"

"No, me!" shouted a third bird.

"Me!" yelled a fourth.

"No! No! Listen to me!" screamed the first bird again above the rising din. "Flap Flap! Flap! I tell you. Flap your wings all together when I say 'three!'"

But no one flapped. They just argued and argued. And as they argued, the hunter came along and found them and their fate, alas, was not a happy one.

But the quail who had gone off deeper into the safety of the great forest learned, under the wise quail's guidance, how to really cooperate. They practiced constantly, until they were, indeed, able to work together without anger or argument.

Though the hunter tried many times to catch them he never could.

And if he never caught them, why, they're still free today.

The Monkey and the Crocodile

Once, there was a lazy and slow-witted crocodile, who liked nothing better than to lie in the sun on the warm, muddy banks of his lazy, green river. He would stretch out at the water's edge and, shutting his eyes tight, open his mouth wide in a great toothy grin. Then the little birds would fly in and out of his jaws, pecking at the scraps of food stuck between his yellowed teeth.

"Ah," he thought contentedly, digging his claws into the soft, gray mud, "but this is the life!"

One day his wife crawled over to him and said, "Dear, have you noticed that monkey swinging around on the island lately?"

"Uh-huh," grunted the crocodile, keeping his eyes shut and his mouth open wide.

"Well," she went on, "he looks large and juicy. I bet his heart is very tender. Oh," she exclaimed at last, "how I wish I had that monkey's tender heart! Dear," she concluded, "wouldn't you go get his heart for me?"

"Uh-huh," sighed the crocodile. Closing his jaws with a *snap!* he quietly opened his cold, yellow eyes and slowly crawled down the bank into the river. He moved his broad tail from side to side and slid through the cool, green water with hardly a ripple. But when he was only halfway across he slowly swung around in the water and swam back to the shore. His wife lay on the bank sunning herself. Her eyes were shut tight and her mouth was open wide.

"Dear," he said.

"Uh-huh?" she said.

"Well," he said, "how am I going to catch that monkey when he's way up in the trees and I'm down here in the water?"

"Well," she answered, "you're big and strong, aren't you?"

"Uh-huh," he exclaimed.

"Well, then, it's simple," she said. "Just offer to carry him across on your back to where all the sweet coconuts are ripening. Be a friend. You can do that, can't you?"

"Uh-huh," he said. And then, once again, the crocodile turned around and slid back into the water. Slowly he swam off, moving his broad tail steadily from side to side.

At this time the monkey was swinging around on the trees of his island. He was eating sweet fruits and enjoying himself in the warmth of the sun. "Ah," he reflected as he sat among the bright green leaves and fluttering orange butterflies, "but life is good!"

Just at that moment the crocodile reached the shore of the monkey's island. Crawling along the sandy beach, he raised his knobbed and scaly head up toward the trees and called out in a very gentle-seeming voice indeed, "Brother monkey! Oh, Brother monkey!"

"Yes," answered the monkey, "what is it? Who is calling me?"

"It's me," answered the crocodile, "your friend from across the deep river, the crocodile. And I was just thinking, as the day is so warm and bright and the sun is shining so gloriously, that I'd like to do something special for a friend today. My wife has told me that the mangos and coconuts on our side of the river are tender and juicy and ripe. And, as it's the perfect day for a swim, I'd be glad to take you for a ride over to where the sweetest ones are growing so you can eat to your heart's content. In fact," added the crocodile, with a great, toothy grin, "I'd be really glad to do it. Won't you come along?"

"Hmmm," said the monkey, scratching his head. "I don't know. Let me think it over. It is a nice day, and ripe coconuts and mangos would be nice." Then he asked, "Will you promise to go slow?"

"Slow?" grinned the crocodile, "Slow? Why, slow is my middle name! Just come along. You'll see."

"All right," said, the monkey, "I'll go with you." Then he hopped down out of the tree onto the crocodile's back, and off they went across the river.

As they swam along, the little waves washed and rippled over the crocodile's leathery hide, splashing among the rough scales and wetting the monkey's hands and feet. "Ooh, it's cold!" he cried.

"Cold?" leered the crocodile. "Cold? You call that cold? Why, that's not cold—that's not cold yet at all!" And with that, he dived down through the green water to the gray, muddy bottom of the river!

The terrified monkey held on tight—*TIGHT!*—and when they broke the surface again in a burst of mud and foam, the poor monkey gasped out from between his chattering teeth, "Friend crocodile, what are you doing? You nearly drowned me with your joke! Please be more careful. Have you forgotten your promise? Remember, my home is in the trees!"

"What joke?" said the crocodile with another nasty grin. "I'm taking you back to my wife. She wants your tender heart. And what she wants, she gets!"

"Oh," said the monkey slowly, "I see. Yes, now I see! Well, friend," he added after a moment, "it's a good thing you've told me. You almost made a terrible mistake."

"I did?" asked the crocodile, concerned. The smile left his jaws. "Please tell me, Friend monkey, how?"

"Why," said the monkey, "everyone knows I don't take something as important as my tender heart with me on ordinary little everyday trips. Oh, no—except for the most special occasions, I always leave my tender heart hanging safely at the top of the tallest tree on my island. A tender heart is a precious thing. Look back, Friend crocodile. Don't you see it hanging there on that tall tree by the shore?"

The crocodile looked and, after a moment, thought that maybe he could see it. Yes, now he was sure of it! He did see it! He had almost made a terrible mistake.

"Listen, Friend crocodile," said the monkey, "now that I know the whole story, why don't we just turn around? I'll go back and get my tender heart. It will be no trouble at all. In fact, I'd love to do it. Really. It will take just a minute. I bet your wife would have been upset," he added, as the crocodile turned slowly in the water and began to swim back toward the island, "if you had brought me all the way over the water without my tender heart. That would have made for a really long delay. We would have had to come all the way back then, but now, you see, there's no real harm done."

"You're right," agreed the crocodile, "she never would have understood. You know," he added, "for a monkey you are a very good fellow."

"Thank you," said the monkey. "Glad I could help. Now, just wait here. I'll be back in a moment!" And with that the monkey took a tremendous leap straight up off the crocodile's back and bounded up into the branches of the tallest tree. Up, up, up he scampered, straight to the very top. Then, dancing on the highest branch he called out, "Foolish, foolish crocodile! Tender hearts don't grow on trees! A tender heart is the heart of compassion that feels kindly towards all things—even silly crocodiles. One day you and your wife will surely have your own tender hearts. But, until you do you won't find me riding on your back. Better head home now, my toothy friend. This joke's on you!"

And with that, the crocodile swam off, embarrassed and confused.

The wise monkey sat in the warmth of the golden sunshine drying his wet fur. Sweet fruits hung from the sturdy branches. Clear waves lapped against the shore below. "Ah," he exclaimed, "how could that foolish crocodile have failed to find my tender heart!?"

Great Joy, the Ox

Once, long ago, a poor brahmin was given an ox calf in repayment for a debt. The calf was the Buddha in an earlier birth. The brahmin delighted in the tiny creature and cared for it well.

And the ox, with the man's care, grew and grew. When fully grown it was a great, powerful ox. Yet, as big and powerful as it was, it was gentle too. Whatever the brahmin asked it to do, it did, and with good spirit. Deeply rooted stumps, big boulders, whatever it might be—if the brahmin wanted it pulled from his fields he had only to tie one end of a rope to his ox's yoke, the other end to the boulder or stump and say, "Pull!" And the ox would pull it up out of the earth and drag it from the fields. Yet the ox was so tame that children could safely ride on its back. So pleased was the brahmin with his great, powerful, and gentle ox that he named it "Great Joy."

One day, Great Joy was thinking to himself, "My master, the brahmin, is so poor, yet he has always been so kind to me. I want to use my great strength to repay him."

So Great Joy walked over to the brahmin's low, sun-baked mud house and put his great, horned head through the open window. There sat the poor brahmin, sitting at a little crooked table, mending the torn page of a book. And the ox said, "My master and my friend, you have always been so kind to me, yet you are so poor, I want to use my great strength to help you. Listen. I have a plan."

And the astonished brahmin, his jaw dropping in disbelief, said, "I have an ox who can talk?!"

"Oh, yes master," replied Great Joy calmly, "there are many more wonderful things than that in this world. But listen."

So the brahmin ceased his work and he listened.

"Tomorrow," said Great Joy, "go into the town. Find a wealthy merchant and bet him one thousand pieces of silver that you have an ox who can pull a hundred carts loaded with boulders, gravel, and stone."

"It's impossible!" exclaimed the brahmin. "No ox has ever pulled so many loaded carts. It can't be done!"

"Trust me," said Great Joy. "Have I ever let you down?"

The Brahmin thought about it and, upon reflection, realized that, indeed, Great Joy had never failed him. So he agreed.

The next day, when the sun rose, the poor brahmin tied on his worn sandals and headed for the town. Entering a tea shop where the wealthier merchants and farmers often gathered during the heat of the day, he sat down alone at a little table. Then, as a wealthy merchant entered, he called out, "My friend, will you join me?"

"Why not?" answered the wealthy merchant.

After pleasantries, a few sweets and tea, the brahmin took a deep breath and said, "I have an ox."

"So," replied the wealthy merchant. "I have many oxen and, let me tell you, they cost me plenty."

"Yes," said the brahmin, "but...but my ox is strong."

"Bah!" said the merchant. "It is an ox's nature to be strong. Every ox is strong."

"Not as strong as my ox," continued the brahmin, now warming to the task. "Why, my ox is so strong he can pull one hundred carts loaded to the top with boulders, gravel, and stone. That's how strong my ox, Great Joy, is!"

"Impossible!" laughed the merchant. "Listen, neighbor—no ox, no matter how strong, can pull one hundred loaded carts. This world is one of weights and measures. Everything has its necessary limits. An ox is after all, just an ox. This can't be done."

"But it can," persisted the poor brahmin.

"It can't!" insisted the wealthy merchant.

"Would you like to wager?" asked the poor brahmin.

"With pleasure," replied the wealthy merchant.

"One thousand pieces of silver?" asked the poor brahmin, somewhat hesitantly.

"You're on!" cried the wealthy merchant. "One thousand pieces of silver it shall be! Tomorrow, when the sun rises to the top of the tallest mango tree in the town square, you bring your ox and I'll have one hundred loaded carts, waiting. Until then, my friend, let us call it a day."

And with that the wealthy merchant rose and, with a flourish of the sleeves of his elegant robe, walked smiling from the shop.

Soon the whole town was alight with the news. "One thousand pieces!" they exclaimed. "One hundred carts," they wondered. "One ox!" they laughed.

Money changed hands and bets were placed. Then all waited in expectation for the morning.

That night the poor brahmin tossed and turned. Would he win? Would he lose? Could Great Joy really pull all those carts? The odds, after all, were entirely against it.

The brahmin awoke early and went at once to Great Joy's stall.

There stood Great Joy, calming chewing the golden straw, flicking his long tail from side to side. His great dark eyes looked out at the brahmin with great good humor, as if to say, "Today's the day, eh? Well, don't worry. All shall be well. We won't lose this bet."

But the brahmin was preoccupied. He couldn't see. He couldn't hear what his ox was so clearly saying.

Picking up a stiff brush the brahmin began to brush Great Joy, slapping and brushing his sides and the muscles of his broad back so that the dust rose up and danced, sparkling in the sunbeams, like bits of silver or gold.

When he had combed and brushed and curried Great Joy, he threw a rope around his ox's neck and led Great Joy through the fields and down the dirt roads to the town.

They arrived just as the sun touched the top of the tallest mango tree in the town square. A noisy crowd already filled the square. And there were the one hundred loaded carts, waiting.

The poor brahmin took one look and his stomach sank down to his shoes. He was shocked! He thought that he had never seen so many carts! And certainly never so many loaded carts! "What a fool I have been," he admonished himself, "for having listened to the words of a beast. I, a man, have listened to an animal, and just see the result! I am lost!" But, putting on a bold front, he led Great Joy through the crowd.

There stood the wealthy merchant, waiting. "So," he asked, "are you ready?"

"Certainly! Of course we're ready," replied the brahmin.

The wealthy merchant clapped his hands together and two strong men stepped from the crowd. They lifted up a heavy wooden yoke and set it on Great Joy's shoulders. Then they tied the ropes from the carts firmly to the yoke, knotting them tight.

The crowd grew quiet. It became so quiet you could hear the birds singing in the trees. It became so quiet you could hear the sweep of Great Joy's tail. It became so quiet you could hear the buzz of the glittering flies.

Unconcerned, Great Joy mildly eyed the staring crowd and watched the white clouds drifting slowly overhead. He shook his huge head and snorted loudly as it to say, "What's all the fuss?"

Then the poor brahmin, feeling all eyes focused on him, walked up to Great Joy's side, lifted up a whip, struck Great Joy on his giant shoulder and cried, "On, you beast! On, you wretch! Pull those carts! Show your strength!"

But, when Great Joy felt the bite of the whip and heard all those harsh words, his eyes opened wide. "Blows and curses, is it?" he said to himself. "Not for this ox!" And, planting his hooves firmly in the earth, he would not move.

The crowd went wild! They yelled and jeered. They threw clods of earth. They threw sticks and stones. But Great Joy would not budge. He wouldn't even try to pull the carts. Not even an inch. He stood resolute beneath all the shouts and blows.

No matter how loudly the crowd laughed and jeered, no matter how hard they threw their sticks and stones, no matter what they shouted and screamed—Great Joy simply would not move.

"My friend," spluttered the merchant, tears of laughter streaming down his cheeks, "that is some—ha! ha! ha!—ox, indeed!"

When the proddings and threats had at last ceased, the crowd drifted away, and the merchant, still dabbing at his wet eyes, been paid ("Better luck next time!" he joked), only then did Great Joy allow himself to be unhitched and led silently away, home.

Once there the poor brahmin put his head down in his arms and wept and wept for grief and loss and shame.

Then Great Joy, hearing his sobs, walked again to farmer's little house, put his horned head through the open window and said, "My master and my friend, why do you weep?"

And the poor brahmin, in great bitterness, between his broken breaths, exclaimed, "You beast! You wretch! You animal! Everything you told me to do I did, yet I have lost everything. What's more, the whole town has laughed at me as well. And it's all your fault!"

But Great Joy said sadly, "Did I let you down or did you let me down? Let me ask you something. Have I ever failed you before? Did I ever crack a plow, break a fence, or smash a pot? Did I ever track filth into some clean place in your home or before some sacred shrine? Did I ever injure a child or fail to pull a load?"

"No," said the brahmin, raising his head, "you were always a great joy to me."

"Then why," asked Great Joy, the Ox, "did you beat me and hit me and call me such names—'wretch' you said, and 'beast?' Was this truly the reward I deserved at your hands, I who only wanted to work hard for you and to serve you?"

Then the brahmin sat up and dried his eyes. He looked at his ox in silence—and he grew ashamed.

"You are right," he admitted at last. "You didn't let me down. It was I who let you down And Great Joy, I...I'm sorry."

"Well," said the ox, "since you now feel this way about it, go back to town, find that merchant, and bet again. Only this time bet two thousand pieces."

"My friend!" cried the brahmin."I will do it. I will bet again and this time I won't let you down!"

"Good," said Great Joy, "for if you don't let me down, I will certainly not let you down."

The next day the brahmin ran to the town and entered the tea shop once again. There was the merchant calmly sipping his tea and eating from a plate of sweets.

"My friend, may I join you?" asked the brahmin.

"By all means," answered the merchant merrily, "for have you not brought me great joy?" And he jingled his bag of coins.

"My friend," said the brahmin, "let us bet again."

"What!?" exclaimed the merchant, "don't you know when you are beaten?"

"Come," said the brahmin calmly, "one more bet on the ox and the carts, just as before. Only this time let us bet two thousand pieces. What do you say?"

The merchant stroked his beard. "Fools like this," he thought to himself, "don't grow on every tree. He is begging me to take his money. So, why not?"

"All right," he shrugged at last. "Who am I to say no?"

"So it's a wager?" asked the brahmin.

"If you wish," said the merchant.

"Yes, I do wish. Tomorrow, when the sun rises to the top of the tallest mango tree in the square, once again have your carts ready and I will bring Great Joy, my ox. Until then, my friend, let us call it a day." And he departed once again, wishing all a good day.

The next morning the brahmin once more curried Great Joy and cleaned him. Then he led the great ox down the dirt roads to the town.They arrived as the sun touched the top of the tallest mango tree.

Once again a noisy crowd was gathered, this time ready to laugh and jeer. Many already held their sticks and stones and clods of earth all ready to throw. But, as Great Joy was led up to the carts spiritedly tossing his great horned head, the sun suddenly shone down upon him and power seemed to pulse from his great, shining back. His horns seemed to grow so wide it was as if they could tear the clouds and his tail now lashed behind him like a dragon's tail. The hairs of his glossy hide stood erect, bristling and crackling with electricity.

As one the crowd gasped: "What an ox! Maybe he will be able to do it!"

Then, as before, the merchant motioned. As before, those strong men set the heavy yoke up on Great Joy's shoulders and the ropes were knotted and tied. Then, once again, all grew quiet. It became so quiet you could almost hear the clouds drifting overhead. Then the poor brahmin, feeling all eyes focused upon him, stepped up to his ox's side, lifted up a wreath of flowers, hung it around Great Joy's neck, patted Great Joy on a giant shoulder and said, "This is the time, my mighty brother. This is the time, my great friend. So pull, pull with your whole heart and let the world see your noble strength!"

And with these kind, encouraging words, Great Joy happily planted his hooves into the sun-warmed earth, stiffened his legs till they stood like ancient trees, and pulled.

And *puuulled.*

And *PUUULLED.*

And slowly, steadily the wheels began to turn, faster and faster and faster. "The ox has won!" cried the crowd. "He's won!" Faster and faster and faster rolled the carts as Great Joy, at a run, pulled those one hundred carts all around the square.

The crowd ran after, laughing and calling for joy! Never had they seen such a wild and wonderful thing! Only one ox it may have been and a hundred dusty carts. Still, Great Joy the Ox, with his dignity, strength, and self-respect, had achieved the impossible.

It may have happened long, long ago, but it's still remembered today.

The Golden Goose

Once a poor man lived with his wife and two children, a boy and a girl, at the forest's edge.

For some reason, the man fell ill. Despite all efforts to restore him to health, he grew weaker and weaker. As he lay dying, one thought filled his mind: "I want to help my family." And then he died.

That night both his children had the same dream. Their father appeared to them and said, "Dear ones, don't grieve. I will return and help you. Though I will not look as I did to you in our life together, still you will know that it is me."

When they told their mother of it, she only laughed bitterly. "Forget this dream, little ones," she said. "Our lives will be hard enough."

So the children didn't mention it to her again. But, together, they spoke happily about it.

One evening months later, as the sun began to sink below the trees, a large white goose with golden eyes and yellow beak and legs walked up the path to the mud-walled little house where this family lived. It approached the children, stretched out its neck, honked loudly, then spoke in a human voice, a voice they knew well! "Children," said the goose, "It is I, your father."

"It is you!" they shouted. "You told us it would be like this. You told us in our dream!"

The goose wrapped its wings around them and held them. Then it said, "I have come to help you. Each day you must pluck a feather from my wings. It will turn to gold. With my golden feathers you and your mother will be able to buy all you need. But you must tell no one, not even your mother, who I am. And you must pluck only one feather each day, pluck it while the sun still shines. And let the sun's light touch the feather. Quickly, children," said the goose, "before the sun has set, pluck a feather."

They plucked a feather from the goose's wing—and, just like that, it turned to gold!

They ran to their mother, crying "Look, mother, look! A feather of gold! And fath—uh—the goose said we shall have all we need!" And joining hands the two children began to dance around and around the astonished woman.

"What are you saying?" she cried. "Where did you get this bright feather?" Then, as she touched it, she exclaimed, "Why, it's gold!"

"Of course it's gold," said the children. "It's gold. Just as the goose said it would be!"

"What goose?"

"Why, the goose in our yard," said the children. "Come, mother. Look!" And taking her hands they led their mother out to the yard. And there, indeed, stood the goose, large and white.

"It's a plump and handsome goose," said the mother. "But its feathers are soft and white. They aren't made of gold."

"No," said the boy, "they only turn to gold when you pluck them and hold them to the sun."

"And," said the girl, "you must pluck only one feather each day. For the goose told us so."

Naturally, their mother found this hard to believe. Still, there was the feather of gold. "We will wait until tomorrow," she said. "We shall pluck another feather tomorrow, and we shall see."

The sun set. The stars came out twinkling overhead. The children petted the goose and spoke softly to it. The goose wrapped them in its wings and lay its head and neck against them. It spoke no human words but only honked and gabbled like any other goose.

The next morning, as the sun rose bright as gold above the trees, the mother plucked a feather from the goose's wing. And instantly, once again, just like that, the feather turned to gold! She gasped and nearly dropped it, so great was her surprise. "It's gold!" she cried. "Gold!"

"Yes, mother!" cried the children happily. "We told you. We told you. The goose is here to help us."

"Well," she said, recovering from her shock, "we must feed this goose well. This goose is our benefactor. We shall take good care of it."

And so it was. They fed the goose and cared well for it. And every day, as the sun rose over the trees, they plucked a feather from the goose. And every day, the feather turned to gold.

With this gold, the mother bought good food and new clothes for them all. She bought shining copper pots and ladles of polished wood. She bought little mirrors and tinkling bells to hang from the roof poles. She bought carved wooden animals for the children. She freshly plastered the walls of their little house and added a new room, and then another. She put a strong fence around the yard. She bought a buffalo to help them plow the fields and to give them its rich, sweet milk. She bought sweet corn and grain to feed the goose.

They were content. And the goose seemed content as well. Every morning, after a feather had been pulled from it, it stretched out its neck, flapped its wings, and honked for joy. Then, after it had eaten and drunk and preened its feathers, it followed the children out into the fields, guarded them through their day, and returned with them to the house when darkness fell again.

Often, at night, the mother would lie awake in the darkness, reflecting on their extraordinary luck. She heard her children breathing peacefully in their sleep. She heard the buffalo as it snorted in its stall and she heard the night birds call. Who, she would marvel, could have ever imagined that a goose with feathers that turned to gold would suddenly appear to save them from hardship? It was a miracle!

But as their life become less burdensome, the mother found it harder to be content. One feather at a time, she realized, had built their security. Yet, if she might only pluck the bird bare, once and for all, they would have a fortune.

Her two children begged her to resist this temptation. "The goose told us," they said, "to pluck only one feather each day. We promised not to take more. Please, mother, please. Let well enough be."

And for a while she agreed. But after a time, the thought of all that gold arose once again within her. "It's only a goose, after all," she reasoned. "Why should I be so concerned? Though children have tender hearts, they will soon forget. And what if the goose should be carried off—by a jackal, perhaps, or a thief? All would be lost! Besides, I will only use the gold for my children's welfare. What harm can be in this? And as for plucking one feather at a time, why, I never heard the goose say that—or anything else for that matter. It's foolish to wait any longer."

So again, she decided to pluck the whole goose. But again, the children pleaded and begged and cried. And again, she held off, confused.

"It's just a goose," she told herself. "A goose! What do children know of life? How can I weigh a single goose against the welfare of my children? It is absurd."

Then, at last she made up her mind, and this time she was determined. "I shall pluck the goose," she said, "and protect my family with the gold."

The next morning, before the sun rose, the mother crept into the yard and caught the goose. While the children slept, she quickly pulled fistfuls of feathers from the uncomplaining bird who shivered uncontrollably, watching her all the while with sad, golden eyes. Feathers flew like whirling snow, but still the woman plucked and plucked, stuffing the soft, white feathers into a sack.

At last she released the bare bird which ran and hid under the bushes in the corner of the yard. From beneath the broad, green leaves came sounds that were almost human, as if someone were softly sobbing.

With a shiver the woman set her jaw and lifted up the sack of feathers, opening it to the sun which was now rising above the trees.

The golden light fell upon the sack of feathers. But the sack stayed light as down. She lowered the sack and peered within. The feathers were all soft and white. Not one had turned to gold. She emptied the feathers out onto the ground and let the sun's light play upon them. But not one showed the slightest sign of change.

The poor woman cried aloud. The children, hearing, ran out to the yard where fistfuls of white feathers now blew like snow from the mountains.

"Oh, Mother!" cried the children. "The goose, the poor poor goose! Oh Father, Father! We promised we wouldn't tell but, mother, it is our own father you have plucked so bare. He is the goose! He returned as he said he would in our dream."

The mother sobbed and sobbed. "Your poor father is gone, children," she said at last. "But feathers grow again. We'll take good care of the goose. Next time I promise you I will pluck only one feather at a time."

But, when the goose's feathers grew in again, they were speckled and grey, and not one ever turned to gold.

One day the goose spread its wings and flew away. The gold they had already gained would be enough to see them through. They could make their way now unaided.

As the woman grew older she became known as a hard worker as well as for the simplicity of her life. "Don't be greedy," she would say to those she met. "Everything comes in its own time."

Those who heard her took her words to heart. Somehow they felt that here at last was someone who really knew what she was talking about.

The Brave Little Parrot

Once, long ago, the Buddha was born as a little parrot. One day a storm fell upon his forest home. Lightning flashed, thunder crashed, and a dead tree, struck by lightning, burst into flames. Sparks leapt on the wind and soon the forest was ablaze. Terrified animals ran wildly in every direction, seeking safety from the flames and smoke.

"Fire! Fire!" cried the little parrot. "To the river!" Flapping his wings, he flung himself out into the fury of the storm and, rising higher, flew towards the safety of the river. But as he flew he could see that many animals were trapped, surrounded by the flames below, with no chance of escape.

Suddenly a desperate idea, a way to save them, came to him.

He darted to the river, dipped himself in the water, and flew back over the now raging fire.

The heat rising up from the burning forest was like the heat of an oven. The thick smoke made breathing almost unbearable. A wall of flames shot up on one side, and then the other. Crackling flames leapt before him. Twisting and turning through the mad maze of fire, the little parrot flew bravely on. At last, when he was over the center of the forest, he shook his wings and released the few drops of water which still clung to his feathers. The tiny drops tumbled down like jewels into the heart of the blaze and vanished with a *hissssssssss*.

Then the little parrot once more flew back through the flames and smoke to the river, dipped himself in the cool water, and flew back again over the burning forest. Back and forth he flew, time and time again, from the river to the forest, from the burning forest to the river. His feathers were charred. His feet were scorched. His lungs ached. His eyes, stung by smoke, turned red as coals. His mind spun dizzily as the spinning sparks. But still the little parrot flew on.

At this time, some of the devas—gods of a happy realm—were floating overhead in their cloud palaces of ivory and gold. They happened to look down. And they saw the little parrot flying among the flames. They pointed at him with perfect hands. Between mouthfuls of honeyed foods they exclaimed, "Look at that foolish bird! He's trying to put out a raging forest fire with a few sprinkles of water! How absurd!" And they laughed.

But one of those gods, strangely moved, changed himself into a golden eagle and flew down, down towards the little parrot's fiery path.

The little parrot was just nearing the flames again when the great eagle with eyes like molten gold appeared at his side. "Go back, little bird!" said the eagle in a solemn and majestic voice. "Your task is hopeless! A few drops of water can't put out a forest fire! Cease now and save yourself—before it is too late."

But the little parrot only continued to fly on through the smoke and flames. He could hear the great eagle flying above him as the heat grew fiercer, calling out, "Stop, foolish little parrot! Save yourself! Save yourself!"

"I don't need a great, shining eagle," coughed the little parrot, "to give me advice like that. My own mother, the dear bird, might have told me such things long ago. Advice! (*cough, cough*), I don't need advice. I just (*cough*), need someone to help."

And the god, who was that great eagle, seeing the little parrot flying through the flames, thought suddenly of his own privileged kind. He could see them high up above. There they were, the carefree gods, laughing and talking, while many animals cried out in pain and fear from the flames below. And he grew ashamed. Then one single desire was kindled in his heart. God though he was, he just wanted to be like that brave little parrot, and to help.

"I will help!" he exclaimed and, flushed with these new feelings, he began to weep. Stream after stream of sparkling tears poured from his eyes. Wave upon wave, they washed down like cooling rain upon the fire, upon the forest, upon the animals and upon the little parrot himself.

The flames died down and the smoke began to clear. The little parrot, washed and bright, rocketed about the sky laughing for joy. "Now that's more like it!" he exclaimed.

The eagle's tears dripped from burned branches. Smoke rose up from the scorched earth. Miraculously, where those tears glistened, new life pushed forth—fresh shoots, stems, and leaves. Green grass pushed up from among still glowing cinders.

Where the teardrops sparkled on the parrot's wings, new feathers now grew. Red feathers, green feathers, yellow feathers—such bright colors! Such a handsome bird!

All the animals looked at one another in amazement. They were whole and well. Not one had been harmed. Up above in the clear blue sky they could see their brave friend, the little parrot, looping and soaring in delight. When all hope was gone, somehow he had saved them. "Hurray!" they cried. "Hurray for the brave little parrot and for the miraculous rain!"

The Banyan Deer

Once, the Buddha was born as a Banyan Deer. When he was grown he became leader of the herd. He guided his herd wisely and led them to the heart of a secluded forest where, sheltered by the giant trees, they lived free from danger.

Then a new king came into power over the land. And, above all things, this king loved hunting. As soon as the sun rose he would mount his horse and lead his men on a furious chase through fields and meadows, forests and glens. Shooting his arrows madly, he would not leave off until the sun had set. Then the wagons rolled back to the palace behind him, filled now with deer, boar, rabbit, pheasant, monkey, leopard, bear, tiger, and lion. And the king was happy.

His people, however, were not pleased. Fields had been ruined by the royal hunt. Farmers and merchants had been forced to leave off their work in order to beat the jungles and drive the hidden beasts towards the waiting king and his men. Affairs of state, too, lay unattended.

The people, determined to bring all this to an end, devised a simple plan. They built a stockade deep in the forest. "We'll trap a herd or two of deer in this stockade," they said. "Then the king can hunt all he wants. Let him hunt to his heart's content. He won't ruin our fields or force us to leave our shops. Then let him be happy."

The stockade was built and two herds of deer were driven within its walls. The gates were closed and the delicate animals, charging and wheeling in frantic circles, sought some way out. But there was none. Exhausted at last, they stood trembling, awaiting their fate.

The men left happily to tell the king of their success.

One of the herds that had been captured was the herd of the Banyan Deer.

The Banyan Deer walked among his herd. Sunlight played on his many-branched antlers. His black eyes shone and his muzzle was wet. "The blue sky is overhead. Green grass grows at our feet," he told the others. "Do not give up. Where there is life, there is hope. I will find a way." And so he strove to ease their fears.

Soon the king arrived to view the newly captured herds. He was pleased. He strung his bow in preparation for the hunt. Noticing the two deer kings below he said, "The leaders of both herds are magnificent animals. No one is to shoot them. They shall be spared." Then, standing on the wall, looking down over the stockade, he sent his arrows flying into the milling herds. The deer became frantic. Racing wildly they injured one another with horns and hooves as they sought to escape the deadly rain of arrows.

And so it went. Every few days the king and his courtiers would return to the stockade. And every few days more of the gentle deer were killed. Many others were wounded by the flying arrows. Still others were injured in the effort to escape.

The king of the Banyan Deer met with the leader of the other herd. "Brother," he said shaking his antlered head sadly, "we are trapped. I've tried every way, but all are barred against us. The pain our subjects suffer is unbearable. As you know, when the arrows fly, many get badly hurt just trying to stay alive. Let us hold a lottery. Each day all the deer, one day from your herd, one day from mine, must pick a straw. Then, the one single deer on whom the lottery falls will go stand near the wall just below the king. That one deer must offer itself to be shot. It is a terrible solution, but at least this way we can keep many from needless injury and pain."

And the leader of the other herd agreed.

The next day, when the king and his courtiers arrived, they found one trembling deer standing directly below them. Its legs and body were shaking but it held its head high. "What is this?" said the king. "Ah, I see. These are noble deer indeed! They have chosen that one deer alone shall die rather than that they all should suffer from our hunt. Those deer kings have wisdom." A heaviness descended on the king's heart. "We will accept their terms," he announced. "From now on shoot only the one deer that stands below." And unstringing his bow, he descended from the stockade wall and rode back in silence to the palace.

That night the king tossed and turned, a radiant deer pacing through his dreams.

One day the lot fell on a pregnant doe. She went to her king, the leader of the other herd, and said, "I will willingly go and fulfill the lottery once my fawn is safely born. But if I go now, both I and my unborn child will die. Please spare me for now. I do not ask for myself but for the sake of the child that is soon to be born."

But the leader of that herd said, "The law is the law. I cannot spare you. The lottery has fallen on you and you must die. There are no exceptions. Justice demands that you go."

In desperation she ran to the Banyan Deer. She fell on her knees before him and begged for his aid. He listened quietly, observing her with wide and gentle eyes. "Rise, Sister," said the Banyan Deer, "and go free. You are right. The terms of the lottery require that only one need die. Therefore you shall be freed from the lottery until your fawn is born. I will see that it is so done."

Too overjoyed for words, the grateful doe bowed and, then, bounded away.

The Banyan Deer King rose to his feet. There was no other he could send to take her place. He had spared her, therefore he himself must replace her. How could it be otherwise?

He walked calmly, with great dignity, through his browsing herd.

They watched him as he moved among them. His great, curving antlers and strong shoulders, his shining eyes and sharp, black hooves, all reassured and comforted them. Never had their Banyan Deer King let them down. Never had he abandoned them. If there was a way he would find it. If there was a chance to save another he would take it. Not once had he lorded it over them. He was a king indeed, and his whole herd took comfort in his presence.

The courtiers were waiting with bows drawn atop the stockade. When they saw it was the Deer King who had come to stand below they called out, "O King of the Banyan Deer, you know our king has spared you. Why are you here?"

"I have come so that two others need not die. Now shoot! You have your work and I have mine."

But, lowering their bows, they sent a message to the king. "Your Majesty, come with all speed to the stockade."

Not long after, the king arrived, riding like the wind, with his robes streaming behind him.

"What is it?" he called. "Why have you summoned me?"

"Come your majesty," his men called. "Look!"

Dismounting from his horse, the king hurried up the rough wooden steps and looked down over the wall.

The Banyan Deer stood below. Then deer king and human king looked at one another.

"Banyan King," said the king of men at last, "I know you. I have seen you gliding through the forests of my dreams. Why are you here? Have I not freed you from my hunt?"

"Great King," replied the Banyan Deer, "what ruler can be free if the people suffer? Today a doe with fawn asked for my aid. The lottery had fallen on her and both she and her unborn fawn were to die. The lottery requires that only one shall die. I shall be that one. I shall take her place. The lottery shall be fulfilled. This is my right and my duty as king."

A stone rolled from the king's heart. "Noble Banyan Deer," he said, "you are right. A king should care for the least of his subjects. It is a lesson I have been long in the learning but today, through your sacrifice, you have made it clear to me. So I shall give you a gift, a teacher's fee for the lesson you have taught me. You and your whole herd are freed. None of you shall be hunted again. Go and live in peace."

But the Banyan Deer said, "Great King, that is, indeed, a noble gift. But I cannot leave yet. May I speak further?"

"Speak on, Noble Deer."

"O King of Men, if I depart to safety with my own herd will that not mean that the remaining herd shall simply suffer all the more? Each day you shall kill only them. They will have no respite. A rain of arrows will fall upon them. While I desire, above all things, the safety of my people, I cannot buy it at the cost of increasing the suffering of others. Do you understand?"

The human king was stunned. "What!?" he exclaimed. "Would you, then, risk your own and your herd's freedom for others?"

"Yes," said the Banyan Deer, "I would. I will. Think of their anguish, Great King. Imagine their sufferings, and then let them too go free."

The king of men paused and he pondered. At last he lifted his head and smiled. "Never have I seen such nobility or such resolute concern. How can I refuse you? You shall have your wish. The other herd too shall go free. Now, can you go off with your own herd and be at peace?"

But the Banyan Deer answered, "No, Great King, I cannot. I think of all the other wild, four-footed creatures. Like them, I have lived my life surrounded by dangers and by fears. How could I live in peace knowing the terrors they must endure? I beg you, Mighty King, have pity on them. There can be no peace unless they too are free."

The king of men was again astonished. He had never imagined such a thing. He thought and thought, and slowly the truth of the Banyan Deer's words grew clear to him. It was true, he realized. There is no real peace unless its benefits extend to all.

"You are right, Great Deer," said the king of men at last. "Never again, in all my realm, shall any four-footed creature be slain. They are all freed from my hunt—rabbit, boar, bear, lion, leopard, tiger, deer—all.

Never again shall they fall to my huntsmen's arrows. So, my Teacher, have you now found peace?"

But the Banyan Deer said, "No, Great King, I have not. What, my Lord, of the defenseless ones of the air? The birds, Great King, live surrounded by a net of danger. Stones and arrows shall greet them now wherever they fly. They shall fall from the skies like a rain throughout your kingdom. They shall know such suffering as can hardly be imagined. O Great King, I beg you. Let them go free. Release them also."

"Great One," said the king of men, "You drive a hard bargain and are determined, it seems, to make farmers of us all. But, yes, I shall free the birds. They may now fly freely throughout my realm. No man shall hunt them again. Then may they build their nests in peace. Now, are you satisfied? Are you at last at peace?"

"Great King," answered the Banyan Deer, "think if you will of the silent ones of your realm—the fish, my Lord. If I do not now speak for them, who will? While they swim the lakes, rivers, and streams of your land, hooks, nets, and spears will be ever poised above them. How can I have peace while they abide in such danger? Great King, I beg you, spare them as well."

"Noble Being," said the King of Men, tears trickling down his cheeks, "Compassionate One, never before have I been moved to think in such a way, but, yes, I do so agree. The fish, too, are of my kingdom, and they too shall be free. They shall swim throughout my land and no one shall kill them again.

"Now, all of you assembled courtiers and attendants," announced the king, "hear my words; this is my proclamation. See that it is posted throughout the land. From this day forth, all beings in my realm shall be recognized as my own dear subjects. None shall be trapped, hunted, or killed. This is my lasting decree. See to it that it is fulfilled.

"Now, tell me, Noble One," he said, turning to the Banyan Deer once more, "are you at peace?"

Flocks of birds flew overhead and perched, singing, from among the nearby trees. Deer grazed calmly on the green grass.

"Yes," said the Banyan Deer, "Now I am at peace!" And he leaped, up kicking like a fawn. He leaped for joy— sheer joy! He had saved them all!

Then he thanked the king and, gathering his herd, departed with his herd back into the depths of the forest.

The king had a stone pillar set on the spot where he had spoken with the Banyan Deer. Carved upon it was the figure of a deer, encircled with these words: "Homage to the Noble Banyan Deer, Compassionate Teacher of Kings."

Then he too lived on, caring wisely for all things.

The Blue Bear of the Mountains

Once, long ago, many ages past, a bear with blue fur, silver claws and ruby-red eyes dwelt among the snow-covered Himalayan peaks. Kings and princes offered great rewards to anyone who could capture this bear. They wanted its blue fur and silver claws. And they wanted to eat of its flesh, which was said to be as sweet as honey. But no one ever brought accurate news of the bear.

One day, a hunter who had come in search of this miraculous bear became lost in a snowstorm. He staggered on through the drifts and whirling snow, calling for help.

The great blue bear, curled up in its den, heard those cries and awoke. It was a beast, but somehow those helpless cries pierced its heart. Rousing itself, the bear raised its paw, and with one blow broke down the snow-wall which blocked its den. Sniffing the air, it shuffled off through the howling storm to find the creature whose cries had awoken it from its winter's sleep.

In time the bear found the hunter. He was near death, half-buried in the snow. Scooping the man up in its paws, the bear carried the hunter to its cave, wrapped its great, furry arms around him, and breathed warmth back into the hunter's near-frozen body.

The hunter's eyes flickered open, and he looked into the face of a bear—the very blue-furred bear he had been seeking. Trembling with fear, he gazed up at the furry face, at the wet muzzle and the ruby eyes. He saw sharp teeth hovering over his own throat. But the bear's eyes were soft and the breath flowing from its mouth was as sweet as lotus honey.

Then the bear spoke in human words. "Hunter," it said, "when I heard your anguished cries, I thought my own heart would break. When you are strong enough to travel you may go freely, friend. Only promise that you will never reveal where my den is hidden."

And the hunter promised.

However, once the hunter had descended safely from the mountain, he thought of the reward, and the desire for riches again grew strong within him. "A man is greater than a bear," he growled. "A promise to a beast cannot compare with a man's welfare and comfort. I alone know where this bear's den lies. The gold is mine." And off he marched to tell the king.

The king was overjoyed. "However, if you are lying," said the king, "I'll have your head. Others have tried to trick me before this. Wait here while my huntsmen seek the bear." And he sent off three of his huntsmen to the den on the mountain that the faithless hunter had described.

The three hunters crept stealthily up to the bear's den, draped a net over the opening and sounded their horns. The bear awoke and rushed out from the darkness of its cave into the bright sunlight. Blinded by the light, it stumbled into the net, and was caught. The hunters tied the bear's silver-clawed paws together and lifted it up, still alive, onto a pole. But, before they tied its jaws shut the bear spoke. "Hunters," it said, "I have been betrayed. Take me to the king and I will reveal the treachery."

The hunters were startled, but they agreed. Then they set off through the snow and down the mountainside. Arriving at the palace, they set the bear before the king, cut its cords, and let it speak.

"Your Majesty," the bear began, "I saved a hunter from death, and in return asked only that he keep the secret of my den hidden. But, for the sake of your gold, he has broken his word, and thrown away his honor and my life. Even a beast knows better. I pity him."

The king was astonished to hear the bear speak. And he was angered by its tale. "Bring the hunter," he ordered.

Surrounded by guards, the hunter was brought to the throne room. Seeing the bear alive he sought to escape. "Hold him!" ordered the king, "and bring him near."

"Man," said the bear, "do you not see that you have done an evil thing? Did I not give you your life, and did you not promise, in return, to protect me?"

But the hunter turned angrily away. "Your Majesty," he said, "you have the bear. Though it may talk, remember, Sire, that you are a king and it is just a beast. You may kill it, cut off its fur, and eat its flesh just as you please. What is that to me? Give me the reward I deserve."

Then the king said, "Release the bear and with all honors escort it back to its home in the mountains. And as for this hunter, he shall, indeed, receive the reward he deserves. Take him from our city immediately. We shall not harm him. The treasure I give him is his own life, a gift greater than all gold. From this bear I have learned a little of honor and kindness."

The hunter's lips snarled and his beard bristled in anger. "I'll be revenged," he roared, "revenged on you all!" But before he could lay hold of his weapons the king's men drove him from the palace and beyond the city walls.

The king bowed to the bear, and with his own hands placed a garland of flowers around the wise beast's neck.

Escorted safely by the king's soldiers, the bear returned to the mountains, where it chose another den and lived in peace for many years.

The Golden Deer

Once, long ago, when Bramadatta was reigning in Benares, a rich merchant passed on his inheritance to his son, and then died.

The young man lived foolishly. Quickly going through his father's fortune, he soon began borrowing and living on the credit of others. One day he awoke to find himself deep in debt, creditors knocking on his door. In desperation, he led them all to the bank of the Ganges River, claiming that he had a treasure buried there in the sandy bank.

As they neared the riverbank he seemed to slip, and suddenly, losing his balance, tumbled in. The current bore him swiftly away. He called for help but not one of the creditors could brave that current, and standing helplessly on the shore they watched the youth as he was washed downstream, supposing he would be carried to his death.

Now, all this had been part of that youth's hastily conceived plan. His creditors, he thought, seeing him washed downstream, would think him dead, and so he would be released, through this trick, from all liability.

But the plan had a flaw. Swept away by the current the youth could not, in reality, regain the shore. His cries grew more and more desperate. He seemed lost, beyond all hope.

A magnificent Deer lay resting in a thicket. This Deer's fur was the color of gold. Its antlers gleamed like silver. Its hooves glistened as if lacquered. Its eyes shone like jewels. The Deer was, in fact, the Buddha in a former birth.

Hearing the cries of that drowning man, the great Deer said to himself, "I hear the voice of a man. While I live I will not let him die! I will save his life for him!" Rising to his feet, the golden-furred Deer plunged through the thicket and leaped into the river. Forging through the swirling water he came to the drowning man, swam beneath him, lifted him up on his back, carried him safely to the shore, and brought him to the security of his own shelter.

For several days the Golden Deer nurtured the young man with wild fruits and nuts. Then, when he had fully recovered, the great Deer said, "In return for my kindness to you, when you return to the world of men, please tell no one of my hiding place. As I have saved you, now you must save me."

The young man, overflowing with gratitude, promised he would tell no one. Then, once again, the great Deer carried the young man on his back, bringing him now to the road. The Golden Deer returned to his hiding place in the forest, and the young man set off, back to the great and ancient city of Benares.

In the city of Benares, Queen Khema, wife to the great king, Bramadatta, had a dream. She dreamed that a Deer whose fur shone like gold, whose antlers were like silver, whose hooves were bright as lacquer, and whose eyes shone like jewels appeared to her and taught her the ways of wisdom. She awoke filled with a longing to hear, in actuality, the wise teaching of this Golden Deer. Though it was only a dream, somehow she was sure that the Deer was real. She went to her husband and, relating the dream, begged that he offer a reward to anyone who might find this Golden Deer for her.

Bramadatta had tablets of gold put up on the walls of the city, offering a great chest of gold and jewels as well as an elephant from his own stable to carry the treasure to any one who could lead his men to the golden-furred Deer.

The young man, re-entering the city, read the tablets and was filled with longing for the treasure. Despite his promise, he went to the king and revealed what he knew.

Then King Bramadatta, accompanied by a great company of men bearing spears and nets, had the young man guide them to the hiding place of the Golden Deer.

Surrounding the thicket, the men cried out loudly. The great Deer, hearing that cry, knew that he was trapped. "Where the king stands I shall be safe," he thought, and dashing from the thicket, he ran straight towards the king.

The king put an arrow to his bow and watched, thinking, "If the arrow frightens him well enough, he will stop. If he is for running, I will wound and weaken him that we may take him."

The Golden Deer ran like fire in the sunlight, straight towards the king, and stopped just before him. "Great King," he said, in a voice like golden honey, "I bear you no ill will. Nor will I run from you. But, tell me, who was it that led you to me?"

The king, enchanted by that wonderful voice, lowered his bow. Pointing to the young man, he said, "It was this one. He guided us here."

Then the great Deer recited this verse,

"Upon the earth are many men of whom the proverb's true
Better save a sinking log than one like you."

At this the king grew frightened and asked the meaning of the verse. "Of whom do you speak, great Deer?" he asked. "Are you talking of some bird or beast?"

"No, Great King," replied the Golden Deer, "I am speaking of a man. This young man here. He was drowning in the Ganges. I leaped in and saved him. I nursed him to health and, on my own back, carried him to the road when he was ready to travel. I asked only that he keep my whereabouts hidden. Now he has betrayed me."

When King Bramadatta heard of this, he drew his bowstring in wrath, ready to send an arrow through the traitor's heart. "Here is fit repayment for falsehood. Here is the treasure you deserve for such kindness to your benefactor," he proclaimed.

"No, Great King," said the Golden Deer. "Shame on this fool indeed, but no good men can approve of killing. Let him go and give him the treasure you promised. He has done what you have asked. Keep your word and I will serve you willingly."

"This Deer is goodness itself," the king thought. "It is worth much treasure, indeed, simply to have met him. That he will come willingly and share his wisdom is our good fortune."

"Go," said the king, to the young wastrel. "Take the reward I have promised and good riddance to all such uncharity."

Then the great Deer spoke again. "Great King, men say one thing with their lips yet often do another. Truly it is hard to trust the words of men."

"Great Deer," replied the king, "this day I offer you a boon. Do not think that all men are alike. I offer you the fulfillment of any wish you may choose. And I, for one, will keep my word to you, even should it mean I lose my kingdom or my life!"

"Then, Great King," replied the golden deer, "I choose this boon of you. I choose that all creatures, from this day on, shall be free from danger. I ask that you give up all hunting."

The king granted this boon, and then led the great Deer back to the city of Benares. Having adorned the city with garlands and having garlanded the great Deer as well, he and the queen and all the people listened to the Great Being's discourse on truthfulness, charity, resoluteness, vigor, and other items of good character. Having strengthened the populace from king to beggar, each in his or her own determination to win mindfulness and attain wisdom, the Golden Deer left the city and returned to his forest where he resided as leader of a deer herd.

King Bramadatta sent a proclamation through the land, and a drum beater marched through the city proclaiming, "Great Bramadatta extends protection to all creatures!" From that time on, all hunting ceased.

Now, after this, herds of deer ate the crops unhindered and all the people suffered. No one dared kill the deer or drive them away. An angry crowd gathered before the palace. "Bramadatta in his greatness has ruined us!" they complained. "Take back your proclamation, so that we may drive the deer from the fields. Do it or your kingdom is lost!"

But Bramadatta replied, "I have given my word and will not go back. Though I lose my kingdom or my life, to the Golden Deer I will remain true. The boon I have given him I will never deny."

The people departed in distress. Word of this spread through the land. The Great Being, the Golden Deer himself, heard of it and, gathering all the deer, gave them this order, "From this time forth, do not devour the fields of men. Bramadatta has, with his word, given us freedom. Let us, in return, repay him with restraint."

And so it was. Even to this day, the deer of that land do not feed in the cultivated fields. Men and animals share the land equally and the crops grow straight and tall in the golden sun.

The Lion, the Elephant, and the Merchants' Cries

Once, the Buddha was born as a lion. Together with his friend, a great bull elephant, he would often travel to explore the caves, forests, mountains, and seacoasts of his island home.

One day, the lion and the elephant were walking at the jungle's edge, not far from the sea. The lion lifted his heavy, golden-maned head and sniffed the salty air. Gulls cried. Waves broke and foamed against the shore just beyond the screen of trees. Suddenly, above the crashing of the waves and the shrieking of the gulls, came the sound of many voices screaming with terror.

The lion gave a great roar and leaped forward out of the jungle, onto the sandy beach. The elephant, too, maddened by those cries, burst from the jungle behind him.

Before them they saw a group of shipwrecked merchants, screaming and running wildly for their lives. A monstrous serpent had come up out of the sea. Having thrown a great loop of its body around them, like a wall, it swayed over them and prepared to strike. Its fangs dripped venom. Its shining scales and cold green eyes glittered like ice.

At once, the lion leaped up on the elephant's domed head. Lashing his tail in fury, he roared his challenge. Then the elephant, trumpeting shrilly, pointed its tusks towards the great snake and charged, carrying them into battle.

The serpent's head rose up into the air higher and higher. With a long, murderous *hissssssss* it released the merchants, who ran at once for the shelter of the trees. Drawing itself coil upon armored coil up out of the foaming sea, the great serpent slid angrily along the beach towards its oncoming foes.

The battle was terrible. The lion's roaring, the elephant's trumpeting, and the serpent's hissing were so loud that they drowned out the crashing of the waves. The merchants, hidden in the jungle, threw themselves to the ground in terror, covering their ears with their hands. Great clouds of blinding sand were thrown up, darkening the sun. To the terrified merchants it seemed as if the world were coming to an end.

Hours later, the last sounds of the battle drifted away. Once again, the murmuring of the ocean and the screeching of the gulls could be heard. As the air slowly cleared, the merchants peered out fearfully from among the trees.

There, belly up, lay the long body of the serpent, bloody and crushed. The once hard, bright scales were dull and torn. The cold green eyes were faded and glazed. It was dead. Beside it lay the two fearless friends, the lion and the elephant—alive, but dying. The serpent's venom had done its deadly work.

Later, the merchants built a great funeral pyre on the beach and, with all honors, consigned the bodies of the lion and the elephant to the flames.

The merchants wondered why two wild creatures should have sacrificed their own lives to save them. They could not imagine two more unlikely saviors—a fierce lion and a great elephant.

Such selfless compassion, the merchants realized, could never really be explained. It would always remain a mystery.

The Doe, the Hunter, and the Great Stag

Once a great stag, the leader of a herd, lived in the heart of a green forest. His doe was a beautiful creature with eyes as dark as forest pools. The great stag and his wife, the doe, lived together in mutual respect and love.

One day, a hunter came into the forest and set a wire snare along one of the deer trails. Later, the great stag, leading his herd, stepped into the snare, which tightened around his leg, just above the hoof. He tried to pull free but the wire noose only cut deeper into his leg. He tugged again, and the noose, cutting deeper, struck bone. With a cry the great stag tumbled into the dust.

His herd, hearing his cry of alarm, turned and ran. But his wife, thinking only, "My husband is in danger!" leaped forward. There lay the great stag, his sides heaving, struggling to rise, one bloodied leg held by the wire noose.

"Get up, my Lord!" cried the doe. "Use your great strength. Snap the snare, before the hunter arrives!"

But the great stag replied, "It is no use; it is beyond my strength. Run now! Run and be free!"

"No," said the doe. "I will not leave. I will find some way to free you." She licked the stag's face, and stood protectively beside him.

Soon the hunter could be heard crashing through the bushes. His spear blade, striking the stones, sounded to the terrified doe like the screeching of the bone-piercing winds that end an eon. The smell of death and of dried blood assailed her nostrils.

"Run!" cried the stag. "The hunter must not find you!"

But the doe only shook her delicate head from side to side. Her eyes were wide. She shivered and trembled. But all she said was, "I will not leave."

The hunter's steps came closer. The leafy branches by the side of the trail swayed violently. They bent, then snapped and broke. Suddenly the hunter, wearing an old scarred buckskin jacket and gripping a short, stabbing spear in his hands, broke through the bushes before them.

"What's this?" he exclaimed. "Two deer with only one snare? I've never seen such a thing!"

But the doe rose bravely and walked towards the hunter. "O Man-Who-Smells-of-Death-and-Blood," she said, "I have not been caught by your cruel snare. I stay of my own free will. It is my husband, leader of the herd, who is trapped. Let him go free, and I will stay in his stead. The whole herd will suffer if he dies."

The hunter was amazed. He looked from the doe to the helpless stag and back again. His face softened. He stabbed his spear point down into the earth.

"Lady," he said, "your words have touched my heart. I have never released a single creature from my snares before. But this day, you and your mate shall both go free. I am a hunter. It is true. But I'm also a man. And here I exercise my choice and say you both shall live."

Leaving his spear he approached the stag, and pulled open the sharp noose with his calloused hands. "Arise, Great Stag," said the hunter, "and go freely with your doe. She has saved you both this day!"

The great stag rose painfully. Then, leaning against the doe's slender shoulder he said, "Friend, virtue is a priceless jewel and, man or beast, it remains our only refuge in times of danger. You have done a noble deed this day. Let me repay you."

Digging his antlers into the earth, he uncovered a priceless gem. "Take this jewel," said the stag, "and buy your freedom. From this day on, you shall never need to kill again. May you and your family live in peace."

Then the great stag turned and, with the brave doe beside him, limped off into the forest depths.

The hunter watched them go. Soon he stood alone beneath the great trees, the topmost branches tossing, the leaves fluttering and turning in the wind. Wild birds were singing freely all around. In his hands he held a single jewel, but it was indeed worth a fortune.

The Brave Merchant

Once, in days long gone by, when the Bodhisattva dwelt as a merchant in the ancient city of Benares, a solitary Buddha—a Buddha who dwells alone, not teaching—entered the city. Walking silently, the Buddha went from house to house, gathering offerings for the midday meal. Arriving at the gate of the merchant's house, he stood quietly. Though his robes were ragged, he radiated both dignity and calm.

The merchant looked up from his work within the courtyard and, seeing the ragged stranger at his gate, suddenly thought, "Now there is someone at peace with himself and with all the world. It must be one of the solitary Buddhas come from the mountains! I will make an offering to him for the sake of the Buddha-knowledge." Gathering some of the best food in the house, he hurried towards the sage who stood at ease, deeply absorbed, quietly waiting.

Suddenly Mara, the Tempter who opposes all goodness, appeared. "If this merchant makes his offering his faith will increase a thousandfold," said Mara. "Someday, he too will find his way beyond my devices and power. I must stop him."

Then Mara made one of the great fiery hells to open up at the merchant's feet. Flames leaped up, hiding the Buddha from the merchant's sight. Instead of the calling of birds and the ordinary noises of the street, the merchant now only heard screams and groans. The merchant's heart beat wildly with terror and with dread. Sweat dripped from every pore. But, mastering his terror, he thought, "This is Mara's doing. He seeks to overcome me. But today we shall see who is stronger. Hell or no, I will make this offering. I am determined." And, he took a step forward, into the flames.

The flames beat against him. Red-hot iron walls rose up around him. Bloody figures writhed in agony.

Terrifying screams rose above the crackling of the flames and voices, hard as iron, laughed horribly saying, "This is the end, the end of all things!" The merchant, his hair standing on end, walked on. He walked on and on. Time seemed to stop. He walked forever.

As suddenly as they had appeared now, just like that, the flames, the screams, and the demonic laughter ceased. Birds were singing sweetly. The sun was shining down from a clear blue sky. Green-leaved trees swayed in a gentle breeze. Men, women, and children strolled along the crowded streets just beyond the merchant's gate. It was over. The merchant had triumphed over the devices of Mara. He was entirely unscathed.

Before him, as before, stood the solitary Buddha with his begging bowl held forward to receive the merchant's offering. Hardly a minute had passed.

Flushed and triumphant but trembling still, the merchant came forward and made his offering. The Buddha smiled and inclined his head toward the courageous merchant. "Well done," he said. "Well done. Know, worthy merchant, this life is like a dream. Gains and losses all pass by swiftly as the clouds. But to those who walk on despite obstacles and fears, success comes at last, a triumph beyond all dreaming and doubt. Walk on, good merchant, walk on. In this dream of a life we shall meet again."

Then the solitary Buddha turned and walked from the city.

The brave merchant, sharing his wealth with others, walked on rightly through the many years of his life. And, although Mara often tried, he never did stop him.

The Hare's Sacrifice

Once the Buddha was born as a tender-hearted hare. One day, he and his friends—an otter, a monkey, and a fox—decided that once a month they would observe a fast day. On this day, they would give the food that they might have eaten to someone hungrier than themselves.

A month passes quickly in the forest. Trees bend and shift in the wind. By day clouds drift across the sun and at night they race across the moon. Clear streams rush on, carrying leaves and twigs and bugs down over the rocks and on, to heaven knows where. Soon another fast day had arrived.

"I will be good," said the otter to himself, scratching his stomach and fluffing up his wet fur. Slipping into the water, he swam across the shining lake. There, on the other shore, he found a fisherman's camp. Seven fish lay on the grass strung in a row on a stick. "Is there anyone here?" called the otter quietly. There was no answer. "Well, these fish must have gotten lost," he decided. Taking the stick firmly between his teeth, he reentered the water and swam home. Just before he reached the shore once more he suddenly remembered the fast day. "Someone is going to have a fine feast," he thought sadly, "but alas, it's not going to be me!" And feeling very righteous he waddled out of the water, shook himself, and sat down in the sun to dry his fur and rest.

The monkey, swinging in the trees, also thought of the fast and resolved to be good. He would give his own meal to another. Hunting around he found beautiful bananas and mangoes. "Why couldn't I have only found these yesterday?" he couldn't help but think. "Well, today they shall be given to another." And, setting them aside, he too rested in his tree, feeling very righteous indeed.

The fox was trotting along, his sharp nose to the wind. Catching the scent of cooked foods, he bounded through the bushes until he came to a farmer's hut. "Ho, ho!" he thought to himself, "What, no one around? Why, look here, someone's left a pot of yoghurt on the ground and some bread baking on a spit!" Slipping his head through the cord attached to the yoghurt pot, and taking the spit of bread between his teeth, he trotted off, the plume of his tail waving with delight as he thought of the fine meal that lay ahead. He had not gone far when he remembered the fast day. His tail drooped. "Oh, well," he sighed, "someone is going to eat well." Then, recovering his spirits, he trotted on, feeling very righteous indeed.

The hare thought, "Today is the fast day. I'm tired of giving what grows of its own in the ground—carrots, cabbages, potatoes and such. I want to give more than that. But what do I have to offer?" He thought and thought, then he leaped up with delight. "I have it! This very day, I shall offer my own body to someone in need. I shall give myself, give all!"

Up in the heavens, Shakra's marble throne grew hot, a sign that somewhere on the earth someone was about to undertake a noble deed. "Aha," said the king of the gods, "a little hare is about to take a big leap. I shall test him."

In less than an instant, the high god appeared in the hare's forest. Taking the form of an old beggar, he hobbled off, leaning on a staff, to where the otter was resting by the lake shore.

"Friend," said Shakra, King of the Gods, his voice weak and shaking with age, "can you spare a little food for me?"

"Of course," said the otter, "sit down right here. Rest." Running to his den, he dragged out five of the fish and lay them at the beggar's calloused feet. "Eat well," said the otter.

"Thank you for your kindness," said Shakra, his voice again full of vigor and strength, "I may be back for these." And off he went, leaving the astonished otter alone by the shore.

He came to the monkey. "Have you some food for a weary traveller?" he asked, extending a trembling hand.

"Of course. Sit down," chattered the monkey as he scrambled up a tree. He returned in a moment, carrying several bananas and a mango. "These are for you. Eat and enjoy. They are fresh and ripe."

"Thank you," said Shakra, "you are very generous. I may be back for these." Striding off, he left the monkey, who scratched his head in confusion.

Next, he approached the fox. "Help me!" he piteously cried. "I am old and very hungry. Have you any food?"

"Of course!" yelped the fox. "Lucky man, I've got just the thing!" Racing off, he returned with the pot of yoghurt and the spit of bread. He threw himself down, grinning and panting, delighted with his own goodness. But, to his amazement, the old beggar rose and marched off into the twilight, saying, "Thank you. I may be back!"

Then the god Shakra came to the little hare, just as the moon was rising. "Friend," he groaned, "I have not eaten for many days. The roads have been hard and I am faint. Have you anything that I might eat?"

"Yes," said the hare, "I do. Just seat yourself and be patient, for tonight you shall have such a meal as I have never offered before!"

Gathering leaves and twigs, the little hare started a small blaze on the rocks of the forest floor. When the fire was burning fiercely he shook himself thoroughly (to save any fleas that might still be in his coat). Then, leaping high, he jumped straight into the flames.

But what was this? The fire was cool! It was like ice. Not a hair or pore of his body was even singed!

"Come out from the flames, brave little hare," said a noble voice. And leaping out from the fire, the little hare found himself facing one of the radiant gods. It was Shakra himself! The old beggar had vanished.

"What? What has happened?" exclaimed the little hare in astonishment.

"You yourself are the great event that has happened," answered Shakra, King of the Gods. "For your noble sacrifice you shall be remembered for an entire eon. Look!" And, reaching up with a finger, he drew a picture of the hare on the shining disk of the moon. "There, noble hare. You shall not be forgotten for as long as the moon shall shine in the sky. Now come with me. Let me show you my home."

Bending down, the mighty god lifted the little wide-eyed hare into his arms. Then, soaring upward, they disappeared together into the vastness of the night sky.

The forest became very still. The flames of the fire died down. A glowing log popped, shooting up a last burst of sparks. The sparks whirled up, rising higher and higher, until they too disappeared, lost at last against the brilliance of the moon and stars.

The three friends—the otter, the monkey, and the fox—lived on in harmony. Seated together in the forest, they often would look up at the moon and remember with amazement the day that the king of the gods himself had walked among them in their forest. And they would recall their friend, the little hare, and his great sacrifice.

All that was long, long ago, but the hare-in-the-moon shines just as brightly today as he did when Shakra first drew him there, as a sign for all to see that compassion is the light that illuminates our darkness. And if you don't believe me, why, just go out some night and look!

King Sivi

Once, the Bodhisattva was a virtuous king, named Sivi. He was wealthy, respected, and his kingdom was at peace, but he was not content.

One day he looked out through the window of his throne room, over the streets of his city and over the tilled fields of his land. "What have I accomplished?" he sighed. "Life is short and even the virtuous gods do not live forever. All that I have given—time, thought, wealth—seem trivial to me now. I have greater strength than I have yet shown. I want to do more. I want to really help another. I want to give of myself."

Shakra, King of the Gods, heard this and thought, "King Sivi has led an exemplary life. The gates of the heavens will open to him when his earthly years end. Yet now he seeks to test his true strength. He seeks to advance further on the Path he chose long ago."

Then the king of the gods transformed himself. Where but a moment before he had sat resplendent on his golden throne—clothed in robes of gold, crowned with a diadem of stars—there perched two birds, a dove and a hawk.

The hawk ruffled its feathers and glared with fierce, yellow eyes. The dove cooed, flapped its wings, then, suddenly, darted down down through the swirling clouds. The hawk launched itself after the dove. Faster and faster and faster flew the little dove, and faster and faster and faster came the sharp-eyed hawk. Turning and twisting, they plunged towards the earth, straight towards the palace of King Sivi.

The dove spied the open window, sped through it and perched, shaking, on the arm of the king's throne.

"What is it, little bird?" exclaimed the king. "How can I help?"

"O Great King," panted the little dove, "I am in danger. A fierce hawk is coming for me and wants to take my life."

"Don't worry," said King Sivi. "I will save you."

The hawk burst into the room, and with a great flapping of wings perched on the throne's other arm.

"Great King," said the hawk. "My lawful prey sits by your side. I am weary with the chase. Let me claim my prize and I will depart in peace."

"I cannot give you this dove," replied the king. "She came to me in danger and I have promised to save her."

"That is all very well," said the hawk, "but what of my rights? I am a hunter. Doves are my food. You have robbed me of what is mine. Without food I shall starve."

"I'll give you some other food," answered King Sivi. "Name what you will and I will have it brought to you."

"Good King," said the hawk. "I need fresh-killed meat to live. Can you kill another creature so that I may live? Consider. Give me the dove. It is the simplest way."

"It's true," thought the king to himself. "I could never kill another being so that the hawk might live. That is no better than giving him the dove. Yet I must find some solution to this dilemma for, if I cannot, either the dove's blood or the hawk's will forever be on my hands. Both hawk and dove have an equal right to live. I must find a way to help them both and yet cause no harm to any other creature."

Then he had an idea. "Fierce hawk," he said, "I have a plan. You shall eat, the dove shall go free, and no other creature need be killed."

"What is your plan, O King?" asked the hawk.

"I will give you a piece of my own flesh," answered King Sivi, "exactly equal to the weight of the dove."

"If it is equal," the hawk replied, "I shall be content."

By the king's order, a set of golden scales was set before the throne. The king's minister's begged him to reconsider. His courtiers pleaded. The women of the court wept. "I am determined," said King Sivi. "Besides," he added reassuringly, "how much can a little dove weigh?"

The little dove was placed in the tray which hung from the scale's balance arm, and a jewelled knife was brought in upon a silken cushion.

King Sivi raised up the knife. Then he bent down, and sliced a piece of flesh from his thigh. A shudder ran through the assembled crowd. Red blood ran from the wound but not a groan escaped King Sivi's lips. He placed the piece of flesh on the other tray. All watched.

But the dove's side of the balance did not rise.

So once again, King Sivi lifted up the knife and again he cut. But again, as before, the balance did not move.

King Sivi cut and cut again. But no matter how much flesh he piled opposite the dove, flesh cut from his own arms, legs, and thighs, the balance would not move. The dove's side of the scale would not rise.

Finally, weak from loss of blood and flesh, King Sivi had his whole body placed upon the bloodied tray.

"Enough!" cried hawk and dove with a single voice. The throne room was lit by a golden light. Both birds vanished. In the center of the room now hovered Shakra, King of the Gods. And beside him, standing whole and unharmed on the polished floor, stood King Sivi.

"Noble king," said the high god, "this day you have been tested as few have ever been. Your resolution to give, to do good, is indeed like iron, is solid as a rock. Be well, Great King, for you have done well, indeed." And Shakra, as is his way, vanished, leaving not a trace.

The kingdom rejoiced in the virtue of their king and gifts of harmony, long life, and peace rained down upon all who dwelt in that land.

Years later, after King Sivi had grown quite old, he left this Earth and went to live among the joyous gods. From their high realm he could look out over the whole Earth, over cities, forests, and fields. He saw how many men, women, and children labored and suffered without relief. He saw the burdens of beasts, the cries of those that must eat and be eaten and he grew determined to return soon. Though much joy was given him in paradise, how could that compare with having a world in which to do good?

The Story of a Sneeze

Once, long ago, when Bramadatta reigned in Benares, there was a Brahmin whose senses were so finely tuned that he could, just by sniffing, tell if a sword blade would prove lucky to its wielder. The king, hearing of this, said, "That Brahmin must be employed by the palace."

And so it was done.

Soon proclamations were sent throughout the land, stating that all swordsmiths were to bring their new swords to the Brahmin for testing. Only blades he deemed lucky would be purchased by the palace.

It was too bad that no one could sniff the Brahmin out, for if he was an honest man at the start, he didn't stay honest long. After a time, only those swords which were accompanied by gifts—gold, silver, jewelry, land, horses, fine cloth—met with his approval. He declared all other blades unlucky.

One honest swordsmith, outraged, vowed to repay the Brahmin in kind. He took his finest new sword, dropped freshly ground pepper down into the scabbard, thrust the sword in, and set off for the palace.

He presented the sheathed sword, without any accompanying gift, to the Brahmin. The Brahmin unsheathed the blade, held it grandly to his nose, and sniffed: "*Aaachoooo!*" And with that he slit the tip of his nose on the sword's fine, razor-like edge.

The king took pity on the Brahmin, and had an ivory-worker carve a cunningly real nose-tip for him. After this he went back to his work of sword-sniffing but, from then on, gift or no, he always told the truth.

Now, this king had a daughter as beautiful as sunlight on the river, and as clever as the moon which floats perfect and full on even the smallest pond. He also had a brave and good-hearted nephew who lived at court, and whom the king himself had raised from infancy. This nephew was heir to the throne. Do you need to be told

that when the daughter and the nephew were both sixteen years of age they fell in love?

Bramadatta went to his councillors. "Look," he said,
"My nephew, the heir, has fallen head over heels in love
with my jewel of a daughter, and wants her as his wife.
She, in turn, has fallen in love with him. I say we
should let them be wed. A finer pair cannot exist. It is a
match made in heaven. What's more, in time they shall
bring joy to all the realm, for their children will not
only be smart, but they'll be beauties as well. He shall be
king and she shall be queen. What do you think?"

And the councillors all said, "An excellent idea, O
Bramadatta. It will be just as you say." So it was agreed.

But after a while the king began to have second
thoughts. "It's all very well that they want to marry. It's
only natural, after all. Still, if my nephew were to marry
the daughter of some other king, and my daughter were
to marry the heir of yet another, the royal line would
continue through not just one, but two realms. And I'd
have twice as many grandchildren. Hmmm. They are
young, and love is, at their age, fickle. Certainly, they
will come to love whomever I choose for them just as
much as they seem to love each other now! At such times
wise minds, mature and rational minds, should prevail."

And calling again for his councillors he said, "Look.
I've been doing some thinking. Now all of you follow me
on this. If my nephew marries some other princess and
my daughter marries some other crown-prince our ties
to two whole other kingdoms will be strengthened. Plus,
I'll have twice as many grandchildren and heirs. Isn't
that so? Shouldn't we make use of our opportunity?
They are young. Wise and mature minds should prevail."

The councillors all agreed. "That is true. Exceptional
thinking, O Great Bramadatta," they proclaimed. "We
agree. It should be exactly as you have stated."

"Well, then," said the king. "I think our duty is clear."

And the king's nephew and his daughter were forced
to remain apart.

Now, when you are sixteen, such forced separations
are not taken lightly. The prince plotted and planned. He

bent his whole mind to the task of discovering some way that he and the princess might overcome the king's edict. But, try as he might, he could come up with nothing. At last, in desperation, one night he went to the hut of an old woman who lived at the forest's edge.

"Love," she cackled. "What would we not do for love?" Her eyes shone in the firelight, and her rings and necklaces glittered. "Tell me, my Prince," she said at last, "would you dare to enter the grave for love?"

"For the sake of the Princess," he declared, "I would do anything. To have her as my own I would descend into the deepest hells and face an army of demons."

"In that case," said the old woman, "I may have just the plan for you. I will tell the king that his lovely daughter, the princess, is in grave danger." The old woman paused and chuckled. "That a demon king has become enamored with her. The only way to free her from this demon's love is for me to take her to the graveyard, and conjure the demon from her. The demon shall enter a fresh corpse and the princess will be free."

"I don't understand," said the prince.

"You, my dear Prince," said the old woman, "shall be that corpse."

"I?"

"Yes, you. Only you shall be a warm corpse, a very warm corpse, indeed." The old woman chuckled. "Now listen well. You must bring with you to the graveyard a little bag of freshly-ground pepper. You will lie on the ground, unmoving and I will set a small, cloth-draped table over you, hiding you from view. When I begin my incantation, you must sniff the pepper and..."

"Sniff the pepper?!"

"Yes, sniff the pepper. And don't interrupt! Now, where was I? Ah yes—pepper. You must sniff the pepper so that you sneeze. Loudly. Then you must jump to your feet."

"Jump to my feet?!"

"Is there an echo? Just listen and listen well, or this old woman shall leave you to your fate, prince or no!"

"O Wise One! Please, I beg you—do not abandon me in my time of need. I promise I shall reward you greatly."

The old woman chuckled again. "Well, so be it. Now where was I?"

"In your wisdom," said the Prince, "you said that I should jump to my feet..."

"Ah, yes. Now I will have let the guards know, (for we shall have an escort of armed guards—palace soldiers), that the corpse, once the demon-king has taken possession of it, shall sneeze, rise to its feet, grab the nearest soldier, tear him to pieces and devour him. And at that moment, the princess shall be free. I guarantee that when the soldiers hear that sneeze and see you rise to your feet they will bolt like rabbits. Then you and the princess can run off and be wed."

"You are truly the wisest woman in all of India. I swear you shall live in luxury forever."

"My prince," answered the old woman, "this old hut is luxury enough for me. I live here because I choose to. Now let me rest. This evening's talk has already proven too much excitement for my old bones."

The next day the old woman went to the king and told him the terrible news.

"Dreadful!" exclaimed the king, "And yet, how true! My daughter has seemed listless and moody lately. Do whatever you must, but free her from this demon king!"

"My Lord," said the old woman. "I shall. I have a plan." And the old wise woman told him of her device.

That night the old woman and the princess set off for the graveyard with a company of armed men. It was a hot, sticky night. A yellow moon floated like a jaundiced eye over the trees, and a pale mist rose from the earth. Bats flitted in the moonlight, and torches gleamed. Wild dogs howled in the distance like restless spirits.

The beautiful, dark-eyed princess and the old, bent woman walked together at the head of the column of soldiers. Moonlight gleamed on helmets, blades, and greaves. Leather belts creaked. Armor softly clanged.

They came to the burial hill. Bones, skulls, and scraps of flesh lay scattered all around. Though the night was hot, the air that rose from that barren ground was cool.

The princess shivered and drew her light robe around her. The soldiers whispered uneasily among themselves.

"This," said the old woman, "is the place we seek."

The prince had been lying atop the hill waiting for the princess, the wise woman, and the soldiers to arrive. The cold dampness of the cemetery had worked into his bones. Yet, cold as he was, he sweated with a strange heat. Fires seemed to burn beneath him. Sweat gathered at the base of his skull, the small of his back, his ankles and knees. Strange voices moaned. Scaled creatures, dripping with blood and with snakes for hair, seemed to dance from the shadows among the trees. His hair stood on end with the snapping of each twig and the rustling of each leaf. One thought filled his mind—*"Run!"*

But the prince would not run. He lay in the silence and, exerting his will, fought to master the wild pounding of his heart and the mad whirling of his thoughts. "Let fear come," he said, "let whatever will come. I await my princess, and I shall not stir from this spot until my task is done and she is mine."

At last, he heard the tread of sandaled feet, muttering voices, clattering armor. His ordeal was over. He had triumphed over fear.

The old woman approached. "Ah," she crooned. "A fresh corpse, still slick with the sheen of fever and death. Bring the table." A soldier hastily brought the low table and the cloth. The old woman placed the table over the prince and draped the cloth, hiding him from view. Then she began her incantation.

Beneath the table the prince drew a bag of pepper from his robe. He opened the bag, sniffed, and... *"Aaaaachooooo!"* He leaped to his feet, tossing the flimsy table aside. He heard such a scream—like that of a banshee from hell—the old woman playing her part. Then what a sight met his eyes! Swords, spears, helmets littered the ground. Screaming soldiers fled wildly down the hill in every direction.

"Aachooo!"

"Enough sneezing," laughed the old woman. "Take your bride, for you have won her, and be off with you."

And the prince and princess descended the hill and ran off, laughing, into the night.

Before long the king learned the truth. "Well," he said, "I always did say they'd make a fine couple. If they had wit and spirit enough to devise this plan and to carry it off, they deserve their good fortune. They have proved their mettle, though I suspect," he added, looking towards the old woman's hut, "that they had some help. Still, who would not rejoice in such a pair, after all? Yes, we shall welcome them back. In time, they shall be crowned king and queen as I myself originally planned."

And all the councillors said, "Excellent thinking. Yes, most excellent, O Great Bramadatta!"

So the prince and princess returned to the palace and, in time, wisely ruled the land.

One day, years later, not long after the prince had become king, he was walking in the garden with the Brahmin, the one with the famous blade-sniffing nose. It was a very, very hot day. The sun burned down, and softened the wax that held the Brahmin's ivory nose-tip in place. The nose-tip drooped, and before the Brahmin could grab it, it fell off. The Brahmin, ashamed, stood with his hands before his face.

But the young king bent down, picked up the nose-tip, and handed it back. "Don't worry," he said "it's nothing of which you need be ashamed. You may have made a mistake, but you learned a hard lesson well. Your honesty is highly regarded these days. Yet how remarkable it is," he said, pausing to reflect. "Just think. A single sneeze lost you a nose and made you a better man, and with a single sneeze I myself won a kingdom and a bride. Isn't it amazing how simple things can alter our destinies? Who can measure the effects of even a single sneeze?"

When the wise old woman heard that, she laughed. "So, that young fool of a prince has learned a thing or two after all!"

Preacher of Patience

Long ago, the Buddha was a sage, a long-haired, dark-bearded rishi who dwelt alone in the mountains and forests, seeking truth.

One day, he entered a vast park, like a small forest, where he dwelt peacefully, striving alone in solitude for wisdom.

A king, surrounded by his 500 wives, consorts and dancing girls, seeking relief from the duties of his station, came into this park. The female musicians played. The dancers danced. The king ate, drank, and at last, growing tired, lay down and slept.

His women, finding their lord now asleep, ceased their entertainment, and being both curious and delighted with the park's beauty, wandered off to explore the beautiful setting. Tiny silver bells on their anklets and bracelets jingled as they walked. Their voices murmured and rose in soft laughter. As they moved through the park they themselves made a gentle and pleasant music. After a time, they came upon the sage seated in contemplation beneath a great tree.

Surrounding the sage, they asked, "Who are you? Why do you sit here so stern and alone?"

The sage ceased his meditation and answered, "I am a wandering hermit. I dwell alone far from all frivolities and distractions. My mind is set on wisdom. And you are...?"

"We are the women of the king," they answered. "Our lord sleeps now, and being free from the need to entertain or comfort him we are delighting in the beauties of this park. But what is 'wisdom'?"

The sage, seeing that their minds were ripe for teaching, began speaking on the perfections of character and the transcendental insight that frees one from sorrow.

The women seated themselves gracefully before the sage and quietly listened. A great peace settled upon them and they grew aware of a joy far beyond the delights of the palace.

Later that day, the king awoke and found himself alone, his women gone. Irritated at their desertion, he girded on his sword and set out in search of them.

Their trail was not hard to follow. Here he found a scarf draped over a bush, there a golden ball. Here was a silver comb, there a drum or tambourine.

Deeper into the forest he followed their path.

Then he heard a voice speaking, a man's voice, steady and clear. Hastening forward, he found all his women seated before a naked, matted-haired ascetic. Their faces glowed with delight.

"What is this?" he roared. "You desert your king to disport yourselves in sin with a filthy beggar?"

"No, no, my lord," said the women. "This man is a great rishi, a wandering hermit. Far from all distractions, he sternly treads the path of wisdom. He has given us valuable teaching."

"Ha!" shouted the king. "I know his sort. I know what he has in mind! Valuable teaching indeed! What sort of 'teaching' has he given you? Tell me!"

"He has taught us of patience, Lord," they answered. "He has taught us how to attain an even mind, a mind that endures all troubles."

The king, drawing his sword, strode towards the sage.

The sage raised one hand, the delicate fingers slender as lotus stems. Raising his dark eyes, he looked straight at the king, who walked towards him with sword in hand. "Patience, my friend," he said steadily, "patience."

"Patience!" yelled the king, "patience! Let us see your patience, you great liar!"

And, swinging his sword, he lopped off the fingers of the sage's upraised hand. There was no blood; only a milk-like substance oozed from the wound.

The sage did not change his expression. Once again in his clear, firm voice, like a parent speaking to a wayward child, he intoned the single word, "Patience."

The king was infuriated. "Patience!" he screamed, "Here's my patience for you, seducer of royal women!"

And swinging his sword, he cut off the sage's arm, crying, "So, are you still patient now, you rogue!?"

But the sage, his dark eyes fixed firmly on the king, calmly replied, "O King, one must always have patience."

Hearing this, the king became like a maddened bull. He stamped upon the earth in fury and tore his garments in rage. Sweat was running from him. His robes were loosened and disheveled, his face puffy, red with anger and the heat.

"Still it's patience, is it?! You'll sing the same dreary song forever, it seems! Well, I'll make you speak the truth. I'll make you sing a different tune." And swearing all the louder, he once more swung his sword, cutting off the sage's other arm.

Not a thought of anger, fear, loss, regret, or self-concern arose in the sage's mind. No pain disturbed the deep calm of his patient, all enduring, steadfast Mind.

Once again, he looked upon the raging king, and with deep compassion spoke a single word. "Patience." Then he added, "Patience frees one from all sorrows."

"Patience," stormed the king, the eyes starting from his head, the veins swelling thickly, "patience! You stealer of the royal women, you foul derider of the royal dignity, you filthy opposer of the royal will, I'll give you patience! I'll send you to your eternal patience! My power is greater than yours. The patience I'll give you is final and it is real!"

And with a last swing of his sword he cut off the sage's head. The sage's body remained upright, seated gracefully still. With a kick, the king knocked it over to the ground.

"Now we shall have true patience," he laughed madly. "My patience has won! We'll never hear that word patience again!"

But a voice rang out over the forest, speaking but one word, "Patience," and the ground opened up at the king's feet. Flames shot up, and he was swallowed by the earth itself which had opened in horror at his deed.

The Black Hound

Shakra, king of the gods, arose from his golden throne and peered down towards the earth. There were shining seas and pearl-like clouds, snow-capped mountains and continents of many colors. It was beautiful, yet Shakra felt uneasy.

His luminous senses expanded through the heavens. He felt the heat of war. He heard the bawling of calves, the yelping of dogs, the cawing of crows. He heard children crying. He heard voices shouting in anger. He heard the weeping of the hungry, the lonely, the poor. Tears fell from his eyes, showering the earth like meteors.

"Something must be done!" said Shakra. And he changed himself into a forester with a great horn bow. By his side stood a black hound. The hound's fur was tangled. Its eyes glowed with crimson fire. Its teeth were like fangs. Its mouth and lolling tongue were blood red.

Shakra and his hound leaped, plummeting down down down from among the shining stars. At last they alighted on the earth beside a splendid city.

"Who are you, stranger?" called out an astonished soldier from atop the city's walls.

"I am a forester, and this," said Shakra, with a gesture toward the animal at his side, "is my hound."

The black hound opened its jaws. The soldier on the walls grew dizzy with terror. It was as if he was peering down into a great cauldron of fire and blood. Smoke curled from the hound's throat. Its jaws opened wide, wider still...

"Bar the gates!" shouted the soldier. "Bar them now!"

But Shakra and his hound vaulted over the barred gates. The people of the city fled in every direction, like waves flowing along a beach. The hound bounded after them, herding the people like sheep. Men, women, and children screamed in terror.

"Hold!" called Shakra. Do not move!" The people stood still. "My hound is hungry. My hound shall feed."

The king of the city, quaking with fear, cried "Quick! Bring food for the hound! Bring it at once!"

Wagons soon rolled into the market loaded with meat, bread, corn, fruit and grain. The hound gobbled it all down in a single gulp.

"My hound must have more!" cried Shakra.

Again the wagons rolled. Again the hound gobbled the food down with one gulp. Then it howled a cry of anguish, like a howl from the belly of hell.

The people fell to the ground and covered their ears in fright. Shakra, the forester, plucked his great bow's string. Its sound was like crashing thunder on a stormy night.

"He is still hungry!" cried Shakra. "Feed my hound!"

The king wrung his hands and wept. "He has eaten all we have. There is nothing more!"

"Then," said Shakra, "my hound shall feed on grasses and mountains, on birds and beasts. He shall devour the rocks and gnaw the sun and moon. My hound shall feed on you!"

"No!" cried the people. "Have mercy! We beg you to spare us! Spare our world!"

"Cease war," said Shakra. "Feed the poor. Care for the sick, the homeless, the orphaned, the old. Teach your children kindness and courage. Respect the earth and all its creatures. Only then shall I leash my hound."

Then Shakra grew huge, and he blazed with light. He and his black hound leaped up, curling like smoke as together they rose through the air, higher and higher.

Down below, in the streets of the city, men and women looked up into the skies with dismay. They reached out their hands to one another and vowed to change their lives, vowed to do as the mighty forester had ordered.

From up above, Shakra looked down from his golden throne and smiled. He wiped his brow with a radiant arm. The countless stars blazed with light and the darkness between them slumbered like a dog by the fire.

The Hungry Tigress

Once, long, long ago, the Buddha came to life as a noble prince named Mahasattva, in a land where the country of Nepal exists today.

One day, when he was grown, he went walking in a wild forest with his two older brothers. The land was dry and the leaves brittle. The sky seemed alight with flames.

Suddenly, they saw a tigress. The brothers turned to flee, but the tigress stumbled and fell. She was starving, and her cubs were starving too. She eyed her cubs miserably and, in that dark glance, the prince sensed her long months of hunger and pain. He saw, too, that unless she found food soon, she might even be driven to devour her own cubs. He was moved to compassion by the extreme hardness of their lives.

"What, after all, is this life for?" he thought.

Stepping forward, he calmly removed his outer garments and lay down before her. He tore his skin with a stone and let the starving tigress smell the blood. Mahasattva's brothers fled.

Hungrily, the tigress devoured the prince's body and chewed the bones. She and her cubs lived on, and for many years, the forest was filled with a golden light.

Centuries later, a mighty king raised a pillar of carved stone on this spot, and pilgrims still go there to make offerings even today.

Deeds of compassion live forever.

Great King Goodness

Once, long ago, when Bramadatta reigned in Benares, the Buddha was born as the child of the queen. They named him "Silava," or "Goodness." He was called Prince Goodness from then on. When he was sixteen his education was completed, and when his father, the king, died he became the king in his place— "King Goodness."

His first act as king was to have six almonries built— places from which to distribute alms to the poor. One was built at each of the city's four gates—North, South, East, and West. One stood at the very center of the city, and one right at the palace gates. From each of these stations, he regularly distributed from the stores of his own wealth to all the poor and needy, to travellers as well as people from his own city.

He kept all the commandments, observed the fast days, and vigorously upheld all the items of good character. He regarded all his people with such loving kindness, that he felt towards each of them as a parent feels towards a beloved only child.

One day, one of the ministers of King Goodness was found to have trespassed within the treasury, as well as with one of the king's wives. The minister's guilt in both matters was obvious; even the common folk of the city knew the details. King Goodness did not punish this man as he might have. Instead, he banished him from the kingdom. The minister, gathering his family and his wealth about him, went to the neighboring kingdom of Kosala, where he rose rapidly in influence and power, until he was that king's advisor.

When this minister had reached this position of eminence, he said to the king of Kosala, "Sire, the city of Benares is like a ripe honeycomb, easy in the taking. Its wealth is great. Its king is feeble. Send your soldiers into the city. Take the palace, the treasury, everything. The king has no force to withstand you. His goodness has made him weak."

But the king of Kosala was suspicious. "You have left Benares recently yourself," he said. "You are a spy for King Goodness! This is a ruse. I can see it. Upon entering the city, my forces will be ambushed and destroyed. You are conspiring with King Goodness to take hold of my kingdom and destroy me!"

"No, Sire," said the minister. "Never. If you doubt me, just send a raiding party across the border. Let them attack an outlying village of King Goodness' realm. Then see what he will do!"

A raiding part was sent. After destroying a village and making off with many goods and much money, they were captured by King Goodness' men, brought to Benares, and set before the king.

"Why," asked King Goodness, "have you hurt my people? Why have you killed, stolen, and despoiled?"

"We were hungry," they said, "and we were paid to do it."

"My children, if you need food, money, clothing, whatever," said King Goodness, "come to me in the future, and I will freely give it to you. You need not harm others." Then, giving gifts to the astonished men, he had them released, unharmed.

"As you see, Sire," said the evil-hearted minister, when the men had returned, "Benares is a honeycomb, a ripe plum. The King is intoxicated with his own goodness. He has no power to resist. Attack, my Lord, and take the kingdom from this weakling."

But the king of Kosala was suspicious still. Sending another raiding party closer yet to the capitol, he awaited their report. And when these men returned, their story was the same. After attacking a village and doing much harm, they too had been brought before King Goodness, given gifts, and set free.

But still, the king of Kosala was nervous. So yet a third group was sent, this time to plunder the very streets of Benares. And once again they returned, telling the same tale. They too had been given gifts by King Goodness, and released.

Satisfied at last that King Goodness was, indeed, a thoroughly good king, the king of Kosala raised his army, mounted his war-elephant, and set off to capture the ripe, golden honeycomb that was Benares.

Now, King Goodness had a bodyguard of one thousand champions, and each one them was an unbeaten warrior—loyal, strong, and disciplined. When they learned of the king of Kosala's approaching army, they came to King Goodness and said, "Give us the order, Lord, and we will rout this army. We will drive them back, take their king captive, and secure the borders of your realm."

But King Goodness said, "There shall be no violence, my children. None. Let them enter the kingdom. Let them enter the city. Let them enter the palace and, yes, even come into the throne room itself. Yet no one shall lift a hand in violence against them. Is that understood, my children?"

And those mighty warriors, so strong in their discipline and their dedication to that great, good king, all said, to a man, "Yes."

When the host of the king of Kosala entered the land, no one opposed them. They marched into the city of Benares. No army of warriors hindered them. They mounted the steps of the palace and shattered the great bronze doors. Still no weapon was raised against them. They marched into the marble throne room of the great King Goodness. There sat King Goodness on his golden throne, surrounded by his one thousand champions. "Remember, no violence, my children," cautioned the king. "Let only thoughts of charity and love fill your hearts." And, even as the men of Kosala laid rough hands upon him, he cautioned his champions, over and over, "No violence, my children. None." And so great was the discipline of those one thousand champions that not a one broke forth in anger to destroy the enemy host.

Then the great King Goodness and his one thousand champions were all taken to the graveyard. Their weapons were taken from them, and all were buried in the earth, up to the neck. The ground was stamped down tight all around them. And, as the sun set, they were abandoned there.

The night grew chill. Towards midnight, furtive shapes gathered, pacing nervously in the shadows. The jackals had come, as was their way, to devour fresh corpses. As they slunk forward, King Goodness said to his men, "Let your hearts be filled only with love and charity, my children. More powerful than any weapon is the desire for goodness."

When the jackals came close, the king and his men gave a great shout. The jackals retreated in terror. But, when nothing more happened, they returned and drew closer again. Once more, King Goodness and his men gave a great shout. And once more, the jackals fled in fear. But, finding no one giving further chase, they slowed, turned, and after a time, once more crept near. Then, for the third time, the king and his men raised their cry. But this time the jackal-leader said, "They are only prisoners, condemned men, trapped and helpless. Let us go forward and devour them."

And this time they came on and did not turn away.

King Goodness, watched the jackal leader approach, its eyes glowing redly, its teeth gleaming in the moonlight, and he raised his head, baring his throat, as if seeking a quick and easy death. The jackal-king, sniffing cautiously, came closer. Then, seeing no danger, at last it lunged forward for the kill.

But before its teeth could grip and close, King Goodness sank his own teeth into the jackal's furry throat and, locking his jaws, held tight. The jackal lunged this way and that struggling to break free. It pulled and tugged desperately, back and forth, from side to side. As it struggled, the earth around King Goodness was loosened by its claws. Its frantic tugging moved the king, loosening the earth around him even more.

At last, the jackal-king broke free and ran off howling into the night, followed by the pack.

Then King Goodness, rocking himself back and forth in the loosened soil, slowly broke the hold of the earth which had been stamped down around him. He worked his arms free and, at last, climbed up out of the burial ground. He was free.

Then he worked to free his companions, loosening the earth around each, until all were also free.

As it should happen, a corpse had been left lying in that graveyard in such a way that it extended across the territory of two goblins. Each claimed the greater portion as its own. Their argument grew more and more heated. Then, at the point of coming to blows, one of the goblins said, "In this graveyard stands King Goodness, a truly righteous man. Let us bring the corpse to him. He will divide it equally for us, without bias." And to this the other goblin agreed.

Dragging the corpse by a foot, they approached King Goodness and asked for his aid in the matter of dividing their spoils equally for them. "Certainly," said the king, "But as I am dirty I must bathe first."

And, just like that, with their magical powers, the goblins made the king's own bath, filled with scented water, appear. Straight from the palace, where the usurper king slept, they brought it magically through the air. When King Goodness was clean and refreshed, the goblins then brought his own robes to him, the very robes which had been laid out for the usurping king of Kosala. They brought him perfumes in a golden casket and fresh flowers laid out on ivory fans. Then the goblins asked if there was any thing else he might require.

"I am hungry," said King Goodness. And just like that, at once, fresh-cooked rice, flavored with the choicest curries, spices, and herbs lay on a golden plate before him. The goblins also brought his own golden bowl, filled with rose-scented water to drink, straight from the usurper's table. Then King Goodness, well satisfied, had but one more thing to ask. "My sword," he said, "rests by the pillow of my bed. Bring it and I will fulfill your request."

At once his great sword appeared. Then, King Goodness set the corpse upright and, with one stroke, split it precisely in half. The goblins were delighted. The king washed the blade and girded on his sword.

The goblins ate their fill and, when they were done, glad of heart and filled with gratitude, they asked King Goodness if there was not something else they might yet do for him.

"If you would set me in my bed chamber where the usurper lies, and bring my men into the palace, I would be well satisfied," said King Goodness.

In an instant it was done.

King Goodness stood once again in his own bed chamber and looked down upon the sleeping form of the usurper, the king of Kosala. King Goodness raised his sword and, with the flat of it, smote the sleeping king upon his side. The king of Kosala awoke and saw, by the dim light of the bedside lamp, his enemy, King Goodness—or his ghost—standing, blade in hand, beside him. And the king of Kosala was terrified!

Summoning all his courage he rose from the bed and asked, "Are you man or ghost?"

"Man," answered King Goodness, "even as you are."

"How did you enter then? It is impossible," said the king of Kosala. "The gates are all guarded. The doors are barred. The halls are patrolled. What's more, you were left as food for the jackals! Yet you stand here, sword in hand, robed in splendor."

Then King Goodness told the whole story in all its detail.

The heart of the king of Kosala was moved and he cried aloud, "Sir, this is wondrous! I called myself a man, was blessed with a man's shape, with a man's heart and mind. Yet, for all that, I did not know the worth of your goodness while even those blood-drinkers, those eaters of carrion flesh, knew it! I will never plot against you again! I swear it!" Then he swore an oath of friendship with King Goodness, swore it on his own sword, and he begged, too, for the king's forgiveness. Then, taking the little couch, he had King Goodness lie down and rest through the remainder of the night on the bed of state.

When the morning came, the king of Kosala had the drum sounded and gathered all his men. Then, in full sight of his army and of all the people, he praised King Goodness' virtue and once more begged his forgiveness. He vowed, too, to use his strength for good rather than evil. "Great King, I pledge you my strength of arms," he said, "to protect you and your people from all dangers! Rule, Great King, in peace. My men and I shall keep watch over your borders." Then, passing sentence on the treacherous minister, he departed with his army and his war-elephants back to his own land.

Seated in splendor upon his golden throne, with its legs carved like those of an antelope, beneath a great white parasol, King Goodness looked with joy upon his people and upon his one thousand mighty men. "If I had not remained true," he said to himself, "if I had not persevered fearlessly in goodness, both the people of my own kingdom as well as those of the kingdom of Kosala would have suffered greatly. At this moment what joy arises in me! How could any victory gained through violence or warfare begin to compare with it?"

And, speaking from his heart, he said to the assembled people, "Never doubt it. Effort in goodness will be rewarded. Even if you don't see how it may work out, persist in goodness. The fruit of such perseverance is sweet indeed!"

The Naga King

Long ago, when Anga was king of Anga and Magadha was king of Magadha, the two warring kingdoms were separated by the Campa River. The great Naga King, Campeyya, lived with his sixteen thousand subjects beneath the surface of that river.

In the fighting, sometimes the king of Magadha won part of the Anga kingdom, and sometimes the king of Anga took part of Magadha. One day, the king of Magadha, having been worsted in battle, fled on horseback from the warriors of Anga. He came to the river, which was running high. Behind him rode the enemy, seeking his life. "Better to die in the river than be vanquished by foes," he thought, and spurring his horse forward, he plunged into the swirling water.

The serpent king, Campeyya, had built a magnificent jewelled pavilion on the river bottom. The river bed was covered with gold and silver grains, fine as sand. Flame-bright trees of branching coral hung with jewels—diamonds, rubies, emeralds, pearls.

That day King Campeyya was relaxing in splendor in his jewelled pavilion. Musicians played instruments of gold and crystal. Naga maidens danced, swaying and turning. Suddenly the music stopped. The maidens grew still. Looking up, King Campeyya saw above him a man on horseback plunge into the river and, after struggling in the current, come drifting slowly down towards them. The serpent king saw nobility in the face of that man and felt a liking for him. He extended his protection over both horse and rider so they arrived safely on the river bottom. Rising from his throne he offered the stranger his own seat saying, "Fear nothing, friend. I have only your welfare in mind. Tell me who you are and why you have entered my realm."

The king of Magadha told him his troubles. King Campeyya said, "Great King, do not worry. I shall make you master of both kingdoms."

For seven days the king of Magadha remained beneath the surface of the river as the honored guest of King Campeyya. Then he rose up from the depths of the river and, with the serpent king's protection upon him, came once more against the king of Anga, and this time he overcame him. In this way he gained dominion over both kingdoms, and the constant warring ceased at last. He ruled fairly and wisely, and peace settled once more on the war-torn land. From that time on there was great friendship between the human king and his friend and benefactor, the serpent king, Campeyya.

The king of the combined realms of Anga and Magadha had a pavilion of gold and precious jewels built on the riverbank. There, each year, he offered tribute to the serpent king who had saved him. And each year at that time, the serpent king, surrounded by a great host of the Naga people, took human form and came up out of the river so that his splendor might be seen.

At this time, the Bodhisattva was the eldest son of a poor family. Each year he stood in the great crowd that gathered to view the alms-giving and the appearance of the Naga king. One time, upon seeing the Naga king's great wealth and splendor, the desire to also live such a life arose within him. Shortly thereafter, still in this condition of desire, he contracted some malady and died. At the same time the Naga King, Campeyya, also died. As the Bodhisattva had led a virtuous and charitable life, his mind-born desire was realized. He came to life as the new king of the Nagas of the river Campa.

When the Bodhisattva opened his eyes, he saw his great glittering body stretched out along a golden couch and thought, "I have been a man and had stored up as many good deeds, like grains of rice in a grainery. Yet now I have become a serpent. Though I have gained riches, I have been foolish. I have lost the path of virtue." And, though he looked around and saw only splendor and magnificence, he was filled with sorrow.

The Naga maiden, Sumana, seeing the Bodhisattva in this serpent form, cried with joy, "A great god, Shakra himself it must be, has taken life among us. Our new king is great in power and in beauty!" Then all the Nagas came, and bowing before the Bodhisattva, played such music in his honor as he had never heard, not even in a dream. So beautiful was this music and so great their joy that his sorrow was dispersed. Putting off his serpent form, he sat on his throne in garments of splendor.

Choosing the Naga maiden, Sumana, as his wife, the Bodhisattva ruled in wisdom. But, after a time, he thought, "Though I now live in magnificence and splendor as a serpent king, I am still far from ultimate Truth. Better to be a man, even a man such as I was, without wealth or power, and master the ways of Truth, than to dwell in luxury on the river bottom. This is not true freedom. I must discipline myself and regain a human state." Then, in order to regain a human birth, from that time on, for one day each week, he fasted to discipline himself and to increase his virtue.

After a time, he found that this was too easy a task. His life was so comfortable, so full of riches and pleasure, that he sought a greater challenge. He decided that each month he would leave the river and go into the human world. There, for the time of the half-moon, he would maintain vows of fasting and non-violence. No matter what might happen to him, he would not raise his strength against any other being.

On the appointed day, he left the river, and taking the form of a hooded serpent with a body like pure silver, he coiled himself on an ant-heap by the roadside. "Let those who want my skin take it," he said. "Let those who wish to find a dancing serpent to display for money in the towns, find me. Let the ants bite if they wish. Though my power is great, I will harm no living thing." And lowering his hood he lay meekly in the dust.

But people passing, who saw the Great Being coiled on the ant-heap, did not harm him. Instead, they offered flowers and perfumes. And, after a time, the village people, seeing him return so regularly to the ant-heap each mid-month, built a cloth pavilion over him. They spread smooth sand for him to lie on, and continued to make offerings of flowers and perfumes. In this way, the Bodhisattva easily kept his vows.

One day Sumana, his wife, said to him, "My lord, the world of men is filled with dangers. While you are there, far from your own kingdom, let me have some way of knowing if you are well or in some distress."

Then the Bodhisattva led Sumana to a clear pool of water in their garden under the river, and said, "O Sumana, look into this clear pool. If anyone should strike me hard enough to hurt me, the water will become cloudy. If a winged garuda carries me off in its claws, the water will disappear. If a snake-charmer seizes me, this clear water will turn to blood. Now you shall know how I fare, though I am far away." Then Sumana was content. Shortly after this, the Bodhisattva left the river and made his way to the ant-hill once again.

At this time, a young Brahmin was returning from the city of Takkasila where he had gone to learn how to master a powerful charm. The Brahmin, passing through that village, heard of the great serpent and thought, "I will see if my charm works on him. If it does, I will use it to make him obey me. I shall gain riches by making him dance in the villages and towns."

The Brahmin gathered the necessary herbs and, repeating his charm, approached the Great Being.

When the Bodhisattva heard the charm, he felt as if his ears had been pierced with burning splinters. His head hurt as if he had been clubbed. He lifted his head and, flicking his tongue in and out, raised his hood. But when he saw the Brahmin snake-charmer standing near, he thought, "My slightest breath could shatter his body. He does not know my power. Yet I have made my vows, and I will not harm him." Lowering his hood, he let his smooth, scaled head sink down onto the dusty earth.

The Brahmin chewed the herb and spit it onto the great serpent's head. Immediately a fiery blister arose. Repeating his mantric charm, the Brahmin smeared his hands with the herb, took hold of the Bodhisattva's body, and stretched him out full-length on the ground. With a forked stick he pinned the Great Being's head, and with a club he beat him along his sides and spine. He spit more of the herb into the serpent's mouth, which now filled with blood. "Snake," he said, "you are now in my power. Do as I say, or you shall suffer much worse!"

Then the Brahmin took hold of the serpent king and, crushing and twisting his body and causing him great pain, pushed him down into a basket woven of reeds. Carrying him to the next village, he used the charm to make the great Naga king perform for the crowd.

And the crowd went wild, tossing jewels and coins. Though it was just a rural village the Brahmin collected a thousand rupees. Why? Because the dance of the snake king was like the dance of no other snake they had seen before. Spreading his hood, the Great Being moved his body with such grace and such speed that his movements seemed to form circles, squares, and lotus flowers in the air. He moved his head so that one, ten, a hundred, a thousand hooded heads appeared; one, ten, a hundred, a thousand flickering tongues.

At first, the Brahmin had planned to release the snake when he had earned a thousand rupees. But now, seeing how easily he might become truly rich, he thought, "If I can gather such wealth in a village, what could I do in a town, or even at some royal court?" And he bought a cart, loaded the snake king in his basket on the cart, and drove on, followed by an admiring crowd. From town to town he went, gathering much money, and heading steadily, all the while, towards the palace of King Uggasena who reigned then in Benares.

All this while the snake king refused to break his fast. The Brahmin killed frogs for him but the Great Being thought, "If I eat these frogs to ease my hunger he will kill more. I cannot allow it. I have taken vows." And he would not eat.

Sumana, the Snake-King's wife, grew more concerned with each passing day. Her Lord had not returned. At last, fearful of what she might find, she went to the clear pool and peered into its depths.

But the pool was like a pool of blood! Then she knew that her Lord had been captured by a snake-charmer! At once, she set out to find him.

Arriving at the ant-heap, she saw that all was deserted and, in the dust of the bare ground, she saw the marks of a struggle. Taking the form of a beautiful woman, like a radiant goddess, she set off through the air. Alighting in the fields outside a nearby village, she heard talk of the serpent's miraculous dance and of the snake-charmer's journey to Benares. Weeping now, she flew to Benares and the king's palace.

By this time, the Brahmin had arrived at the palace of King Uggasena. All the preparations had been made for the serpent king to display his dance. Galleries had been built and the crowds had gathered. The king was already seated in anticipation, on a dais covered with fine carpets, and the courtyard had been spread with white sand, and a fine carpet had been placed in the center.

The Brahmin carried a jeweled basket to the carpet, took off the basket's lid and charmed the snake king forth. The Great Being began to dance, forming circles, squares, and lotus flowers with his twining body, making one, ten, a hundred, a thousand hooded heads appear. The crowd was ecstatic. Thousands of kerchiefs waved in the air and jewels fell like rain all around the dancing serpent king.

But, slowly, the snake king grew strangely quiet, and ceased his magical dance. The crowd called, "Dance, royal serpent! Dance! You have won our hearts!" The king called, "Why have you stopped, great snake? Dance on. You shall be rewarded." But the serpent king, his length held erect, only gazed solemnly up, into the sky.

Then the crowd looked upward, as did the brahmin and the king. And all were filled with wonder. High overhead, standing all alone in the bright air, was a beautiful, shining woman. A golden light radiated from her. And she was weeping. It was Sumana, who had found her lord at last. Then tears fell from the Great Being's eyes too and, feeling ashamed, he crawled into the basket and lay hidden from sight.

Then King Uggasena called, "Surely, you are a goddess. Not human, at any rate, is your shining beauty. Tell me who you are, and why you weep. Is it rage, or sorrow?"

"I am no goddess," answered Sumana, "but a Naga queen. I weep for rage and for sorrow. My great Lord, whose power, like that of Shakra, king of the gods, is fierce as fire, whose single breath might destroy a province or turn your city to cinders, now dances harmlessly before you. Such is his love of goodness and so great his vowed restraint he will not strike out to gain his freedom. His body is bruised and blistered; his sides are caved-in, bony, and thin. Yet, beneath the Campa River, sixteen thousand Nagas call him King. This snake charmer has taken a great lord for his own profit. He does not know what he has done. But you, O King, desirous of merit, will you not set my great Lord free?"

And, still hovering in the air, she recited this verse:

"Justly, gently, set him free,
Buy, Great King, a Serpent's liberty.
Giving gold and cattle, jewels and rings
Will win great stores of merit for thee."

The king thought and replied:

"Justly now and gently see
I'll buy this Serpent's liberty.
With gold and cattle, jewels and rings
To win vast stores of merit for me."

And King Uggasena, turning to the Brahmin, offered him the finest bull of his herds, one hundred of his finest cows, one hundred coffers filled with gold and with gems, a princess to marry, and a golden throne made in the form of a flax flower set with silken cushions of blue. "Release this holy Naga Lord," he said, "and all shall be yours."

"There is no need, Great King," said the Brahmin. "I will release the Naga Lord." And he offered this verse:

"I want no gifts, Great Majesty,
But release this Serpent willingly.
Naga Lord, please pardon me.
This deed will to my merit be."

Then he bowed before the Great Being, who still lay coiled in the basket. The Serpent King came forth and crept into a flower, where he changed from his serpent shape to the form of a young man arrayed in robes of shining gold. There he stood, handsome as a god, and Sumana, descending from the skies, stood beside him.

Indeed, all those who had come that day thinking to see a serpent dance felt themselves well rewarded.

After that, the King Uggasena travelled with the Bodhisattva and Sumana in great splendor to the river Campa. "Allow me one request, Great One," he said. "Please, take me to see your palace beneath the waters."

Then King Uggasena and all his retinue descended with the Bodhisattva and Sumana to the river bottom. Uggasena had never seen such magnificence and, great king though he was, he was still awed. "Great Being," he asked, " why did you leave such unearthly magnificence to lie on an ant-heap by a dusty roadside?"

"This vast treasure is nothing compared with the treasure of human birth," answered the Bodhisattva. "Through human birth full Enlightenment itself may be achieved. It is for this that I would labor. As to this treasure, take it. I renounce it all. Hills of pearl, groves of flame-colored coral trees and clusters of jewelled fruit— diamonds, emeralds, rubies, sapphires; mountains of gold, lakes of silver. Take what you will and use it for good." Then he had the Nagas of his realm fill countless coffers with treasure for the King Uggasena who returned, strengthened in virtue, to his own kingdom.

The king had been given so much gold, however, that as he travelled home the excess, spilling continuously from his over-laden treasure carts, stained the earth. And that is why the ground extending from the shores of the Campa river to the ancient city of Benares remains golden colored even to this day.

Section III:
Later Stories

Most Lovely Fugen

About three hundred years ago, in Japan, there lived a Buddhist priest named Shoku Shonin. For many years, he had been a devotee of the Bodhisattva Samantabhadra, or Fugen, the Bodhisattva of Wise and Compassionate Action. Day and night, Shoku Shonin focused his mind on the Bodhisattva. Day and night, he recited the verses from the sutras which promised Fugen's protection.

Shoku Shonin had only one wish. He wanted to *see* Fugen.

One day, as Shoku walked through the streets of a local village, he happened to overhear two merchants talking about a courtesan who lived in the town of Kanzaki, several days walking distance away. This beautiful woman, they said, attracted large crowds each evening by dancing while dressed as the Bodhisattva Fugen. Shoku was outraged.

That night he had a dream. He heard a voice that said, "Go to Kanzaki and watch the courtesan dance."

"What foolishness!" proclaimed Shoku upon awakening. "So, *that* is still with me! Well, devil's promptings will never move me." And he didn't go.

The next night the dream-voice came again. "Go to Kanzaki and watch the courtesan dance."

"Never!" said Shoku.

The third night, the same dream came again. "Watch her dance," said the voice. And that morning when Shoku awoke, he said to himself, "Perhaps I am called to end the sacrilege."

So he tied on his straw sandals, set the wide, deep bowl of his monk's travelling hat upon his head, and with his ringed staff in his hand he set off along the roads to Kanzaki.

After two days of brisk walking, he entered the town. It was early evening. The sky was just beginning to darken. A few stars glittered faintly overhead. A crowd of men had already gathered at the courtesan's home, waiting for her to appear. Torches were lit. Then, as the sky grew dark, as if by magic, the woman appeared on a small stage which had been set up in the courtyard. She was breathtakingly beautiful and she was dressed in the flowing, Indian-style robes and necklaces which, in paintings and sculptures, adorn the Bodhisattva Fugen. Keeping time with a small hand-drum, she began to dance. Her jewels sparkled in the torchlight and all the men, except for the priest Shoku Shonin, entered into a trance of delight.

Shoku Shonin's rage grew. This was blasphemy! But, gradually, an inexplicable change overcame him.

He grew calm, and a deep peace spread throughout his limbs, rising from the soles of his feet up through the crown of his head.

The night sky shimmered and the ground seemed to drop away beneath his feet. What did he care? The dance! The dance! Such joy radiated through the entire universe from this courtesan's dance. The stars were dancing, the Earth was dancing. His eyes seemed to penetrate the darkness, and it was as if the trees, the animals in their holes, the people of the town, were all somehow moving with, breathing with, all were part of this wonderful dance. Even the beating of his own heart, the rush of air in and out of his lungs, the ticking of his pulse were elements in the miracle of this perfect dance.

A slender ray of golden light shot from between the eyebrows of the dancing courtesan. Dazzled, Shoku Shonin closed his eyes. When he opened them there, before him on the little platform in the courtyard, he saw, not the courtesan, but the radiant figure of the Bodhisattva Fugen, seated on a great six-tusked white elephant, golden beams of light shooting all around.

Tears of joy trickled down Shoku Shonin's old face. His lifelong dream had been fulfilled. For how long he stood there gazing, drinking in the scene before him, he never knew. When he came to himself at last, the stage was bare. The torches had burned low. The last of the men were leaving. Coins and favors littered the dancing platform.

Shoku turned and stumbled out into the street. As he left the village, he heard a faint tinkling of little silver bells. There before him stood the courtesan in the robes of Fugen. "Tell no one," she said, "of what you alone have seen this night. Go in peace, old friend." And she was gone. A faint scent, like some heavenly incense, lingered on the night air. Then that, too, was blown away on the wind.

In a daze, Shoku started walking again. Two days later, he discovered that he had arrived back at his own temple. Of his two days' journey on the roads he remembered nothing.

Shoku told no one of his strange experience. But just before his death, he related the whole incident to a brother monk. His last words were, "Free for compassion's sake, to take endless forms throughout the limitless universe, they do not despise the lowly and ignoble." And putting his palms together he chanted this verse:

Buddhas sell the Dharma
Patriarchs sell the Buddha
The courtesan sells herself
All to ease the passions of men.

Form is only Emptiness
Emptiness only Form.

And then, Shoku Shonin peacefully died.

The Dog's Tooth

Once, as a Tibetan trader was preparing to leave on his travels, his mother asked him if he would bring her back a relic from India, the land of the Buddha.

"I'm too old to make such a pilgrimage now," she said.

The son assured his mother that he would find her a holy relic.

But months later, when he returned, he was dismayed to discover that he had completely forgotten his mother's request. So he promised her that next time, he would not be so careless.

But, when he returned from his next trip, he was once again ashamed to find that, what with all his travelling, buying, and selling, the thought of his mother's request and his promise had slipped his mind.

He vowed he would not be so forgetful again. The following year, when he set out, he was determined to find his mother an especially holy relic.

Time passed. The trader spent busy months buying and selling. At last, pleased with his efforts, off he headed with a train of laden ponies for the mountains of Tibet and home. He left the hot plains behind and rose higher into the mountains. At last, as he was coming through the final pass that led to his village, he remembered—it struck him like a thunderbolt! He had forgotten his mother's relic for a third time!

Just at that moment he happened to notice a dog's skull lying by the roadside. The jawbone, with several brownish teeth still attached, was nearby. The trader had an inspiration. He jumped down from his horse and pried loose one small, brownish tooth from the dog's jawbone. After polishing the tooth on his sleeve, he wrapped it in a piece of fine brocade.

When he got home, he gave the tooth to his mother. He told her it was an especially sacred relic—a tooth of Sariputtra, one of the Buddha's greatest disciples.

Beside herself with joy, his mother placed the dog's tooth on the altar and prostrated herself before it again and again.

The next morning the son left to begin selling his goods—spices, silks, and herbs from India—promising to be back within the month. Of course, he planned to find a genuine tooth-relic to replace the dog's tooth, but in the meantime, he had made his mother very happy.

Weeks passed. Then, one day just before nightfall, the son returned. His trading had again been quite successful. But what was this? There were crowds in the courtyard of his house! He slid off his horse, hurriedly tied the ponies, and hurried inside.

Many people were also inside, neighbors and lamas and strangers—pilgrims, by the look of them. His mother was beaming. "My son!" she cried upon seeing him enter. Then, taking his hands in hers, she said but one other word: "Look!"

He looked. There on the altar was a small brownish tooth. It was lying on the piece of brocade in which he had wrapped the dog's tooth. Beams of light emanated from the tooth and rippled through the crowded room. The trader had never, in all his travels, seen anything like it. It was a holy relic, undoubtedly genuine.

"Mother," he asked, "where did you find such a relic?"

"Foolish son," she answered, "modest child! This is the holy tooth of the Buddha's own disciple, Sariputtra. You yourself brought it to me!"

The trader went closer and looked again. It was indeed the dog's tooth after all; of this he could have no doubt. Even as he looked, golden beams of light leapt from the tooth and, shining through the open window, seemed for an instant to touch the most distant stars.

Spontaneously, the trader prostrated himself before the tooth.

So great was the power of that old woman's faith that, deluded as she was, she had, indeed, turned a dog's tooth into a holy relic.

A Legend of Avalokitesvara

The Bodhisattva Avalokitesvara looked down into the many hells and saw that they were filled with suffering beings.

A great vow spontaneously arose in his heart. "I will liberate all beings from the sufferings of the hells," he said. And so through countless ages he labored, descending into and emptying hell after hell, until the unimaginable task was at last done.

The great Bodhisattva ceased then from his eons of heroic exertion. He wiped the glistening diamonds of beaded sweat from his brow, and, looking down into the now empty, silent hells, smiled. It was done. Here and there a curling wisp of smoke still rose up. Now and then, in some vast cavern far below, faint echoes sounded as a loose brick shifted on a pile of rubble. But the raging fires had been quenched and the great iron cauldrons were quiet. Sweet silence flowed through the dark halls. Even the demons were gone for they too, in the end, had been released, liberated to the heavens, by the mighty efforts of the Compassionate One.

But what was this? Suddenly, there came a wailing scream, then another, and another. Flames leapt, clouds of smoke whirled, blood-filled cauldrons bubbled madly. The radiant smile faded from the Bodhisattva's face. Once again the hells were entirely filled. In less than an instant all was exactly as before.

The heart of the Bodhisattva Avalokitesvara filled with sorrow. Suddenly, his head split into many heads. His arms shattered into many arms. The one thousand heads looked in all directions to see the sufferings of every being. The one thousand arms were enough to reach into any realm, to save those in need.

Rolling up his one thousand sleeves, the great Bodhisattva settled down once more to the unending task.

Stilson's Leap

On a gray day in late November 1941, a squadron of
Spitfires was flying back towards Britain across the
English Channel. The sky was low, with few breaks in
the clouds. They had just broken up a formation of enemy bombers and, while most pilots were now low on
fuel, all would make it back safely to the base if luck
held.

Then flames leaped out from beneath the cowling of
the commanding officer's plane, and thick, black smoke
spewed from his exhausts. The whirling propeller
slowed, then froze, and his aircraft, trailing smoke, began hurtling down toward the sea.

The cockpit canopy slid back, and the commanding
officer tumbled out. His parachute opened. The others
watched him drift down through the wind and silence
toward the ocean, which splashed and foamed, tilting
yawningly below.

Dropping lower, they saw him hit the sea, sink, then,
supported by his life-vest, rise up and swim away from
the entangling parachute lines. He waved them off, but
awkwardly, as if he were injured. Despite his signal,
they circled over him until their fuel was dangerously
low. They would wait for his life raft to bob up to the
surface before they left him.

But the raft never surfaced. A shard of metal had torn
it, perhaps—or a bullet had pierced it, or the flames had
destroyed it. No matter. Without a life raft he could
never survive in those cold waters.

The other pilots radioed his position over and over,
though several were flying with almost dry tanks.

The new acting squadron leader, until moments before the CO's wingman, knew there was nothing more
they could do. It was his job to bring the squadron home.
Cursing the foul luck that had caught them so close to

home, he gave the order for them to continue back to their base.

But a man named Stilson, ignoring all orders to leave, and refusing to acknowledge any radio contact, only gained altitude while still circling over their downed commander. At three thousand feet, Stilson's canopy slid back, the graceful green-and-brown fighter arched over, and Stilson tumbled from the warmth and safety of the cramped little cockpit, falling free.

His parachute blossomed above him, as he floated down towards the foaming sea. The sun broke through the clouds, and a mile away his empty plane ploughed into the waves, kicking up a long plume of rainbow spray, and, settling in the water, sank from sight.

The other pilots saw Stilson float down, strike the choppy, glinting surface of the Channel, sink, then come frothing up into the sunlight. They saw him cut loose from the shroud lines and kick free of the billowing, sinking chute. They saw his inflated raft pop up to the surface, saw him pull himself in and paddle over to where the CO was still struggling feebly in the bitterly cold water. They saw him haul the CO into the tiny raft with him. On their next pass—their last—the others saw both men bobbing in the life raft together. Then the clouds closed in, obscuring all.

The others all made it back safely—just barely. They filled out their reports and waited. No word came. In the morning the sky was peaceful and clear, and they flew out over a bright, blue, calm, sparkling sea.

But no trace of either man was ever found.

Digit

Digit yawned and swung to his feet. Powerful muscles rolled beneath his shaggy black hair. With hands strong enough to tear a leopard in half or snap a four-inch thick bamboo stem, he gently pulled a single leaf from an overhanging branch. Resting on the knuckles of one broad hand, he rolled the leaf and placed it between his pursed lips. His canines, which could rip logs apart, delicately separated the fleshy leaf from its stalk. Chewing thoughtfully, Digit sat down again, leaned against the bole of the tree, crossed his arms, and peered into the gathering light. His deep-set brown eyes took in every shadow, every movement, every minute flash of light reflecting off the green, misted leaves.

Digit lowered his head to the Old Man, the great silverback, who now walked calmly, with a rolling, sailor's gait, across the glade. The others slowly rose from their nests, shimmied, slid, and swung down from the trees and began to follow. Digit let them pass, then, rising to his feet, responsible and alert, took up his guard's position at the rear.

The early morning mists burned away and the twisted, moss-covered hagenia branches, wide as velvet armchairs, glowed serenely in the golden light. The full, rich odors of the moist earth and rotting vegetation filled the air.

The Old Man led them on, thrashing through the thick vegetation, rustling the long grasses as they went. Not a gorilla could be seen. Only the shakings of the tops of the slender grass stalks and the deep, contented belch-grunting of their feeding marked their passing.

The Old Man led them on at a leisurely pace, through thickets of tender young bamboo and patches of wild celery and blackberries, eating as they went. The family moved steadily ahead, splitting the limbs of trees to strip out the pith, nibbling berries, and selecting, with a connoisseur's eye, the tastiest leaves. They came to an old banana tree. The broad, dark-green leaves, shot with streaks of yellow, gleamed in the mid-morning light.

The silverbacked Old Man strolled up to the tree, reached up with both great, black-furred fists and calmly took hold of a main stem. Then, without visible effort, he slowly, almost lazily, pulled. With a terrific, slow-motion *rrrrrrrrrip!* a whole section of the fibrous bole tore evenly away. Pale yellow strands of tough woody fiber, strips of hard, mottled bark, years of accumulated dirt and debris rained down onto his massive shoulders and high-crested, fur-capped head. Contentedly, he began digging out the soft, yellowish-white pith.

One by one, the whole family joined in. In a few minutes only a stump of the tree remained.

As the day warmed, the family moved on, nibbling and browsing still. The sun shone down, casting deep shadows beneath the green trees, as the Old Man led them to a glade high upon the mountain. Just beyond the glade stood a crested ridge making a kind of bowl open to the sky. Soon the family was stretched out in the sunshine. Some lay on the earth among the long grasses while others perched up among the branches of the trees.

Digit sat up, sleepy and dreaming, his great silvery back propped against the bole of a tree. His hands lay cupped, open and relaxed, on the earth beside him. The sunlight streamed down into his palms, warming the skin, the bones. He felt absently at the ridge of scar which encircled his right wrist and disappeared into the root of the badly twisted third finger—his bracelet of memory left long ago by a poacher's wire snare. The Old Man had used his great teeth to free Digit from the trap. The hand had been mangled.

Digit did not forget.

Digit rubbed his scarred hand. He looked up. Immense white clouds piled up high overhead in the clear blue sky. He looked around. The shaggy bodies of his family lay slumbering in the glade. Slowly Digit's own eyes closed. His great crested head nodded forward and, in a moment, he too was asleep.

He had a dream. He dreamed he was high up in the air, like a hawk soaring on the wind, balanced on its pinions. The wind blew freely all around. Down below on a dusty plain gigantic animals stirred into life. They stretched and yawned. A great wind came soughing through the trees. The leaves fluttered like hands and Digit heard a voice calling his name. "Digit! Digit!"

"Here I am," he answered. "Who calls?" But the voice on the wind kept calling, calling.

Now a great dog, spotted like a leopard, leapt into the sky and gnawed the sun. Crimson drops sizzled and fell and wherever one touched the earth a dark red flower sprang up, nodding and bending its heavy, sweet-smelling blossom on a slender stem. Then...

Digit awoke with a start. It was mid-afternoon. Shadows stretched like fingers across the darkening glade. He rose to his feet, rested his great bulk on his knuckles, and sniffed the air. All seemed peaceful, yet he grabbed the bushes and shook them grumpily. The sun shone with deceptive brightness overhead. Yet, it was as if he could feel storm clouds gathering somewhere nearby. He grunted in annoyance and slapped his tense chest, *pok! pok! pok!* The sound rang out. As his family awoke Digit set off through the glade towards the trees.

Digit stopped, alert and poised, on all fours. The long grasses and bushes on the ridge before him trembled. He rose angrily to his feet, tearing up fistfuls of vegetation, flinging them towards the sky, a pungent fear-warning odor rising around him.

Five poachers, wearing torn T-shirts and greasy khaki shorts, burst through the bushes, their wiry dogs bounding before them.

A terrible, roaring scream burst from Digit's throat. At once his terrified family rose and, barking and screaming, hurried off. Digit wanted to run, too, but he would never abandon his post to let the poachers pass.

The startled poachers paused. Then, as their dogs advanced, jaws snapping, they lifted their heavy spears.

Digit stood his ground and became huge, monstrous in his fear and rage. His knotted muscles stood out like ropes. Screaming he hurled his great fists at them like clubs and reached out towards the frenzied dogs to gather them to him and save his family forever.

Five spears tore into his chest. Digit stood still, almost puzzled, like a man struck by lightning on a cloudless day. Only this lightning bolt illuminated every pebble, stone, and leaf in this world and in every other, etching them all into his brain with an intense, neonblue electric flame. Every fleeting emotion and flickering thought stood out, scored forever on the plain of his heart. Time froze. *NOW! NOW! NOW!* clanged a giant bell whose tolling split the sky. And Digit's body, its heart stopped in mid-beat, toppled forward upon the earth.

But Digit was ascending a ladder of light. He climbed with as much agility as he had climbed the great trees of the forest, moments, days, years, seemingly lifetimes ago. Up and up and up he went. Higher and higher, his great arms moving effortlessly.

Though the sun was just setting and it was still light, somehow the stars were also already out, shining in the velvety blackness directly overhead. Great petals of incandescent flame leapt from the setting sun. Each distant star, Digit now saw, also gave off its own stream of light, like petals or like tongues of flame—rose, amethyst, icy-blue, blood-red. There was humming, like the music which rises up off sun-baked rocks at midday. It was like the sound of many voices, too.

Down below, Digit could see the poachers hacking with their sharp-bladed pangas at a great black shaggy corpse. They chopped off the head, hands and feet, while the dogs snarled and worried the shaggy trunk.

"How strange," thought Digit, rising higher and higher. Now he saw his family sheltered safely once more beneath the green forest leaves. He saw the mountains spread below. He saw cities filled with women and men. He saw blue, foaming seas.

"Go on, Digit," said a kindly voice. "Don't stop." And Digit, light as a feather, as a green forest leaf, went on rising higher and higher into the great, starry, African night.

Kogi the Priest

The whale skeleton:
I kneel to pray in it, as
in a temple.

—from "Three Whale Haiku" by Sen Akira

This is the story of Kogi the priest. Actually, his given name was Eizo, and as a child he loved the sea. He grew up in a fishing port and the sea, the waves, the beaches, filled his childhood. As a child he was something of a dreamer. He could sit for hours and watch the waves roll in and back out again, while the seabirds circled overhead.

When he was grown, he learned of opportunities in the whaling fleets and, because it meant a chance for him to be at sea, he signed on. They taught him how to be a harpooner. They taught him how to kill. And for the next seven years, he worked the whaling fleets, killing the great whales—the blues, the fins, the rights, the sperms. But in the seventh year of that slaughter, his story—the story of Kogi the priest—suddenly began. It was as if Eizo's life started over. This is how it happened.

One day Eizo stood, as he always did when whales were ahead, behind the heavy swivel-mounted cannon. A cold, gusting, 25-knot wind blew against his face and chest as he squinted out into the grey, heaving sea. The sun was setting below the rim of clouds, but there was still time to make the kill. A small pod of sperm whales was not far ahead. The ship was gaining on them. Soon they would be close enough. He could make out the whales' ridged backs sliding through the sea. He could see the foam beating around them. Yet, for all their panicked speed, they seemed to move effortlessly, like great birds in flight.

Eizo released the safety catch on the cannon. The two-hundred pound explosive harpoon was already loaded and, gripping the cannon's polished handles, he slowly swung the massive device to sight on the whales ahead. Steady. *Steeeaddy.* Closer, closer...

NOW! A sudden, terrible, explosive blast, and both sea and sky were hidden behind a cloud of black smoke. The air stank of gunpowder. The inch-thick line flew out, uncoiling rapidly. It was a hit! Then, in a few seconds, from ahead, a second, muffled, *boom!*—the harpoon head exploding. The line twisted as the agonized whale writhed, rolling in the bloodied sea.

Though men were shouting all around him, Eizo hardly heard them. The cannon had been reloaded and once again he sighted along the cannon's heavy barrel. Again he grew ready. A dark shape rolled before him.

Again the cannon roared. Sea and sky were obscured by a screen of smoke. The heavy rope uncoiled. It was another hit! But, as the air cleared, he saw that it was smaller than he had thought—an adolescent calf. They'd be lucky to make the limit on it. But there was nothing he could do. The harpoon head exploded, *boom!* And the whale died.

He paused as the crew raced around him, reloading the cannon with a third harpoon. Once more he steadied his legs. Took aim. Then, what was this? The great bull sperm whale had turned in the water and was now swimming directly towards the prow of the ship. Foam rose up in great white crests, like breakers before it, as on it came.

Time slowed. The clouds parted as the sun shone down upon a blue and sparkling sea. Eizo's vision grew telescopic, preternaturally clear. He could see the pale, mottled patches around the whale's jaw and mouth as the bull's great square head lifted from the rippling, bubbling water and planed on the waves like the prow of a fast-moving ship. He saw how its wet, rubbery skin shaded from a glossy, jet-black to the softest iron-gray. He saw the delicate pink lining inside the whale's open mouth. He saw the ivory teeth glistening in the silvery-white foam, and how the bright blue-green of the sea flared like flames.

As the whale approached, its wet, inky skin flashed red in the dying sun, and each of the thousands of wrinkles and scars crisscrossing its length seemed to run with blood. Water droplets sparkled along its immense body like diamonds, rubies, emeralds, pearls—and the whale, rearing through the waves, seemed to Eizo like one of the great Naga kings, who dwell, he remembered, in jeweled palaces beneath the rivers, lakes, and seas, according to Buddhist legends of old.

The sound of water pouring into deep rocky pools filled Eizo's ears. Then a voice, thunderous as the surf, spoke to him, saying "Eizo, do not kill. Never, never kill! Never kill again!" It was the voice of the bull sperm whale.

"Am I mad?" thought Eizo. "What is happening? I must be going insane!" He stood as if frozen, shaking and trembling, sweat streaming from every pore.

Boom! Without knowing or meaning to, Eizo had gripped the trigger. The cannon had fired. He took a step, slipped on the wet deck and fell with a crash against the iron floor. A crimson spear tore through his brain as he sank down into darkness and knew no more.

He was flying, soaring, rising weightlessly through an emerald sea. A thin, swirling, pearl-and-silver curtain danced above his head. He arched and rose towards it, poured through it into bright sunlight, air, and warmth. His pleasure burst into breath, a vast whooshing exhalation and slow drawing in, in, in of breath. He didn't have hands, he had two great flippers at his side. He didn't have a face or nose or hair. His great square featureless head projected smoothly forward, eyes set far back on either side, a fifteen-foot long, toothed jaw hanging directly below. His body was sixty feet long, weighed sixty tons, and ended in a great fluked tail. He was a sperm whale.

For several moments he was scared, confused. But gradually he realized that he had never felt so powerful, so alive and free. And his fear left him.

He hung weightlessly, breathing, listening to the waves lapping against the shoreline of his own huge body. The ocean was alive with squeakings, twitterings, raspings. From hundreds of miles away came the deep, resonant calls sent out by others of his kind.

The surface of the sea was like a carpet of jewels, light pouring down and disappearing into the darkening haze. Leisurely, Eizo turned his fins, arched his ridged back, and pushed down with his flukes. His immense bulk hurtled ripplingly down into the darkening sea. He pressed forth his power and the dive deepened. Slowly, steadily, the light green of the sea darkened. Emerald green became pine green, became dark evergreen. The darkest of all possible greens was tinged now with purple, became black, became inky-black, became absolute *BLACK*. Still he plunged, down and down and down, into the unending darkness and cold. The weight of one mile of ocean pressed upon him. His aching ribs bent. His lungs collapsed. He grew as long and sinuous as a grinning serpent. The air hummed in the cavities of his body like bees trapped in a bottle. He hunted breathless and without physical sight along the icy bottom of the world.

Though the darkness was absolute, with sound he could "see." He could see in his mind, in images formed by the echoes of his own voice bouncing back through the icy darkness. He glided over and through a vast undersea world of spiring mountains, of caverns and canyons, sound-visioning it all with luminous clarity.

He sensed a strange tangle of movement and was irresistibly drawn. His lower jaw swung open and, turning his massive body with a final gliding push, he ran headfirst into the body of an immense squid.

Suddenly, ten long, cold, powerful arms writhed around him. Strong suckers gripped at his two-foot thick skin, and a sharp beak sliced and tore. Gripping the squid in his teeth, and pushing with all his strength, he swam up through a mile of sea as tentacles thick as trees strangled and frantically squeezed, the squid's great, staring, unlidded foot-wide eye pressed up against his own. Up he rose, his jaw clamped upon the furiously struggling squid, unerringly following the beacon of sound that led to his pod.

Gradually, light and warmth and color returned. When he broke the surface again in a burst of clotted breath and foam, the squid was dead. He had been a mile under the sea without air or warmth or light for over an hour. He tore at the squid, gulping it down in chunks, breathing through the single nostril on his head in long, sweet, easy breaths.

He swam on protectively behind his females and calves. In the vast, languid emptiness of the glittering afternoon sea, there was neither house nor tree nor flower nor bird nor object of any kind. He had nothing now, not even hands to grasp with and, yet, he had never before dreamed of such contentment. He felt richer than a king.

The falling sun touched the waves. The whales blew, breathing together, and flew, weightless as birds, over the ocean floor hidden far below. Their broad, wrinkled heads, ringed with fleecy foam, shone like ebony in the slanting sun. The water tingled electrically between them and rang like glass chimes.

Slam! Bang! Slam! Bang! Something beat loudly against the surface of the sea behind them.

The whales grew nervous, and quickened their pace. But *Slam! Bang! Slam! Bang!* on it came quicker yet, like iron footsteps striding behind them. Then Eizo the whale was filled with a sudden and terrible dread. It was as if he had dreamed this all, horribly, before. He rolled his eyes back—and there was a ship, his own ship, its black iron hull streaked with rust like dried blood, smashing through the waves, coming after them. And the cannon was loaded.

BLAM! the cannon roared. A cow was hit. Eizo heard her scream, so high no human could hear her. Then, *Boom!*, the harpoon head exploded and she died, her blood staining the sea.

And the chase went on. Again the cannon roared. And now, amidst the smoke and sudden, terrible noise, an adolescent calf was thrashing wildly in agony.

A great protective determination arose in Eizo's whale-heart. He turned in the sea and swam directly on, on towards the oncoming ship. Waves broke and foamed against his mountainous brow. "Do not kill!" he proclaimed, "Never, never kill! Never kill again!" He could see men he knew standing high up near the point of the iron prow pointing down at him. "Don't kill!" he repeated in a thunderous voice, his great toothed jaw open wide.

Boom! A blinding flash and a sharp and terrible pain drove him down against the sea. He gathered his immense strength, rose, and swam on, once more straight at the oncoming ship. "Do not kill..." he began, and with a muffled roar, sea and sky ripped and, in one horrible burst, tore completely apart. Eizo's scream was lost in the thunder. And he knew no more.

He floated up to consciousness like a drowning man given up by a repentant sea. He lay in a narrow bunk. A single dim, wall-mounted ship's lamp burned above him. He was covered with sweat and every muscle and bone in his body ached. He was alive. He was a man once more. He flexed his fingers and stared at them in amazement. He touched his own hands, arms, head in astonished disbelief, and felt fingers, eyes, nose, hair.

He rose dizzily and looked in the mirror. A thin, haunted, sweat-shining human face peered back at him. His own face. And, yet, something else too. He was a man and had dreamed that he was a whale. Or was he a whale even now dreaming that he was a man?

He showered slowly and dressed. Weak, and trembling with the effort, he climbed the spiralling metal stairs to the deck. *Clang, clang, clang,* his steps echoed hollowly as he rose, lurching with the ship's movement. He pushed the iron door open.

He was on the deck of the factory ship. The deck ran red with blood. Mountainous slabs of gleaming, dark-purplish meat, reeking entrails, glistening blubber towered above him. A sperm whale's long lower jaw lay before him, the white teeth shining in the sun. The bodies of three sperm whales, a female, an adolescent calf, and a great bull lay before him. They were being rendered down into bone, meat and oil. One of those huge dis-membered bodies, he knew, had just recently been his own.

Saws whined, hoses hissed, chains clanked; dark, oily smoke curled across the decks and great iron cauldrons bubbled madly. Wrapped in their black rubber aprons and high, open-top boots, men were shouting, hacking, chopping, while winched steel cables screamed and mas-sive iron hooks swung just over their heads. It was a scene from hell.

"I won't kill. That's it," said Eizo. "Never again." And he returned to his cabin below deck.

Eizo lay in his narrow bunk. Once again he saw the clear, sparkling sea of his childhood. He recalled a summer night, long ago. "I have heard it said," his mother was saying, "that the Buddha gave his highest teachings into the care of the Nagas. Deep down, in their jewelled palaces beneath the seas, they guard this trea-sure of Perfect Wisdom. They keep it safely for us, until the day when we shall be wise and humble enough to re-ceive our inheritance."

The memory passed. In his mind's eye he now saw, swimming in silent procession before him, the hundreds of whales that he himself had slain. They spouted red blood and swam in a crimson sea, white birds fluttering and calling all around them.

Eizo relived his own brief life as a whale. Dream or not, the memory was sharp and clear. The instinctive courage and wild, oceanic joy of his whale-life flooded him. He saw again the vast, elusive beauty of the sea. Alone in his narrow bunk, he wept bitterly.

Eizo kept to himself through the rest of the voyage, and he refused to return to his position at the gun. When the ship neared port, he reemerged from his room with his head shaved like a monk's. As the ship docked, he collected his pay and left. He sought out a Buddhist tem-ple he knew of that stood near the shore. It was an old place, with few believers still supporting it. The abbot, a

lean-faced, serious man, lived there, training three or
four black-robed novices and several senior monks.

Eizo entered the temple with his sea bags slung over
his shoulder and asked to speak with the abbot. The
monks eyed him curiously with his shaved head and
seaman's clothes, but he was announced to the abbot,
and admitted. The tide was already coming in on the
beach below when, several hours later, he emerged
clothed in the black robes of a Buddhist monk. And his
name was Kogi—a name he took from an old folktale
about a Buddhist priest who dreamed he was a fish and
who, upon awakening, found indications that his dream
had, in fact, been true.

That was years ago. The sea rolls on as it has since
the earliest times. The whales that survive still live
their mysterious lives. And the whalers still kill.

Kogi is the abbot of that little temple now. Some of
the whalers have been going there to talk with Kogi.
Some, like him, have left the fleets and started their
lives over. It has not been easy for them or for their
families, but they persist, slowly finding their way into
lives that do not require killing.

Behind the temple, on a hillside overlooking the sea,
is a small burial plot covered with stone markers,
memorials, and tablets. Some have on them the names
of deceased whalers. Most are inscribed with the numbers and species of the whales these men have themselves slain.

Kogi has said of his own experience: "Not to kill, but
to cherish all life, is the essence of the Buddha's teaching. Some come to understand this through formal meditation. Some find it as petals blossom, or as petals fall.
Some see it in the stone lying in the dust by the roadside. Mothers have told me they hear it in the cries of
their newborn. These words came to me from the mouth
of a bull sperm whale. It does not matter where or how
one hears. But having heard, one should follow the im-
port of these words to the best of one's abilities. There
are no more important words on this or on any world."

On the altar in that temple by the sea is a figure of the Buddha, flanked by the Bodhisattvas Manjusri and Samantabhadra. These figures were carved by Kogi from cedar logs which washed up on the beach below the temple. Though the carvings are rough and simple, they radiate honesty and power. Kogi's Buddha sits, as is customary, on a carved lotus-throne. But his Manjusri and Samantabhadra are unique. Manjusri, the Bodhisattva of Wisdom, with his delusion-cutting sword usually sits on the back of a lion. Samantabhadra, the Bodhisattva of Action, should sit on an elephant's back. But Kogi's Samantabhadra sits on the back of a diving blue whale, and his Manjusri is on the back of a great, open-jawed sperm whale.

The ex-whalers appreciate that. And so, perhaps, do the whales.

Section IV:
Commentaries

Commentaries

A Note on 'Rebirth'

Accepting the idea of rebirth, or re-becoming (on which the jatakas depend) can sometimes prove difficult for Westerners. Technically speaking, rebirth is not the same as reincarnation. Reincarnation implies that there is some fixed entity, some being or soul that is reborn. Rebirth, however, suggests that there is no such fixed entity, being, or soul. Simultaneously, no energy—physical, mental, emotional, or spiritual—no effort, including one's moral exertions, can ever be wasted or lost. Nothing we consciously do is without consequences. Rebirth holds that each effort of will, each action from each thought, gives rise to future thoughts, actions, and efforts. This causal conditioning is what creates, and is at the same time a manifestation of, our life in time and space; this is the world of relativity and of the workings of karma (cause and effect on the moral plane).

But ultimately, the doctrine of rebirth insists that there is no limited "doer" behind these deeds. In reality there is only the Self, or Buddha-Nature (the Absolute, the Void, Emptiness). Paradoxically (to our modern, logical, intellectually-trained way of looking at things), this Absolute Self-Nature is not separate from our conditioned, causal existence.

The Buddhist teaching of rebirth also holds that our bodies are the physical manifestation of our own past thoughts. After the final disintegration of this body-mind, a new body-mind will arise out of the subtle workings of the karma we have created and are now creating by the way we live and think. The being we will be in our next birth stands upon the shoulders, so to speak, of who we are now. The present moment is the birthing ground of all future selves.

So those who feel that there is no rebirth and that we are only here on this Earth once are correct, in a sense. The specific "I," the person we are now—with the unique biography, personality, family, possessions, and so forth—will never be again. This lifetime, then, is a one-time-only experience and needs to be cherished as such, even as it also needs to be respected as the vehicle through which we establish our future existences.

According to this teaching, there is no way to coast comfortably to some beneficial future life. Ineluctably, coasting will generate a less-than-ideal future karma. We need to live wisely in this present life, for out of this present life will arise our next existence. This process begins in the endless past and extends into the endless future.

In Buddhism, rebirth is also understood as occurring countless times in the course of a single lifetime. Thoughts flow endlessly through the mind. Ideas, beliefs, questions, and understandings change. Friends may become enemies—enemies, friends. Individual cells die and are regularly replaced. An adult of sixty has little physically or mentally that can identify that person as the six-year-old or six-month-old child he or she once was. Yet there remains an underlying continuity.

A thorough, lucid, and contemporary examination of the Buddhist vision of karma and rebirth can be found in *The Wheel of Life and Death: A Practical and Spiritual Guide* by Philip Kapleau.

Beginnings (p. 3)

References to this jataka, "Subhasa Jataka," appear in *The Sanskrit Buddhist Literature of Nepal*, by R. Mitra, published in Calcutta in 1882. I have not come across any versions in the Pali *Jataka*, or elsewhere. Still, it remains an interesting story. There is a wonderful psychological acuity to this brief and relatively unknown tale: the images of training, the lapses from training, the desire for freedom from a half-realized life. It also marks the conscious beginning of the Buddha-to-be's religious career. The training-path of the Bodhisattva (literally, "Awakened-being") will extend, according to traditional sources, through four periods of $(3 \times 10^{51})x$ (320×10^6) years, or four times nine hundred sixty thousand million billion billion billion billion years—an unimaginably long (and for all ordinary purposes, endless) period of time. We are being told, in the cosmic, mythic language of the Indian imagination, that this is an eternal, time-transcending effort. Therefore, it is not an exertion which one makes in the future. It is the exertion one makes now, in the present.

The twelfth century Zen Master Dogen, one of the greatest of all the Japanese Zen masters, described this Path as one of "sustained exertion," and added that "to attempt to avoid exertion is an impossible evasion, for the attempt itself is exertion." To quote Dogen more fully:

> The great way of the Buddha...involves the highest form of exertion, which goes on unceasingly in cycles from the first dawning of religious truth...It is sustained exertion proceeding without lapse from cycle to cycle...It is through the sustained exertions of the Buddhas and Patriarchs that our own exertions are made possible, that we are able to reach the high road of Truth. In exactly the same way it is through our own exertions that the exertions of the Buddhas are made possible, that the Buddhas attain the high road of Truth. Thus it is through our exertions that these benefits circulate in cycles to others, and it is only due to this that the Buddhas and Patriarchs come and go... attaining the Buddha-mind and achieving Buddhahood, ceaselessly and without end. This exertion too sustains the sun, the moon, and the stars; it sustains the earth and sky, body and mind, object and subject, the four elements and the five compounds.
>
> This sustained exertion is not something which people of the world naturally love or desire, yet it is the last refuge of all...[1]

Elsewhere in this famous passage, Dogen wrote: "The exertion which brings the exertion of others into realization is our exertion right at this moment."

It is said that Shakyamuni himself, having completed this entire process and perfected himself to the fullest, is still "only halfway there." From the Buddhist point of view, spiritual development is limitless.

In considering the beginning of this vast and profound process as presented in this jataka, the twelfth century Japanese Buddhist monk-poet, Saigyo, has an appropriate verse:

> The mind for truth
> Begins, like a stream, shallow
> At first, but then
> Adds more and more depth
> While gaining greater clarity.[2]

Yasutani-Roshi, one of the most highly respected contemporary Japanese Zen masters, has said, "Man fancies himself to be the most highly evolved organism in the universe, but in the view of Buddhism, he stands midway between an amoeba and a Buddha."[3]

The tale, while not a formal jataka, is part of the "Bodhisattva Avadana," a collection of Buddhist tales and legends purportedly told by the Buddha for the edification of his disciples while in residence at Sravasti near the water tank of Anavatapta. 'Avadana' is a general term applying to a vast body of traditional "noble-giving" literature, i. e. to stories of the Buddha and other great Buddhist figures and their sacrifices in this and earlier lives.

One traditional appellation for a Buddha is that of *jina*, or "Conqueror." This is so because a Buddha is one who has conquered all egoistic delusions, all greed, anger, ignorance and selfishness of even the subtlest sort. Most fundamentally, a Buddha has conquered the delusion that self and other are separate. The wisdom and compassion which are inherent to our True Nature, or Buddha-Nature, can then flow forth.

According to Buddhist teaching, there have already been many full Buddhas on this Earth, and endless Buddhas—that is, fully awakened, fully spiritually developed, wise, compassionate beings—already exist throughout the endless sentient worlds of our infinite universe.

When used as a proper name, the Buddha is the historical person, born Siddhartha Gautama, who realized profound Enlightenment and became the Awakened One, the Buddha of our historical time. The traditional (and therefore mythic) view which this simple tale begins to express, is that the Prince Siddhartha Gautama, who was born in Nepal some 2,500 years ago and who then attained Enlightenment, must have actually begun working towards the realization of such an incredibly lofty condition in the far distant past. The depth of not just his realization but his character, it was believed, could not be the result of just one lifetime of effort.

Myth is not simply another kind of literal reality, but a way of trying to say something more "true" than mere fact can convey. It is not real, but it is true. Mythic perception puts us intimately in touch with a powerful and suggestive kind of truth.

In *The Power of Myth*, Joseph Campbell says that "the basic theme of all mythology [is] that there is an invisible plane supporting the visible one."[4] Myth *suggests* this truth, gives us insight into it by mobilizing our deepest imaginative and intuitive forces. Mythic thinking unites us with a deeper level of experiencing and being. The truth of myth, then, does not efface personal, psychological, or literal levels of reality, but embraces all of them

Too often, however, stories and myths degenerate into dogma, and the mythic level becomes entirely bound to the literal. When this happens, the tale's profound, liberating power—its essential appeal to the mind, imagination, and spirit—is lost, and its creative force entombed. Mythic thinking, when allowed to function freely, tends to open the mind to what is highest, to what is possible. It restores us to the deep, creative wellsprings of wish and dream. This brief, artless little tale, whether created or literally true, manages to open many suggestive vistas on the depths of human character and personality.

Sumedha and Dipankara (pp. 4-7)

The legend of the meeting between the hermit Sumedha (the historical Buddha of our world cycle in an earlier birth) and Dipankara (the Buddha of that distant time) is a key story in the jataka tradition. It comprises the major event in *The Nidana-Katha,* "The Story of the Lineage," the traditional introduction to the Pali *Jataka.*

Set in the inconceivably distant past, the story reveals a crucial moment in the Bodhisattva's career. Having already achieved a high degree of self-mastery, he now gives up the prospect of a personal liberation, and aligns his future destinies with the welfare and liberation of all living things. Rather than enter Nirvana as he is, he realizes that the full development of all moral, spiritual, psychic, and intellectual faculties and their dedication to the welfare of all living beings (i. e. full Buddhahood) is possible. The meeting with the Buddha Dipankara, who has attained such perfection, inspires Sumedha to walk this ultimate Path of selfless exertion as well. Not until he has been able to aid all beings will he himself enter Nirvana; not until all are freed will he cease working for the welfare of others.

(See "The Legend of Avalokitesvara." Also see "The Brave Little Parrot." Free from the flames he could have flown to safety—but the plight of others still suffering and in danger prompts him to act. Also see the story of "The Banyan Deer," who risks his personal freedom and the freedom of his herd to plead for others.)

As it will obviously be a vast period of time before all beings, down to the last blade of grass, have attained full liberation, this vow of renunciation suggests a limitless dedication. The jatakas are a record of all the subsequent lives of Sumedha, from this moment of decision through his historical birth as Siddhartha Gautama and the attainment of Buddhahood. These vows underlie and define the Path of the Bodhisattva as it is understood from the viewpoint of Mahayana Buddhism, (Mahayana is Sanskrit for "Great Vehicle"; so named because it carries all beings).

According to Theravadin ("Teachings of the Elders") Buddhism, one on the path to Buddhahood is a fledgling Buddha, a bodhisattva regardless of whether such a vow has arisen or not. The distinction is probably, more a matter of emphasis than real difference. Somewhere along the line, a vow of this type is going to arise in the heart of any spiritual aspirant. If the world and oneself are *not* separate, then working to liberate oneself is going to lead to a deepening sense of one's profound interrelation with others.

The desire to fulfill this selfless and heroic vow is the heart of Mahayana Buddhism. In Zen monasteries and training centers throughout the world, four vows are chanted at the conclusion of all formal periods of seated meditation (*zazen*). These four Bodhisattva vows, are:

> All beings without number I vow to liberate.
> Endless blind passions I vow to uproot.
> Dharma gates without measure I vow to penetrate.
> The great Way of Buddha I vow to attain.

It is such a set of vows which spontaneously arose in the heart of Sumedha.

Buddhist cosmology holds that, on this Earth, there have been twenty-four Buddhas (or seven Buddhas; both numbers, really, symbolize something beyond all numbers—a limitless number), including the historical Shakyamuni Buddha. The Buddha just prior to Shakyamuni, but many ages after Dipankara, is said to have been the Buddha Kasyapa. A curious traveller's tale is related by the great seventh-century Chinese Buddhist pilgrim, Hiuan Tsang, concerning this previous, nonhistorical Buddha.

At a distance of two hundred li to the West the traveler comes to a mountain that is enveloped in clouds and vapors. Its sides rise extremely high. They appear to be on the point of collapse and remain as it were in a state of suspension. A number of years ago the thunder roared and a piece of the mountain fell away. In the caves which were thus exposed sat a religious with eyes closed. He was as tall as a giant; his body was wasted and his beard and unkempt hair fell down to his shoulders and obscured his face. He was seen by some hunters or woodcutters who ran to inform the king. The king hurried to the spot and, the news having spread, he was soon joined there by the entire populace. A monk explained what had to be done:"The man who has entered a state of ecstasy can remain in this condition for an indefinite period. His body is supported through mystical power and escapes destruction and death. Exhausted as he is by his long fast, were he to emerge from the state of ecstasy abruptly he would die in the very instant and his body might crumble to dust. First his limbs must be moistened with butter and oil to make them supple again, then the gong can be struck to wake him." This was done, and when the saint heard the gong he at last opened his eyes and looked around him. Then, after a long pause, he asked those present: "You who are so small in stature, who are you?" Receiving a reply from one of the monks who was standing around he asked for news of his master, Buddha Kasyapa, Sakyamuni's predecessor who had passed away hundreds of thousands of years before. The monk replied, "Long, long since did he enter the great Nirvana." Hearing these words," Hiuan Tsang goes on, "the saint closed his eyes like a man in despair; then suddenly he asked, 'And has Sakyamuni appeared in the world?' 'He was incarnate,' they replied, 'he gave guidance to the age, and he entered Nirvana in his turn. ' At these words the sage lowered his head. Then he lifted his flowing hair with one hand and rose majestically into the air. By a divine miracle he was transformed into a fiery sphere which consumed his body and let the calcined bones fall back to the earth." The king of the country had a stupa erected to him in the heart of the mountains."[5]

When Sumedha returned to his isolated retreat, he exerted himself in deepening his wisdom through intense meditation as well as through profound contemplation of the *paramitas*, or perfections. While ten paramitas are often mentioned, there is also a concise formulation of six paramitas in the Mahayana, which is as follows: (1) charity (*dana*); (2) moral conduct (*sila*); (3) patience (*ksanti*); (4) strength (*virya*); (5) contemplation (*dhyana*); and (6) intuitive wisdom (*prajña*). These are the perfect qualities of character which express the nature of a Buddha. Their full realization requires long and dedicated training, and so in order to master them, Sumedha could not remain in isolated meditation. The jatakas show his subsequent exertions in the world, working lifetime after lifetime, to attain this mastery of the perfections.

A kalpa has been described in this way. It is that period of time in which, if a deva (a god or angelic being) were to descend once every hundred years from the highest heavens and lightly brush the top of the tallest mountain with the sheerest piece of cloth and continue to do so, once every hundred years, in one kalpa the mountain would have been worn down smooth to the earth. Modern science gives us many ways of measuring time on this eonic scale, but none so poetic.

For more on devas see note for "Leaving Home."

The Birth of the Buddha (pp. 8-9)

Legends of the Buddha's birth, like those of other great religious figures, include miraculous elements. Perhaps this reveals something of the workings of the human mind in attempting to explain the birth of a child, whose destiny proved so remarkable, to otherwise ordinary parents. As with all symbolism, there is an underlying effort here to verbalize what there are no words for. The result is a language of symbol and myth.

So, while these miraculous events need not be seen as literal occurrences, neither should they be viewed as untruths. Profound truths are being expressed, but in a language of a different order. Maya's dream and the other miraculous elements (the Buddha's walking and talking at birth; the appearance of devas and devic music, etc.) have their traditional root in the first, most seminal and perhaps finest biography of the Buddha, *The Buddhacarita* or, "The Acts of the Buddha," of the first century Indian poet, Asvaghosha.

The Buddha's sounding of the "lion's roar" is a traditional expression, signifying that the utterances of a Buddha have great potency, filled as they are with the power of Truth. A Buddha's words, like the lion's roar which stuns all lesser beasts, transcend all speculation and are majestic in their Truth.

The birth takes place countless lifetimes after Sumedha's meeting with the Buddha Dipankara, and fulfills Dipankara's prediction that Sumedha would become a Buddha after four *asankheya kalpas* and one hundred thousand world cycles.

Leaving Home (pp. 10-16)

The Buddha's leaving home brings history and legend together. The prince Siddhartha did leave home 2,500 years ago to seek Enlightenment. The mythic imagination, however, was obviously at work in the tradition which followed, finding, as is its way, the universal in the historical. In this story of one person, then, is the story of all people. At some point each of us does awaken from innocence to see the cruelties and imponderable injustices of life. And we all, too, eventually leave home to find our own way

That in such a few days the Prince would literally see for the first time sickness, aging, and death as well as a renunciate is, historically speaking, unlikely. That he actually *saw* them—realized their actual meaning and was profoundly moved by it—for the first time is very possible, even likely. Who has not had a similar experience? Roshi Robert Aitken states, "If it could be shown that Shakyamuni never lived, the myth of his life would be our guide. In fact it is better to acknowledge at the outset that myths and archetypes guide us, just as they do every religious person. The myth of the Buddha is my own myth."[6]

The gods who guide Channa's speech and who, in some versions of the story, take the form of the old man, the sick man, the dead man and the homeless truth-seeker, are the devas of higher-than-earthly realms and are part of the traditional Buddhist cosmological world-view. According to Buddhist thought, there are six realms—hell, hungry ghost, animal, human, the asuras (or "warring spirits"), and the blissful devas, or gods. These six realms are arranged like a kind of Ferris wheel, with hells and their denizens at the bottom, heavens and the devas at the top. Two of these realms are ordinarily visible to us—the human and the animal realms. The six realms may be viewed mythically or psychologically, or both. Certainly it is not hard to accept the psychological reality of one's daily wandering through these six realms of being. Hateful, demonic thoughts give way to greedy, ghostly ones, which in turn are replaced by clouded, animalistic thinking and so on.

Devas generally lead lives of great freedom and pleasure, lives of wish-fulfillment won through positive karma of the past. But it is no ultimate condition, and it is said that when their good karma is exhausted, such beings may then fall—in terrible anguish—into realms of great suffering. The human realm is considered in Buddhism to be most advantageous—even more so than life in heaven—for it is only within the human realm, through the vehicle of a healthy human body and mind (which are extremely hard to attain, in terms of rebirth), that one may gain enlightenment. (See "The Naga King.")

In each of these realms, even in the lowest of the hells, are said to reside Buddhas and Bodhisattvas resolved out of their great, selfless compassion, to help all suffering beings. (See "Most Lovely Fugen.")

In Buddhism, no one is condemned eternally to hell or heaven, or any state in between. All such states are causally-created by one's own thoughts and actions (i. e. , karma) and, as one's karma changes, the realm in which one resides must also change. From the viewpoint of myth, beings are reborn in one realm after having died, their karma exhausted, in another. Viewed psychologically, we shift from states of suffering and inadequacy to conditions of great confidence and security, and vice-versa, in the course of a lifetime; in the course of a day, an hour, even an instant. In the jatakas we see the Buddha himself moving, spiritually evolving, through his experiences in different realms—human, animal, or deva. Sometimes, in Buddhist legends, other realms—hungry ghost, warring spirit, and demonic realms or beings—may appear. These various mythological types also tend to appear throughout the traditional literatures of the world.

Devas appear often in the jatakas and in Buddhist tales and legends. In this collection also see, "Sumedha Meets Dipankara," "Birth of the Buddha," and "The Brave Little Parrot." For appearances by Shakra, king of the gods, see "The Steadfast Parrot," "The Hare's Sacrifice," "Shakra's Black Hound," and "King Sivi."

An especially good examination of the six realms (and of the wheel of rebirth formed by them) appears in *The Three Jewels* by Bhikshu Sangharakshita, as well as in Lama Govinda's classic *Foundations of Tibetan Mysticism*.

Enlightenment (pp. 17-22)

The Buddha's struggle to gain Enlightenment is the heart of Buddhist teaching, practice, literature, and art. The intense efforts of this one person reveal the potential in us all. Myth and history—symbolic, spiritual, and actual experience—are wonderfully blended in all the accounts which have come down to us. This version, like most, draws much from Asvaghosha's classic first century work, *The Buddhacarita*, or *Acts of the Buddha*.

The twelfth century Japanese Zen Master Dogen, writing about exertion (see notes for "Beginnings"), says of the Buddha himself:

> Shakyamuni Buddha began his exertions deep in the mountains...At the age of thirty he labored to achieve the Enlightenment which embraced all sentient beings. Until the age of eighty he labored in the forests and monasteries, without any thought of returning to his royal palace or of sharing in the wealth of his kingdom. Not once did he put on a new robe; not once did he exchange his bowl for another...His whole life was one long exertion...a life that knew nothing but sustained exertion. [7]

In all traditional accounts of the Buddha's Enlightenment, this quality comes through. He undertook, with great faith and courage, a life-and-death struggle with the delusive forces of his own mind. He is not to be seen as divine, but fully human. But as, "the state of a Buddha is one of the highest possible perfection. It seems self-evident to Buddhists that an enormous amount of preparation over many lives is needed to reach it...."[8] The Buddha's Enlightenment reveals the meaning of the jatakas; they are the record of his "enormous amount of preparation."

While the bibliography contains many different versions of the Buddha's life and Enlightenment, Beyer's strong and poetic rendering of Asvaghosha's *Buddhacarita* in *The Buddhist Experience* is one of the most dramatic. Sangharakshita's *Three Jewels* also contains a well-balanced, intelligent, and useful brief account of the Buddha's entire life and his Enlightenment.

The Earth's response to the Buddha's touch is quite traditional. This mythic element imparts a beautiful depth and resonance to the moment of the Buddha's Enlightenment. At the crucial instant, the Earth itself becomes the Buddha's witness, revealing its age-old, ever abiding awareness. It is said that there is no spot on Earth where the Buddha, in some lifetime, did not sacrifice himself for others. From the mythic perspective of the Buddhist tradition, the entire Earth is a sacred place.

The scene of the approach of Mara's hosts—his daughters of desire, his monsters of anger and hatred—is the kind of temptation scene found in many religions and cultures throughout the world.

There is something eerily suggestive about the Naga king. The previous Buddha, Kasyapa (see comments on "Sumedha Meets Dipankara"), had attained Buddhahood and passed into Nirvana (see "Parinirvana" and commentary) many long ages in the past. Yet, to the Naga king, it is as if only a single day has passed. The long row of identical Buddhas' begging bowls resting quietly in his submarine chambers, too, seems to raise a curtain in our minds. Suddenly we are looking across staggering vistas of time. The mysterious Naga king gives us a wonderfully mythic perspective on the phenomenon of time.

The obeisance of Mara's elephant, "Mountain-Girded," in the Enlightenment account interestingly prefigures the later submission of the maddened elephant, Nalagiri. (See "Nalagiri").

For more on Nagas (but no more, alas, on Kala Naga Raja, the ancient and mysterious Black Snake King), see "Parinirvana," "The Naga King," and "Kogi the Priest," tales and notes. For more on Mara, the tempter, see "The Brave Merchant," story and note.

In Japanese (and American) Zen Buddhism, the Buddha's Enlightenment is celebrated and honored by holding a particularly intense seven-day meditation retreat, or sesshin, called the *rohatsu* sesshin. It usually takes place on or near December 8th, which—according to Japanese Buddhism—coincides with the Buddha's own breakthrough into Truth. Other Buddhist traditions, however, set the date of the Buddha's Breakthrough in April or May.

Angulimala the Robber (pp. 23-29)

This story is said to have occurred during the Buddha's lifetime. The conversion of the murderous robber Angulimala remains one of the most poignant of traditional Buddhist tales. Angulimala, the jataka tradition says, was the sticky-haired monster in an earlier life, who was converted by the Buddha in his life as

Prince Five-Weapons (Jataka No. 55—see "Prince Five-Weapons"). In the Sutano-Jataka (No. 398), he who is to become Angulimala is identified as being, in a birth after that of the sticky-hair monster, a yakka (yaksha), or flesh-eating (sometimes man-eating) spirit or demon, who is converted by the Buddha to the ways of virtue.

In the Maha Sutasoma-Jataka (No. 537), the being who is to be Angulimala is identified as having evolved further yet, having attained to the condition of a human king. Unfortunately, a memory of his taste for human flesh (stemming from the king's past life as a yaksha) remains within his karmic stream. This king, through no fault of his own, has the cooked flesh of a dead man served to him at a meal. He delights in the taste, and becomes a cannibal. He is saved from this wrong action by the Buddha, who was at that time a prince named Sutasoma.

A complete, traditional version of the story of Angulimala (which appears in *An Anthology of Sinhalese Literature up to 1815*, by Christopher Reynolds) is of particular merit and was a major source for this re-telling.

The story of Angulimala is a tale of karma. Because Ahimsaka goes so far wrong, he must necessarily undergo a dreadful purgation to free himself from the effects of his own delusive actions. No one can do it for him, not even the Buddha. He must reap what he has sown. But he does it willingly, consciously. The great Tibetan poet and mystic-saint, Milarepa, says something similar about the path of his own life.

> I started by accepting and understanding the Doctrine of Karma long before I grasped that of the Void: that's why I felt so deeply about [the] evil I had done... with the destruction of so many lives and so much property. I knew that by Karmic Law, I would go down to the plane of Hell when I died. That's why I held so firmly to my Guru through thick and thin and persevered so rigorously in meditation. I had to. [9]

Interestingly, the story of Angulimala also makes clear that the innocent boy, Ahimsaka, takes his first step towards becoming the robber Angulimala when he fails to trust his own intuition and judgement. Buddhist tradition asserts that one must use one's own intelligence and reason to decide on the merit of all things— even the Buddha's own Teachings!

An often quoted exchange between the Buddha and Sariputtra, one of his most advanced and devoted disciples, clearly expresses this spirit of reasonableness:

> "Lord," said Sariputtra, "such faith have I in the Blessed One that I think there has never been, nor will ever be, nor is there now any other who is greater or wiser than the Blessed One as regards the higher wisdom."

> The Buddha replied: "Grand and bold are the words of your mouth, Sariputtra. You have burst forth into a very song of ecstasy! Surely you have known all the Blessed Ones who in the long ages of the past have been Buddhas?"

> "Not so, O Lord!" said Sariputtra.

> And the Lord continued: "You have then perceived all those who in the long ages of the future shall be holy Buddhas."

> "Not so, O Lord!"

> "Then surely, O Sariputtra, you must now know me truly and have penetrated the depths of my mind."

> "Not even that, O Lord."

> "You do not know the minds of the Buddhas of the past or of the future. You do not even truly know my mind. Why then, Sariputtra, are your words so grand and bold? Great, indeed, is your faith, Sariputtra," concluded the Blessed One, "but take heed that it be well grounded."[10]

Since ancient times, near-total devotion to and reliance on one's spiritual teacher has been strong in the

Indian mind. When the teacher is deeply realized and compassionate, such a method can obviously produce powerful results. On the other hand, the possibilities for wrong-doing can also be extreme.

Perhaps, at the time of the Buddha, this story served as a comment on a teaching tradition which, even then, had a long history. The emphasis on personal experience and accountability is one of the most significant ways the Buddha's teaching differed from the older spiritual traditions of ancient India and, in part, may help account for the spiritual revolution it was to bring about at that time. Later, the flowering of Chinese Zen Buddhism was to extend this revitalization of spiritual practice and training even further.

One thousand is essentially an unimaginable number, beyond the range of literal possibility. This is in keeping with the often cosmic scale of the Indian imagination.

The story also reinforces some of the final words traditionally ascribed to the Buddha at the time of his Parinirvana. At that time, he stated that, "Salvation cannot not come from the mere sight of me. It demands strenuous effort in actual spiritual practice." (See "Parinirvana.")

Nalagiri the Elephant (pp. 30-35)

The Buddha had two well-known cousins. Ananda, famous for his loyal, gentle, generous, and sensitive nature as well as for his extraordinary intelligence and memory, was the Buddha's attendant for many years.

It is through Ananda that the sutras (which are essentially the teachings of the Buddha himself) have come down to us. Tradition holds that he heard the Buddha's discourses, remembered them perfectly, and passed them on (the opening words, "Thus have I heard..." of each sutra are a reminder of this oral transmission). Many stories attest to the intimate ties between the Buddha and Ananda. In this collection, see "Parinirvana," and notes for "Great Joy the Ox," "The Black Hound," and "The Hungry Tigress."

The other cousin, Devadatta, was infamous for his evil and wrongdoing. In the many stories which include Devadatta (in this collection see "The Falcon and the Quail," The Lion, the Elephant and the Merchants' Cries" "The Golden Deer," "The Blue Bear," "Preacher of Patience"; in "Nalagiri the Elephant" both relatives of the Buddha appear), he is seen as the unconverted and unrepentant evil-doer, the one still completely addicted to the poisons of selfishness, anger, and greed. Devadatta and Ananda appear together in many of the jatakas, Devadatta always doing evil and Ananda always doing good (or learning to do so). In the endless future, however, as all things are ultimately destined for liberation and Buddhahood, even Devadatta, after condemning himself through his own evil actions to countless life-times in the lowest hells, will rise, his negative karma expiated at last, and attain what he has actually always had—Perfection. Such stories ultimately serve to reveal the profound idealism of the Mahayana vision. Even Devadatta, the one who embodies the most spiritually retrograde elements of the cosmos, is assured of Buddhahood—but obviously it will take an incalculable, unimaginably long time!

Stories abound in many religious traditions of the power of deeply realized sages over wild animals. In *Empty Cloud*, the autobiography of Zen Master Hsu Yun, the greatest of the twentieth century Chinese Zen masters, many such incidents are related. (In one incident, a tiger enters the meditation hall and peacefully receives the precepts—much to the consternation of the monks). There are other, considerably older Chinese stories of certain great, but eccentric, Zen masters, sometimes portrayed in Zen paintings fast asleep, completely at ease, with their heads cradled on the side of a sleeping tiger. Or there is the Zen master of T'ang era China whose two attendants, it is said, were not human but tigers, named "Big Emptiness" and "Little Emptiness," "emptiness" being a Zen expression for one's True, empty-of-all-limiting-concepts Nature.

As miraculous as this tale is, the Buddha is certainly not alone in this territory. St. Francis of Assisi, for one, would certainly have appreciated the tale.

Sources abound for this story. The most complete version is in Reynolds, *Sinhalese Literature* and there is a good, brief one in Coomaraswamy's *Buddha and the Gospel of Buddhism*. Many accounts of the life of the Buddha include a re-telling of this famous incident as well.

Kisa Gotami (pp. 36-38)

One source for this story is the traditional commentary on the Anguttara-Nikaya composed by Buddhaghosa in the early part of the fifth century C. E. , quoted in *Buddhist Parables*, Burlingame, pp. 92-94. This is one of the most famous and beautiful of all the teaching stories of the Buddha. It is direct, to the point, and eminently practical. It also makes clear why one of the traditional appellations for the Buddha was "The Great Physician." His wisdom and skill in, not simply explaining about, but actually leading others to the understanding that heals all sorrows, was said to be unparalleled.

In the well-known twelfth century Zen Ox-Herding pictures, which demonstrate the successive stages of spiritual development in Zen, the greatest sage is shown, in the final picture of the series, as one who does not hold aloof from life but, rather, mingles freely and unselfconsciously with all people. Part of the verse accompanying this final illustration reads, "without resorting to magical powers/ withered trees he swiftly brings to bloom." In other words, the fully enlightened person, through his or her own unique spontaneity, vitality, and understanding, can help us to blossom into life once again without consciously trying to do so. This is demonstrated in the story of Kisa Gotami.

Parinirvana (pp. 39-44)

The Buddha's passing or entrance into Nirvana, after 45 years of sustained teaching, is perhaps the most moving incident recorded of the Buddha's life. Teaching until the end, surrounded by monks and nuns, laypeople of all classes, Nagas (great serpent-beings), devas (god-like beings), and animals, spiritually very strong yet simultaneously old and physically weak, it is a powerful and fitting final scene to an active and generous life. Many carvings and painted scrolls exist which depict this moment in all its intensity. Seventeen centuries after the Parinirvana, the Japanese Buddhist monk-poet Saigyo wrote this verse:

> I saw in Yoshino's
> Billows of Blossoms that long-ago
> Time of Great Passing
> When the Sala trees surrounding Him
> Suddenly turned as white as cranes.

Though almost two thousand years had passed, Saigyo looked at blossoms and *saw* the Parinirvana. The moment of the Buddha's Parinirvana is unrivaled, except for the Enlightenment itself, in the depth of feeling it evokes from the Buddhist imagination.

The two events are complements of each other. With his Enlightenment the Buddha breaks through to Permanence, the sub-stratum of all existences, and what is eternal and abiding is brought dramatically to the fore. At the time of his Parinirvana, the impermanence of all created forms is given preeminence and becomes, in effect, the Buddha's final teaching. The Enlightenment and the Parinirvana, permanence and impermanence, taken together, reveal the essence of the Buddha's "life-as-teaching."

In *Foundations of Tibetan Mysticism* Lama Govinda writes:

> Those who keep aloof from the contacts of life, miss the opportunities of sacrifice, of self-negation, of relin-

quishing hard-earned gains, of giving up what was dear or what seemed desirable, of service to others, and of the trials of strength in the temptations and ordeals of life. Again: to help others and to help oneself go hand in hand. The one cannot be without the other.

However, we should not force our good deeds upon others from a sense of moral superiority, but act spontaneously from that natural kind of selflessness which flows from the knowledge of the solidarity of all life and from the indescribable experience of oneness, gained in meditation, and experience whose universal character was expressed...in the general religious attitude of the Mahayana.

It was this knowledge of solidarity...which, however imperfect in its first dawning, led the Buddha in his former existences upon the path of enlightenment, and which made him renounce his own immediate liberation (when meeting the Buddha of a previous world-age), in order to gain perfect Buddhahood through the experiences and sufferings of countless rebirths in the practice of the *Bodhisattva* virtues, which would enable him to reach the highest aim, not only for himself, but for the benefit of innumerable other beings as well.

It was this knowledge which made the Buddha return from the Tree of Enlightenment in order to proclaim his Gospel of Light, according to which the faculty of enlightenment (*bodhicitta*) is inherent in every living being. Whenever this faculty becomes a conscious force in any being, a *Bodhisattva* is born. To awaken this consciousness was the life's task of the Buddha. It was this that caused him to take upon himself the hardships of a wandering life, for forty long years, instead of enjoying for himself the happiness of liberation. [11]

The appellation *Tathagatha* (literally, "He-Who-Is-Thus-Come") is another traditional title for the Buddha.

Nirvana literally means "extinguished," or "blown-out," or, according to some sources, "cooled down," implying that all causes leading to conditioned, limited existence (i. e. , greed, anger, and ignorance), have at last been extinguished, like a candle's flame. It may also suggest the complete stilling of breath (hence, "blowing out") which is said to occur in deep meditation. A full Buddha, Buddhist tradition holds, being completely freed from all limited existence, does not die—but enters fully into Nirvana.

This version of the Buddha's Parinirvana is drawn from Coomaraswamy's *Buddha and Gospel of Buddhism* as well as from Asvhagosha's classic *Buddhacarita*, as it appears in Conze's *Buddhist Scriptures*. The Parinirvana moments themselves are mostly quoted from Conze, with some adaptations and editing.

Give It All You've Got (pp. 47-50)
(Vanupatha-Jataka; No. 2)

An encouraging, straightforward jataka of persever- ance and steadfastness. From this jataka, one can see the ease with which these tales have been used to teach— used by the Buddha, of course, but also by subsequent Buddhist teachers, preachers, and wandering story- tellers. The traditional opening and closing of each jataka is ascribed to the Buddha and establishes a context, in the present, for the tale of the past (the jataka itself). The opening for this jataka tale essen- tially goes like this:

> Once a young monk came before the Buddha and said that he could not go on, that the training was too diffi- cult. "I am like a dry well, O World Honored One. This image returns to me over and over. I have tried and tried but I am thoroughly disheartened. I cannot go on. It is pointless. There is no water down the bottom of this well-shaft. I feel I should quit and return again, still unenlightened, back to my home."

> The Buddha replied. "This is not the first time you and I have spoken in this way. What you did in an ear- lier birth you can do again now. Let me tell you an old story."

And a version of its closing:

"Now, long ago," said the Buddha, "ages past, you were that youth, strong but without full confidence in your own strength, and I was the merchant who encouraged you to go on and try once more to split the rock. Son," he added, "the rock of ego is hard to crack. But you can do it. Give it one more shot and give it all you've got!" And the young monk, heartened, returned to his practice with vigor and achieved a breakthrough into Truth.

The Brave Lion and the Foolish Rabbit (pp. 51-56)
(Daddabha-Jataka; No. 322)

Much kinder than the later European tale of "Henny-Penny" or "Chicken Little," this jataka, often known as "The Flight of the Beasts," shows the strength and functioning of compassion. In the Western European versions of this tale, the powerful animal, a fox, uses his strength to take advantage of the other animals (whom he gobbles up). It is a cautionary fable.

But the brave lion uses his strength and courage to help those endangered by their delusive fears. One can't help but wonder about the comparative effects on the psyches of children who grow up exposed to one version of this universal tale, and not the other.

While ostensibly a tale about rumors and "groundless" fears (no pun intended), the central image of the soil breaking up beneath one's feet remains a potent image of impermanence. *The Tibetan Book of the Dead* lists the sensation of the earth crumbling beneath one's feet as one potential experience in the death process. The anxiety this charming little story faces head-on, then, is not negligible. In one sense, the message of the Buddha—indeed, the whole point of Buddhist training— can be summed up in one word: *fearlessness.* This should not be interpreted as a rigid or aggressive attitude toward an external and threatening universe, but rather a simple readiness to live and grow from a true understanding of the inseparability of oneself and the universe.

Yasutani-Roshi says:

> When you truly understand...[the] fundamental princi-
> ple you will not be anxious about your life or your
> death. You will then attain a steadfast mind and be
> happy in your daily life. Even though heaven and earth
> were turned upside down, you would have no fear. Even
> if an atomic or hydrogen bomb were exploded you
> would not quake in terror. [12]

Laughing ultimately at all fears, even fears of death,
this simple jataka reveals its deeply Buddhistic vision.

The Buddha is traditionally known as "the lion
among men." In accounts of the Buddha's birth, he
sounds "the lion's roar." (See "Birth" and notes.) In
"Enlightenment" he strides like a lion towards the bo
tree—i.e., his stride is confident, fearless, royal. In "The
Lion, the Elephant, and the Merchants' Cries" the Buddha is once again a lion, the king of beasts. In this story,
the lion's touching of the earth seems to prefigure the
Buddha's later calling of the Earth to witness (see
"Enlightenment").

A version of this story has been published for children as *Foolish Rabbit's Big Mistake.*

The Quail and the Falcon (pp. 57-59)
(Sakunagghi-Jataka; No. 168)

Tales in which the small and weak triumph over the
big, strong, and proud are among the most universal and
timeless of all stories. Such tales express the essence of
all the more complex stories of good versus evil and
may, it has been conjectured, be deeply rooted in the
structure of the human psyche.

Perhaps this is a consequence of our evolutionary
roots? Millions of years ago, after all, we *were* small,
weak, and almost helpless. We were surrounded by huge,
powerful, dangerous animals—animals much bigger and
tougher than anything around now. Cleverness, and the
connecting of mental agility with goodness, as well as an
abiding faith that the small will triumph over the large

(and a tendency to root for the underdog) may be our psychological inheritance from these ancient times.

So much for speculation.

This little jataka bears a remarkable resemblance to the classic Hopi tale, "Field Mouse Goes to War," in which the tiny mouse destroys an attacking hawk by the same essentially nonviolent, nonaggressive stratagem— at the last moment he leaps aside and lets the hawk destroy itself. Why should a Native American story and an Indian Buddhist story be so similar?

The archetypal view is essentially that the Mind of peoples all around the world is One. Given this fundamental identity, as well as the fundamental similarity of human experience, similar story patterns must emerge. Just as people everywhere are recognizable as human (two eyes, a head, a nose and mouth, arms, legs, etc.) there is a recognizably human shape to the mind.

The other view, that of cultural dissemination, suggests that in the depths of history there have been cultural exchanges now unknown. Perhaps the truth admits both possibilities, and others as well.

What is the underlying ground that saves the little quail in this jataka? In Buddhist terms it must be the ground of Being—unlimited, unconditioned Mind itself. Relying on it, drawing strength from it, we can safely face all dangers. In the Pali *Jataka*, the Buddha comments on the tale he has just told of the falcon and the quail, interpreting it more specifically for monks, saying "Brethren, when people leave their own station, Mara finds a door...What is foreign ground, Brethren, and what is the wrong place for a brother? I mean the Five Pleasures of Sense. What are these Five? The Lust of the Eye...[and so on]. This, Brethren, is the wrong place for a brother."

This brief, Aesop-like animal fable, also recalls elements in the well-known African-American story, "Br'er Rabbit and the Briar Patch." Having tricked Br'er Fox into tossing him back into the briar patch, the resourceful Br'er Rabbit escapes once more, singing out, "Born and bred in the briar patch, Br'er Fox! Born and bred in the briar patch!" For more jataka connections with tales of Br'er Rabbit, see "Prince Five-Weapons."

The Steadfast Parrot (pp. 60-61)
(Mahasuka-Jataka; No. 429)

Often the jatakas embody Buddhist ethics, showing believers how to live properly in the world, while simultaneously showing the future historical Buddha defining his own Path. In this beautiful and simple jataka we can see this combined process at work. Both the qualities of the mind of any fledgling bodhisattva as well as the resolute mind the historical Buddha himself must display to win complete enlightenment are revealed. This testing of the paramitas is consciously undertaken in the jatakas as early as the Sumedha-birth (see "Sumedha and Dipankara"). In addition, one of the fundamental story-patterns of the jataka tradition is established—the testing of the Bodhisattva's mettle by Shakra, king of the gods. (See also "The Hare's Sacrifice," and "King Sivi.")

Prince Five-Weapons (pp. 62-67)
(Pancavudha-Jataka; No. 55)

This lively jataka seems to be the earliest known version of the well-known Tar-Baby story. Burlingame, in his *Buddhist Parables*, identifies the story as such.

This particular written version grew out of telling it, and its oral flavor owes a great debt to the many children (and adults) with whom I've had the chance to share it. Like "The Brave Lion and the Foolish Rabbit," "Great Joy the Ox," and to a lesser extent, "The Monkey and the Crocodile," "The Wise Quail and the Foolish Quail," and "The Banyan Deer," "Prince Five-Weapons" is a story that I have often told. I hope other adults will continue to pass on these tales, and others like them, to children today.

Storytelling is a wonderfully potent tool for counteracting the negative effects of television. Through it, lan-

guage is charged with deep feeling and the tales really
live, emerging in our own minds with our own images in
ways that are uniquely alive. We are empowered by the
oral telling. What's more, the experience is communal,
not private. Such contexts of oral telling should be always kept in mind when thinking of the jatakas in general, but this particular group of stories bears the clear-
est stamp of such oral telling.

Cowell describes the tale like this—"How Prince Five-
Weapons fought the ogre Hairy-Grip and, though de-
feated, subdued the ogre by fearlessness." See, also, the
note for the story of "Angulimala" for how this brief
jataka connects with that much more complex tale.

The Wise Quail and the Foolish Quail (pp. 68-71)
(Sammodamana-Jataka; No. 33).

The theme of harmoniously working together for the
common good is clearly stated in this parable-like tale.

The Monkey and the Crocodile (pp. 72-75)
(Sumsumara-Jataka; No. 208. Also Vanara-Jataka; No.
342)

A humorous and clever jataka that has long func-
tioned in the West as a popular children's story—and
one not without depth. The story asks, what *is* a tender
heart? Is it the physical heart that hangs like a red fruit
among the branching veins of the body? If not, then,
what is it and where is it to be found?

There are a number of traditional jatakas in which
the Buddha appears as a monkey. In the most famous of
these, (Mahakapi-Jataka; No. 407. Also in Aryasura's
Jatakamala), the Buddha is a heroic and self-sacrificing
monkey king. With his own body he forms a bridge so
that his tribe can escape from the king's hunters who
are waiting below. In the Pali version, one monkey
(Devadatta in an earlier birth) is jealous of the monkey
king's power, and stamps upon his back as he is crossing. The monkey king falls, badly injured. The human

king runs to him and learns a lesson in kingship. Repentant, he buries the body of the monkey king with great honors and, inlaying the skull of the monkey king with gold, sets it up upon a spear as a royal reminder of wisdom and goodness.

In this collection there is an echo of the monkey calling out to the crocodile, "Who calls?" when Digit, the gorilla who sacrifices himself for the welfare of his family-group, answers the voice calling in his dream with essentially the same words. (See "Digit.") The true story of Digit, which I have used as an example of a modern jataka, also carries with it, in Digit's noble self-sacrifice, a suggestion of the beautiful traditional tale, "The Monkey King."

Great Joy the Ox (pp. 76-82)
(Nandivisala-Jataka; No. 28).

In telling this jataka, the Buddha reveals, "Ananda was the brahmin of those days and I myself Nanda-Visala [the ox]." Also, in Great Joy's resolute stand under the shouts, the hurled clods of mud, the sticks and stones, there seems to be a prefiguring of the Buddha's steadfastness during the time of his temptation by the forces of Mara, just prior to his great enlightenment.

Golden Goose (pp. 83-87)
(Suvannahamsa-Jataka, No. 136)

To kill the golden goose, the one that lays the golden eggs, is an image we all know well from Grimms' fairy tales. Though no goose is killed in this story, (which may well be the source of the later Western European tale), and no golden eggs are laid, the plucking of the goose symbolizes this kind of impatient greed well enough.

In this version of the tale, I found it interesting to allow the mother to grow through her error. Rather than ending at her low point of failure or with the goose's later departure, by continuing the story one finds that error itself may be the precursor of wisdom. It all depends on where one ends the story. Stories are ways of exploring and presenting possibilities.

The Brave Parrot (pp. 88-90)

Sources for this animal-birth jataka are not clear. In *The Jatakastava*, or "Praise of the Buddha's Former Births," we find the following verse:

> The vehement fire whirled in the thick forest, rushing swiftly on its path, escorted by noise. Smoke whirling like death was thrown out; it boiled...with long arms, with hands of flame.
>
> The flame was blazing over the...trees; it seized the many birds and wild animals in the forest, tossing the trees with its roaring fire...
>
> You then in that forest, as a bird...a young partridge on a tree, were unyielding, as one full of virtues. You fetched the water; then you checked the flames. By your merits the whole fire assuredly was quenched.
>
> Because you exhibited this heroism...sympathy and compassion towards all beings, therefore...you quenched the fire. [13]

Some liberties have been taken with the story as I originally heard it years ago (in which the god actually makes rain to fall, rather than spontaneously bursting into tears), but the bodhisattvic vision remains clear. A bird that could itself fly to safety from the burning forest does not leave, but risks its own life to save others. In the Lotus Sutra, the Buddha uses the image of a "house on fire" to stand for this world; in the famous and dramatic "Fire Sermon," he describes all conditioned things as burning with the flames of greed, anger, and ignorance.

In a beautiful legend about Avalokitesvara, the Bodhisattva of Compassion, something similar gets expressed. Having worked hard to empty all the hells, the bodhisattva's labors seem at last done. He looks down into the now empty hells. After centuries of unending work he has saved them all. But, to his great dismay, when he looks down he sees that the hells have filled once again! His head splits into many heads, his arms shatter into many arms, and in the palm of each hand opens an eye of wisdom. The spontaneous response of the Bodhisattva of Compassion is not to turn away in defeat, but to respond, beyond limit or comprehension. (See "The Legend of Avalokitesvara" and its notes).

The little parrot, too, does not consciously know how he can possibly succeed. But he does not turn back. And his spontaneous, selfless, seemingly hopeless activity becomes successful. (See "King Goodness.")

The Banyan Deer (pp. 91-97)
(Nigrodhamiga-Jataka No. 12; Also Nandiyamiga-Jataka No. 385. In *The Jatakastava* as well.)

A beautiful and classic jataka which is part of the Pali canon, but which also gained great favor in the Mahayana tradition. Like the story of *The Hungry Tigress*, it is one of the pillars of the jataka vision. A spontaneous determination to risk oneself for the sake of others forms the core of the tale, and gives it a strong Bodhisattvic flavor. It is one of the finest teaching tales of the tradition. Whoever originally told this story must have been not only wise but a gifted storyteller as well. The tale is deceptively simple yet embraces much.

Similar stories, sayings, and religious injunctions can be found in all religious traditions. One of the most poignant and powerful is from the Talmud—"He who saves a single soul; it is as if he saves the whole world." What makes the Buddhist jataka vision unique, and allies it strongly with our contemporary, ecologically alert world-view, is that these highest spiritual principles are shown at work among, not just human beings, but animals as well. Indeed, in many cases, the animal is teacher to the man. (See "The Blue Bear," "The Golden Deer," and "Great Joy the Ox," stories and notes.)

The Blue Bear (pp. 98-100)

The Blue Bear is a straightforward, classic jataka. One source for the tale exists in an English translation from the Indo-Scythian text (Khotanese) of *The Jatakastava*, or "Praise of the Buddha's Former Births." In the three paragraph summation of this jataka which appears there, the Buddha is presented as a noble, blue-furred bear who saves a hunter from freezing in the snow. The hunter then betrays him to those who would kill him. In response to his own evil, the betrayer's hands fall off. Another source for this story can be found in the *Abhidharma Mahavibhasa Sastra*. A scene from this jataka also exists among the famous paintings of the Ajanta caves of India.

Generally, in this type of jataka, the Bodhisattva is the animal who, demonstrating great compassion, saves a man from danger. The Bodhisattva-animal is then betrayed by the man he saves. Another man, a king, ultimately recognizes and honors the wise beast's true worth. Many lessons are woven into this simple and oft-repeated pattern.

A variety of such stories and their permutations are scattered throughout the Pali *Jataka*. One such tale which appears both in the Pali *Jataka* (Mahakapi-Jataka No. 516—not to be confused with Mahakapi-Jataka No. 407, the story of the Monkey King) and in *The Jatakamala* of Aryasura, where it is titled "The Great Ape," is about a monkey who helps a man escape from a deep pit. Once out, the man tries to kill the monkey with a rock so that he may eat its flesh. But the wise monkey, although wounded, escapes the fatal blow and, in the *Jatakamala* version, teaches the evil-doer another lesson in charity and compassion. Eventually, the man feels such burning remorse that his body breaks out in a fearsome leprosy. In time he is seen by a king who, enquiring about the cause of his illness, learns from him about the necessary effects of both good and evil actions. (For another tale in which a transformation of character is brought about through suffering the consequences of wrong-doing, see "The Golden Goose.") In the Pali version, the ground opens up, and the wrong-doer (identified as Devadatta in an earlier birth) is swallowed down to hell.

"The Golden Deer" is another version of this same jataka type. In both "The Golden Deer" and "The Blue Bear" jatakas, Devadatta is the man who, less than a beast, fails to recognize the responsibilities of gratitude. The Buddha is, of course, the wise beast. An interesting implication of this story type is that an animal may be more spiritually developed, more "human," than a human being. (In the story "Great King Goodness," a similar recognition by the King of Kosala—that the blood-drinking goblins have actually been more sensitive and perceptive, more human, than he—prompts his conversion).

The Golden Deer (pp. 101-105)
(Ruru-Jataka, No. 482; also in Aryasura's *Jatakamala*, and the *Jatakastava* or "Praise of the Buddha's Former Births")

This story seems to draw much from its better known cousin-jataka "The Banyan Deer" (in its liberation motif), as well as from "The Blue Bear" (in its central incidents of the animal savior who is then betrayed). This is a normal part of the oral tradition—motifs and incidents wandering naturally back and forth across story lines which are not fortified, but remain quite permeable. What is so interesting about this story (the version here is based on the Cowell translation of the Pali text), in addition to its motif of universal liberation, is the very realistic dilemma the tale poses. Instead of simply giving us a happy ending, the implications of the Golden Deer's request and the human king's promise are explored. The king's vow is tested and the deer themselves must learn the responsibility that comes from a promise kept.

A most interesting story, and hauntingly similar to an actual newspaper account which appeared in 1987, Gannett Newspapers, Rochester, N. Y.

Six more bodies recovered from river after bus accident
The Associated Press and Reuters

COMFORT [Texas]—Searchers found six more bodies in the churning waters of the Guadeloupe River yesterday, bringing the death toll to eight after a church camp bus and van tried to skirt the swollen river and were washed away.

Two people were still missing late yesterday after the seventh, unidentified victim was found 18 miles downstream and an eighth victim was found two miles downstream. Helicopters scoured the river while National Guardsmen and scuba divers searched the banks.

One frightened teenager hurled down the churning flood waters said he owed his life to a ride aboard a swimming deer that guided him to safety.

"The deer just came up under me and I held on tight," said Chris Ray, 17.

This tragic yet remarkable little news article uncannily echoes such traditional jatakas as "The Golden Deer" and "The Blue Bear." Real life and the jataka perception can, it seems, come eerily close.

One of the greatest of the writer-storytellers of our time, Nobel prize-winner Isaac Bashevis Singer, has mused that perhaps stories are events that actually do take place at some level, on some other world in a different dimension of the universe. The brain, he suggests, creates nothing truly new and the universe is so vast that truth cannot be bound to what is simply acceptable at current societal levels. The truth admits many possi-bilities—some as yet undreamed, others simply unac-knowledged. (See also "The Brave Parrot," "The Blue Bear," "The Lion, the Elephant and Merchant's Cries," "Digit," "Stilson's Leap," and "Kogi the Priest.")

The queen's desire, in this tale, to hear the teachings of the Golden Deer is an interesting echo of the crocodile-wife's misplaced desire (in the jataka of "The Monkey's Heart") for the wise monkey's tender heart.

Verses, such as those spoken by the Golden Deer to the king, are a traditional part of the Pali *Jataka*.

The Lion, the Elephant, and the Merchants' Cries (pp. 106-107)

The Nepalese *Bodhisattva Avadana-Kalpalata* is a storehouse of legends from the fifth century, document-ing the Buddha's former lives. (*Kalpalata* means, liter-ally, "a wish-granting tree"—i. e. , a tree yielding what-ever is wanted of it.) In this text we learn:

> One evening the Lord was conversing familiarly with all his Bhiksus at the Jetavana grove. The conversation turned on an inquiry about the origin of philanthropy. Is it a natural propensity, the result of accumulated deeds or merit, or of constant practice? The Lord said, "Even ferocious animals like lions are susceptible to that feeling. For instance, a company of merchants were on the point of being devoured by a large venomous serpent, on the seashore. They screamed aloud at the prospect of instant death; their screams were heard by a lion and an elephant. They fell from a high hill on the serpent and crushed him to death. But they themselves lost their lives from the poisonous breath of the dying reptile. I am that lion, Sariputtra [one of the Buddha's great disciples] is the elephant, and Devadatta is the reptile."[14]

Why should a lion, a flesh-eater, help men? Why should a bear or a deer come to the aid of those in dis-tress? Why should a dolphin rise from the depths of the sea and carry an exhausted swimmer to shore? Such things occur regularly in the jataka-world. And sometimes they also happen in real life. (See "The Blue Bear," "The Golden Deer," "The Brave Parrot," "The Banyan Deer," and their notes. Also "Stilson's Leap," "Digit," "Kogi The Priest," and notes.)

Mention of this jataka also appears in the verses of *The Jatakastava* or "Praise of the Buddha's Former Births":

> The merchants, surrounded by a serpent, in great distress, whom you saw then in a forest, in your compassion, as the lion king you called your friend, the elephant. You roared together with him; you offered up your life.

> Upon the elephant you mounted; standing on the top of his head with your claws you surely split his forehead by your clutching it. The merchants escaped, they all found life. You, however, lost it with your beloved friend.[15]

The Doe, the Hunter, and the Great Stag
(pp. 108-109)
(Suvannamiga-Jataka No. 359)

It is unclear from the tale itself which deer was the Buddha in an earlier birth. The most admirable and decisive character is the doe. It is she who manifests the compassionate and heroic Bodhisattva mind. However, the traditional introduction and conclusion, which form the "tale of the present" in which past life roles are identified, tells us that this story was told by the Buddha about "a maiden of gentle birth in Savatthi," who had married into a family with heretical views. By inviting the Buddhist Elders regularly to her new home, however, she effected a change of heart in her husband and in-laws. Eventually both she and her husband attained complete enlightenment.

The Buddha, overhearing the monks discussing this case said, "Brethren, not only did she set her husband free from the bonds of passion; formerly, too, she freed free from the bonds of passion; formerly, too, she freed even sages of old from the bonds of death. ' And with these words he held his peace, but being pressed by them he related a story of the past." Then, once the tale is told, the conclusion follows. "The Master here ended his lesson and identified the Birth: At that time Channa was the hunter, the female novice was the doe, and I myself was the royal stag."

Channa, by the way, was the name of the Buddha's charioteer, when as the prince Siddhartha he was first moved to leave his home (see "Leaving Home"). Perhaps, by this time, he had, like many other of the Buddha's former acquaintances, become a monk. Cowell's note on this simply identifies Channa as "A Brother who was suspended for siding with heretics." It is unclear.

The Brave Merchant (pp. 110-111)
(Khadirangara Jataka; No. 40. Also *Jatakamala*)

Another of the testing jatakas. In this one, however, it is not Shakra, but Mara himself who tests the Bodhisattva's resolution and courage. That the Buddha, long ago, as a merchant, was able to overcome the challenge of Mara sets the stage for his final defeat of Mara with his profound experience of Enlightenment. Interestingly, *The Vimalakirti Sutra* states that:

> ...the Maras who play the devil in innumerable universes of the ten directions are all Bodhisattvas dwelling in the inconceivable liberation, who are playing the devil in order to develop living beings through their skill in liberative technique.
> ...only one who is...a bodhisattva can harass another bodhisattva, and only a bodhisattva can tolerate the harassment of another bodhisattva. [16]

Compassion, it seems, takes many forms.

The "solitary Buddha" in this jataka is a reference to a being of high spiritual attainment who has attained enlightenment on his or her own (usually through an understanding of the interrelation of cause and effect)—

and who remains alone, not teaching others. Traditionally, such a being is termed a *pratyekabuddha* (Sanskrit) or *paccekabuddha* (Pali). The great Mahayana Buddhist text, *The Lotus Sutra*, however, says this is an illusion. In reality, there is only one Path—the Path of the Bodhisattva who, realizing Truth, continues with his or her own spiritual development even while working for the welfare of others. Since the very idea of an isolated self is an illusion, *pratekyabuddhas* are really Bodhisattvas in disguise. (See *Scripture of the Lotus Blossom of the Fine Dharma (The Lotus Sutra)*, translated from the Chinese of Kumarajiva by Leon Hurvitz, pp. xix-xx).

In the *Jatakamala* there is a much more involved version of this dramatic tale, and much of the testing takes place in discussions between Mara and the merchant before the crucial walking through flames is ever begun. The differences between the spare, oral style of the Pali *Jataka* and the more literary style of the *Jatakamala* can be clearly discerned by comparing these two versions of the tale. The early thrust of narrative is replaced by a testing discourse in the later version. One might also compare versions of "The Golden Deer" in both collections, as well as versions of "The Monkey King" (Mahakapi No. 407), and "The Great Ape" (Mahakapi No. 516).

The Hare's Sacrifice (pp. 112-115)
(Sasa-Jataka; No. 316. Also, *Jatakamala* and verses of
    The Jatakastava.)

Another classic and widely known jataka tale. The famous nineteenth century Zen monk-poet, Ryokan, wrote a beautiful, tender verse based on this jataka, which concludes:

> From that time till now
> the story's been told,
> this tale
> of how the rabbit

> came to be
> in the moon,
> and even I
> when I hear it
> find the tears
> soaking the sleeve of my robe. [17]

In Ryokan's version, based on a version of the tale found in the *Konjaku Monogatari,* a collection of Japanese stories, many of them Buddhist, compiled around the twelfth century, the hare dies from his sacrifice and it is his dead body that is, in the words of the poem, "laid to rest/ in the palace of the moon."

King Sivi (pp. 116-118)

In the Pali *Jataka* there is a story of a King Sivi, numbered 499. In it a beneficent king gives away his own eyes, and is then restored by Shakra. This story also appears in the *Jatakamala,* but in neither of these works is there a story of a King Sivi who gives away the flesh of his own body. This particular version is based on a recounting of the tale which was told to me some eighteen years ago. A translation from a Tibetan text of this jataka, in which King Sivi gives away his flesh, appears in Beyer, *The Buddhist Experience: Sources and Interpretations.* Also, in Burlingame, *Buddhist Parables,* there is a full translation of the tale from Aryasura's poetic Sanskrit work, the *Sutralamkara.*

Some verses based on the story (the one in which King Sivi gives away his flesh) appear in *The Jatakastava:*

> For the pigeon's sake by your virtues you tore the skin
> and flesh upon your limbs for a ransom. You did not
> long for the pleasures...which [were] yours. [18]

In these versions, as in the story of Rupavati (see notes on "The Hungry Tigress"), it is not until Sivi is asked by Shakra if he experienced any regret during or after his sacrifice—and he answers that he experienced none whatsoever, only the great joy of doing good—that he is restored.

For all its tender-heartedness, the story of King Sivi is remarkably unsentimental. Its ecologically sound view of the equal rights of predator and prey makes especially clear sense today. Indeed, its grasp of deep ecology seems nothing less than prescient.

The conclusion of this particular version—"How could that compare with having a world in which to do good?"—may seem paltry. Simply to do good suggests the vague aspiration of a childish mind. It must be taken in its traditional context. The Three General Resolutions of Buddhism which, along with the Precepts, form the foundation of Buddhist action and life are:

> To do good
> To avoid evil
> To liberate all sentient beings.

There is an interesting story in relation to these resolutions. The governor of a province once came to a famous Zen master (who had the habit of perching up in a tree to meditate), and asked "What is the highest teaching of Buddhism?"

The Zen master answered, "To do good and avoid evil."

The governor responded, "Why, even a child of three knows that!"

"Yes," replied the Zen master, "but a man of seventy can still find it hard to put into practice."

The Story of a Sneeze (pp. 119-125)
(Asilakkhana-Jataka. No. 126)

This traditional but relatively little known jataka is both humorous and sophisticated. Yet, even in this comic and entertaining tale, one senses, as in the story of Great Joy the Ox, something of the tradition's interest in showing the Buddha-to-be's efforts toward developing the strength of character and will, as well as the insight

he will need, in his final quest for Enlightenment.
Triumphing over fears while lying waiting in the char-
nel ground especially prefigures some of Siddhartha
Gautama's austerities.

In the Buddha's own words, he says about some of
these experiences:

> Then...I thought, 'Suppose now that on those nights...I
> spend them in shrines of forest, park, or tree, fear-
> some and hair-raising as they are...that I may behold
> for myself the panic, fear, and horror of it all. '
>
> So...I did so...As I stayed there a deer maybe came
> up to me, or a peacock threw down a twig. Or else a
> breeze stirred a heap of fallen leaves. Then thought I,
> 'Here it is! Here comes that panic, fear, and horror!'
> Then...there came to me this thought: 'Why do I re-
> main thus in constant fear and apprehension? Let me
> bend down to my will that panic, fear, and horror...'
> Then...just as I was...I bent that panic, fear, and hor-
> ror to my will.[19]

There is a fairy-tale-like quality to this jataka, too,
with its king and prince and princess and wise old
woman. And there is all the richness of the Indian style
of storytelling, with the sneeze itself being woven in, beginning to end, in unexpected ways.

The surprising conclusion, in which the brahmin returns and the prince is brought to a deeper appreciation
of the essential mystery of things, suggests that the orig-
inator of the tale was wonderfully conscious of his or
her aims in telling the story.

Many of the stories in the Pali *Jataka* open with
lines to the effect that the events of this story occurred
when Bramadatta was reigning or still reigned in
Benares. Benares (or Varanasi) is said to be the oldest
continuously inhabited city on the earth. Perhaps, even
in the Buddha's time, such an opening suggested something of antiquity, like saying "In the old days," or
"Once upon a time."

Preacher of Patience (pp. 125-127)
(Khantivada-Jataka [Sanskrit *Kshanti-Jataka*], No. 313
in the *Jatakamala*; Also in the brief verses of *The
Jatakastava*).

A brief yet remarkable jataka, and one, along with
"The Hungry Tigress" and "King Sivi," likely to seem
bizarre to Western tastes. Yet these jatakas, in their extremity, make their lessons all the clearer. Patience
means real patience; compassion means real compassion—to the limit of all possible testing. Like cubism in
painting, these stories distort ordinary reality enough to
make their meaning, not their surfaces, come through
all the more clearly. Like "The Hungry Tigress,"
"Preacher of Patience" offers neither solace nor magical
intervention. These two tales are the strongest "stuff" of
the jatakas. The modern jataka, "Stilson's Leap" is also
like this, as is, with some tempering, the story of
"Digit," in which we metaphysically go backstage, behind the curtain of death, and see some of the between-
life processes and directions forming.

For similar tales, but ones which turn on a final magical restoration—as if, at the end of *King Lear*, the dead
Cordelia were to begin to breathe and all became well
again, see "The Hare's Sacrifice," and "King Sivi." Such
tales, with their magical endings, are no less true than
"Preacher of Patience" and "The Hungry Tigress".
Rather, they emphasize a different perspective—not realistic, but certainly no less Real.

Myth and legend, it has been said, reveal a truth too
great to be limited by mere fact. These two types of tales
let us look into the structure of mythic thinking. In literature, these two types of tales underlie the respective
visions of tragedy and comedy. They are two different,
but actually quite connected, ways of looking at the real
facts of ordinary life.

There may also be the suggestion of a very ancient
and universal tradition of religious experience lying behind this jataka. Mircea Eliade, in his classic work
Shamanism—Archaic Techniques of Ecstasy, reveals that

a ritual death and often a symbolic or hallucinatory experience of dismemberment are traditional aspects of the neophyte shaman's initiation. The shamanic tradition, built on an ecstatic experience of death and rebirth, extends far back into the Paleolithic Age. It may also underlie and connect with certain yogic traditions of ancient India.

So, something of a very archaic, inner, visionary experience may have been captured in this jataka which presents the dismemberment of the yogi-sage as if occurring in literal, albeit non-historical, time and space.

Mention of this jataka is made in the famous *Diamond Sutra*.

The Black Hound (pp. 128-129)
(Maha-Kanha-Jataka, No. 469)

The principle here is that great Bodhisattvas can take any form in order to aid suffering mankind—even acting in ways that might seem contrary to what one would expect. The Bodhisattva, in this tale, had himself attained the state of the high god Shakra, who appears often in the jatakas to test those on the path of virtue. (See "The Steadfast Parrot," "The Hare's Sacrifice," and "King Sivi." Also related are "Most Lovely Fugen" and "A Legend of Avalokitesvara.")

The black hound is a transformation of Shakra's charioteer, the god Matali. The Buddha declares at the conclusion of this jataka that at that time (in the days of the Buddha Kasyapa—the Buddha in the world cycle prior to this one) he himself had been Shakra and Ananda had been Matali.

This is a powerful and resonant jataka, and in this re-telling I aimed for the sparest presentation. Such a tale has special implication for our own times. Nuclear and environmental dangers may indeed force us to make positive changes in our lives.

The Hungry Tigress (p. 130)

This is perhaps *the* classic jataka. Aryasura placed it first in his classic *Jatakamala*. While Aryasura's telling is elaborate and complex, the jataka nonetheless clearly conveys the profound mystery of compassion, without sugar-coating it.

"The Hungry Tigress" is also a particularly relevant jataka for our own times. Almost daily, we grow more aware of our intrinsic responsibilities to the welfare of non-human beings. Here is a religious drama, 2,500 years old, in which this very modern perception is actualized to the most extreme limit.

Compassionate self-sacrifice for the sake of another being—and not simply another human being—is vigorously upheld by this unusual jataka. In part, this is what makes the jataka tradition so interesting and so unique. The jatakas dramatize the ultimate worth of each living thing—even the worth of something so threatening to humanity's self-interest as a powerful and dangerous carnivore. As natural habitats disappear, and tiger populations are threatened (as well as the populations of so many other animal species), we might want to consider again the ancient message of this tale.

Which is not to say that, literally, we need—or even should—offer our bodies to a tiger! From a Buddhist point of view, such sacrifice would occur spontaneously, at the right time. It is *not* the result of an anguished and lonely process of ethical examination and reflection, culminating in a final steeling of oneself to the decision. Rather, it springs lightly, out of the depths of one's being, from a sense of connection, freedom, and joy.

In our world, there are many actions which can alleviate suffering, and so express the underlying spirit of this jataka in a variety of ways. These might include the dedication of some portion of one's personal time to environmental action; the choice of a vegetarian life-style (which both reduces killing and significantly lessens dangerous stresses on the environment), as well as a whole range of jobs—such as working in education or with the homeless. In short, anything that permits us to give ourselves willingly to tasks that benefit our society, our planet, and our fellow beings.

As the jataka is a literary form, we should also see in it the artistic effort made to express something for which we may have no words, something that can be only communicated by the patterning of story-form, or myth itself. What, after all, does pure compassion look like? What does it feel like? What is a love that is not fettered by likes and dislikes, by appearances, desires, or self interest? By its very extremity, this jataka tries to show something of what such pure love and compassion, the compassion of a bodhisattva, may be like.

This tale of the Prince Mahasattva ("Great Being") and the hungry tigress did not appear in the canonical Pali collection of 547 jatakas and their verses, but found its way into written record during the uprising of the Mahayana, where it gained tremendous popularity over the centuries. In Nepal today, a tree is still said to mark the spot where this jataka occurred, and pilgrims still go there to festoon the tree with offerings to the Buddha—scarves, prayer flags, and locks of pilgrims' hair.

The pillars referred to in this story (and in "The Banyan Deer") are the pillars of the great third century B.C.E. Indian King Ashoka, who made a dramatic conversion to Buddhism after years of bloody conquest. Thereafter, he devoted his life to the welfare of his people, and helped promulgate ethical and socially conscious policies, whose edicts he carved on pillars of stone.

In the Nepalese jataka tradition, there is much supplementary material on the tigress and her cubs as well as on the contexts of this brief but powerful jataka. They are as follows. The *Sanku and Sandhidatta Avadana*, like the *Subhasa Jataka* (see note, "Beginnings)", is from the *Bodhisattva Avadana*.

> Sanku and Sandhidatta, two brothers, lost their father
> Arthadatta, a merchant of Rajagriha, when they were
> very young. Their mother brought them up with great

difficulty, and, when they grew up, employed them in pilfering. The thieves were detected by the vigilant police of Ajatasatru [the king] and sentenced capitally. At the place of their execution the Buddha interposed in their favor, rescued them from the gallows, and carried them to his hermitage, where soon they rose to the exalted rank of Arhat.

The Lord said, "In one of their former existences, they were the cubs of a hungry tigress from whose jaws I preserved their lives by offering my own."[20]

And the following is from the "Suvarnaprabhasa," section XIX.

A Bodhisattva should sacrifice his own body for the good of others. The Lord in the course of his perambulation through the country of the Panchalas, entered a forest. He sat upon a grass plot, and struck the earth with the palms of his hands and the soles of his feet. Thereupon a great stupa made of gold, rubies, sapphires and precious stones rose like an apparition. The Lord ordered Ananda to open the doors of the stupa and found bones covered over with gems. The Bhikshus honored them with a salutation at the command of the Lord, and then the Lord, at the request of Ananda, gave the following history of the holy bones.[21]

There follows an account, by the Buddha, of the Hungry Tigress jataka, which concludes, "I am, O Ananda, that prince Mahasattva. I obtained, by means of these bones, the great Bodhi knowledge which nothing can equal."[22]

There is another interesting and especially bizarre (to Western sensibilities) version of this tale. The version that follows reflects the remarkable lengths to which the jataka tradition will go in valuing compassionate, selfless action. It also reflects something of the cultural heritage of the time. Rupavati, the woman, must become Rupavata, the man, in order to proceed towards Buddhahood. Yet *The Vimalakirti Sutra*, as well as other traditional writings, make it clear that women and men are equal in their ability to attain Enlightenment, and ultimately gain Buddhahood.

In a previous state of existence the Future Buddha was reborn as a woman of great beauty and virtue named Rupavati. Once she came upon a starving woman who under the uttermost pangs of hunger was about to eat her tiny infant son. Immediately Rupavati cut off her own breasts and gave them to the woman to eat as food. Her husband, making an Act of Truth, declared "If it is true such a sacrifice was never made willingly before, may your breasts be restored." Immediately the breasts were restored.

Shakra, King of the Gods, fearing that by the merit of her sacrifice Rupavati might displace him from his high seat, went in disguise to Rupavati to test her. "Is it true," he asked, "that you sacrificed your breasts for the sake of a child?"

"It is true."

"Did you not, either in the act or afterwards experience regret?"

"No."

"How could anyone believe you?"

"I will make an Act of Truth. If it is true that neither in the act nor after at any time did I experience the slightest regret; if, further it is true that I acted without any desire whatsoever for gain—that I yearned not for worldly dominion, or that I might become either a great monarch or Shakra, King of the Gods, but rather, acted only out of spontaneous compassion and for the sake of the Supreme Enlightenment of all beings, then may I on this instant cease to be a woman and become a man."

Immediately she ceased to be a woman and became a man, named Rupavata, who became, in time, King of the city of Utpalavati. After a reign of 60 years Rupavata was reborn as the son of a merchant and was named Chandraprabha because of his beauty which outshone the moon. When he was eight years old the desire to offer himself for the welfare of others, without making distinctions of high or low, arose strongly in him. He went to the cremation grounds and cutting his flesh, bit by bit, gave it to the vultures to feed upon. He was next born as the son of a Brahmin named Brahmaprabha on account of the great radiance which shone from him. When he was sixteen he retired to the forest to undergo rigorous austerities. Near the hut one day he saw a starving tigress who, in desperation, was about to eat her newborn cubs. The youth immediately gave his own body to the tigress and saved the cubs.

The Buddha said, "The town of Utpalavati is the town of Pushkalavata now. She who was Rupavati before is now myself. The starving woman became the tigress. Those who were the parents of the youth Brahmaprabha became my parents Suddhodhana and Maya. The two cubs are now my attendant Ananda and my son, Rahula."[23]

The hungry tigress jataka, in all its versions, powerfully dramatizes the advice which the Buddha gave to his monks—"Even as a mother regards her only child, so should one regard all beings."

A complete and lovely re-telling of the hungry tigress story can be found in Conze's *Buddhist Scriptures.* Conze's source is the *Splendor of Gold,* a Mahayana Sutra which he describes as having been "slowly composed over many centuries."

In *The Jatakastava,* this jataka is summarized in two verses:

> [When] a tigress, weak by hunger and thirst, with blazing eyes, savagely growling, seizing them in her mouth was about to eat her cubs, you did for them a great, noble favor.
>
> For the tigress you fell then from the mountain lest she should eat her beloved young cubs. You suffered distress for the world, as a giver of security. To you homage, O gracious one.[24]

Great King Goodness (pp. 131-137)
(Mahasilava-Jataka. No. 51)

This remarkably Gandhian tale of the transformative power of active non-violence closely follows, with some adaptations, the Pali *Jataka* text. The scene of the king's meeting with the goblins and the corpse adds an entirely unexpected yet fascinating (and very Indian) dimension to the story. The conclusion, on the rewards of persistence in goodness, are reminiscent of the conclusion of "The Brave Parrot," who persists in goodness not knowing how he can possibly succeed. Yet he does.

While this kind of story may seem preposterous, like some naive fairy-tale, it still has the power to touch us deeply. Perhaps this is because it draws so clearly upon mythic-archetypal, wish-fulfilling territory—territory common to us all. Stories are not true the way history is true. They are not true about what happened at one time or at one place. They are true the way wishes and dreams are true. They speak for what we hope may be, and so give us a true picture of the often unrealized dreams of the human heart. In stories, then, we can fulfill our deepest wishes, and make them visible and real through our imagination.

Then, too, there is the reality of Gandhi's non-violent triumph in India.

At the conclusion of this story, the Buddha reveals that Devadatta was the evil minister, the one thousand heroes his (the Buddha's) present disciples, and King Goodness the Buddha himself. Like "Give It All You've Got," the telling of this jataka was occasioned by a monk's temporary loss of faith.

The Naga King (pp. 138-145)
(Campeyya-Jataka No. 506)

This is an unusual jataka. So many magical elements come together in it that its richness startles the mind.

The Nagas, wise and powerful serpent-spirits, are connected with water, and generally viewed as benign. They live in jewelled palaces beneath the ocean, rivers, lakes, and streams. Kala Nagaraja, a very ancient and wise Naga, even knew of the Buddha-to-be's impending Enlightenment. (See "Enlightenment.")

There is a famous legend that after the Buddha's Enlightenment, a terrible storm arose. The serpent-king, Mucalinda, rose up out of the earth, and encircled the Buddha with his great body, opening his cobra hood to shelter the Enlightened One from the storm. Sculptures and paintings of this legendary event are especially popular throughout Southeast Asia.

The seemingly innocuous conclusion to this story—"and so the ground is gold even today"—is a traditional kind of story ending and is found world-wide. The point is not so much literal belief in this fantastic explanation (which seems to make the whole tale simply a kind of "pourquoi" or "just-so story"), as the validation of the real emotions and values brought to life through the story. The conclusion returns us to literal reality, yet a reality transformed. When we look at the earth we now see not just its form, but something of its meaning.

The story's real meaning for traditional listeners, then, would be that, having heard the story, from this point on, whenever we see the golden-colored earth, we too will remember the preciousness of our own human birth—a treasure worth more than even the most vast amounts of gold—and strive, like the Naga king, for greater purity and wisdom. The apparent fiction of the story actually alters the reality of our own lives. This is the story's (and the traditional storyteller's) job. This kind of ending is one of the tools of the profession.

To attain human birth and use it well—i.e., use it to further develop one's wisdom and compassion—is seen as the worthiest of all possible aims and accomplishments in Buddhism.

The brief verses in *The Jatakastava* describe the Naga king as a treasure himself—"pure and tranquil, the skin upon you was like gold, inlaid with precious stones."[25]

There is magic in this jataka. The many transformations, the rising of Sumana into the air like a goddess, her rage and sorrow as she hovers shining in the air, as well as the beautiful and astonishing touch of the great Naga king hiding himself in a flower and then reappearing as a handsome youth, give this tale unique distinction. Also noteworthy is the immediate willingness of both the King Uggasena and the Brahmin snake-charmer to freely release the Naga king.

Magical, treasure-filled, underwater realms appear in the mythologies of many widely separated cultures, such as Ireland and Japan.

Most Lovely Fugen (pp. 149-151)

This story is based on a tale first put into English by Lafcadio Hearn. (Hearn identifies his English version as being from "the old story-book, *Jikkun-sho*" and titles his story, "A Legend of Fugen Bosatsu.") "Fugen" is the Japanese for the Sanskrit, "Samantabhadra," the Bodhisattva of Compassionate Action. "Bosatsu" is the Japanese equivalent of the Sanskrit, "bodhisattva." As this is a Japanese tale, I have kept the title "Fugen."

The verse which concludes this version is not from Hearn's story, but from an incident recounted in *Zen: Merging of East and West*, by Roshi Philip Kapleau. A Zen master, asked to inscribe some words of wisdom on the back of a picture of a prostitute, spontaneously wrote a verse. The conclusion—"Form is only Emptiness/ Emptiness only Form"—is famous in Zen. It is part of the "Heart of Perfect Wisdom" (*Prajña Paramita Hridaya*), which is chanted daily in the Zen tradition.

> The Heart of Perfect Wisdom...is considered the most potent formulation for piercing the delusive mind. It is the kernel or core of the Buddha's teaching, the condensed message of the wisdom sutras he gave over the course of twenty-two years. Also referred to as the Heart Sutra, it is to be grasped not through the intellect but with the heart—that is through one's own deepest intuitive experience.[26]

In *The Lotus Sutra* the Buddha reveals that this ordinary, material universe is filled with countless bodhisattvas. No longer constrained by limited notions of Reality, they are free to appear in whatever form is necessary to alleviate suffering and to help spiritually mature those bound by egoism and delusion. (See "The Black Hound" and "A Legend of Avalokitesvara." Also the notes for "The Brave Merchant.")

The Dog's Tooth (pp. 152-153)

A traditional Tibetan tale about the transformative power of belief and faith. Though simple, the tale makes a profound point. Our faith, and the force of our creative imagination, are essential aspects of reality, and have their effects on the so-called "real world." What we think about and what we dream does, after all, influence our behavior, etc. This little story, however, quietly suggests that the mind's relation to the world goes quite a bit deeper than that; Mind is an essential component of reality. All seemingly separate things are related, for all are, in reality, Mind.

This is one of the central teachings of the 2,500 year-old Buddhist tradition. For a fascinating account of this concept applied to modern science, read Fritjof Capra's *The Tao of Physics.*

The Legend of Avalokitesvara (p. 154)

The path of the bodhisattva is given dramatic expression in this tale of Avalokitesvara, Bodhisattva of Compassion. There is a Zen saying which likens the task of universal liberation to trying to fill a well with snow. Hercules' cleansing of the Augean stables seems almost child's play in comparison.

Throughout the traditional Mahayana countries (China, Japan, Vietnam, Korea, Tibet), paintings as well as cast and carved figures of the 1,000-armed Avalokitesvara bring this legend vividly to life. Iconographically, the endless heads of the Bodhisattva in the legend are usually represented as a tiered tower of eleven heads. In the palm of each of the thousand hands is an opened eye. Lama Govinda explains the iconography in this way: "...in the palm of each hand an eye appeared; because the compassion of a Bodhisattva is not blind emotion but love combined with wisdom. It is the spontaneous urge to help others flowing from the knowledge of inner oneness."[26]

Avalokitesvara, or Avalokita (Sanskrit for "The Lord Who Looks Down from on High" or "Hearer of the Cries of the World"), is known as *Kannon* in Japan, *Kwan-Yin* in China, and *Chenresig* in Tibet. Many gentle, tender, and lovely forms of this bodhisattva exist. The most dramatic however, is that which is thousand-armed.

The unending task of Avalokitesvara, like all Buddhas and bodhisattvas, is to liberate sentient beings from the sufferings of greed, anger, and ignorance. Ultimately, as Avalokitesvara is nothing other than the compassion of one's own Self, his exertions (or her exertions) are one's own. (See note for "Beginnings" and for "The Brave Little Parrot." Also see "Most Lovely Fugen," story and note. Also "The Black Hound.")

The famous *Surangama Sutra* devotes an entire chapter to the saving power of the Bodhisattva Avalokitesvara.

Stilson's Leap (pp. 155-156)

The stories "Stilson's Leap" and "Digit" are based on actual events. "Stilson's Leap" grew out of some reading I did years ago on the Battle of Britain.

The Battle of Britain is itself an example of the remarkable synchronization of inner story, or archetype, and outer, literal story, that seems to periodically surface, like some bright silver thread running through the dark, chaotic tapestry of human history. Outnumbered, outgunned, and, seemingly assured of defeat, the small British Royal Air Force turned back the tide of Hitler's invasion. Good triumphed over evil and the underdog won.

These are ancient stories, seemingly at the very core of human existence. We love to read (and view movies of) such stories, and sometimes they seem to actually happen in real life (perhaps when the need for such stories is greatest). In any case, I cannot place the exact source for this story. However, the story itself, of an unnamed pilot's spontaneous self-sacrifice, stayed with me. I began to see something of what a jataka, occurring today, might look like. ("Digit" is a kind of modern animal jataka—a contemporary version of "The Monkey King" [See note for "The Monkey and the Crocodile."]) Viewed in this way, it comes close to being a modern analog of "The Hungry Tigress."

There is a profoundly universal element in certain jatakas, i. e. , the classic tales of self-sacrifice, that remains mysterious and inexplicable. (In this collection see "The Lion, The Elephant and the Merchants' Cries," jataka and notes; also "The Hungry Tigress," "The Banyan Deer," "The Golden Deer," "The Blue Bear" jatakas and their notes). In these jatakas, a spontaneous and overwhelmingly altruistic desire to aid others comes to the fore and is given literary shape. This selfless desire is not the sole possession of Buddhism, but permeates all peoples, all nations. In times of crisis and danger it arises over and over—as has been well-documented. Both animals and humans seem to share this impulse.

Although scientists have tried to explain such behavior as an evolutionarily derived safety device (a clever stratagem of the "selfish gene," through which the individual's sacrifice insures the continuity of the gene pool of the species), this no more explains the matter than a spectral analysis explains the joy we feel upon seeing sunlight breaking through clouds. Nor does it satisfactorily explain inter-species compassion and self-sacrifice—dolphins coming to the aid of swimmers; dogs risking their own lives to save endangered humans, and so on. In the vision of the jatakas animals and humans equally share the same fundamental heart-mind of compassion, the same fundamental Buddha-Mind of no-separation. Science has its stories, literature and religion theirs. None of these stories need necessarily be incorrect.

The following long quote is from the book, *Flight To Arras* by the famous French author and aviator, Antoine de Saint-Exupery. The book is the record of an almost suicidal reconnaissance flight he piloted during the Second World War. It was such a mission that later claimed his life. He is writing here about flying towards the target through a barrage of deadly flak.

Somehow those explosions...did not really count. They drummed upon the hull of the plane as upon a drum. They pierced my fuel tanks. They might have drummed upon our bellies...But who cares what happens to his body? Extraordinary how little the body matters.

There are things we might learn about our bodies in the course of everyday living if we were not blind to patent evidence...

I used to wonder as I was dressing for a sortie what a man's last moments were like. And each time, life would give the lie to the ghosts I evoked. Here I was, now, naked and running the gauntlet, unable so much as to guard my head or shoulder from the crazy blows raining down upon me. I had always assumed that the ordeal, when it came, would be an ordeal that concerned my flesh...It was unavoidable that in thinking about these things I should adopt the point of view of my body. Like all men I had given it a good deal of time. I had bathed it, fed it, quenched its thirst...I had said of it, 'This is me. ' And now of a sudden this illusion vanished. What was my body to me?...

Your son is in a burning house. Nobody can hold you back. You may burn up but do you think of that? You are ready to bequeath the rags of your body to any man who will take them...

The flames of the house, of the diving plane, strip away the flesh; but they strip away the worship of the flesh too. Man ceases to be concerned with himself: he recognizes of a sudden what he forms part of. If he should die, he would not be cutting himself off from his kind, but making himself one with them. He would not be losing himself, but finding himself. This that I affirm is not the wishful thinking of a moralist. It is an everyday fact. But a fact...hidden under the veneer of our everyday illusion. Dressing and fretting over the fate that might befall my body, it was impossible for me to see that I was fretting over something absurd. But in the instant when you are giving up your body, you learn to your amazement—all men always learn it to their amazement—how little store you set by your body...Here in this plane I say to my body...'I don't care a button what becomes of you...There is no hope of surviving this, and yet I lack for nothing...'

Man does not die. Man imagines it is death that he fears; but what he fears is the unforeseen, the explosion. What man fears is himself, not death. There is no death when you meet death. When the body sinks into death, the essence of man is revealed. Man is a knot, a web, a mesh into which relationships are tied. Only those relationships matter. The body is an old crock that nobody will miss. I have never known a man to think of himself when dying. Never.[28]

This version of the story leaves this modern jataka, like "The Hungry Tigress" jataka and "Preacher of Patience," in a realistic mode, i.e., there is no "answer." No healing restoration occurs, no god magically descends from the skies to set all right—as does happen in jatakas like "King Sivi" and "The Hare's Sacrifice." Both are equally traditional approaches. In the original version of the story "Stilson's Leap" which first appeared in the first edition of *The Hungry Tigress*, there was a kind of restoration. It takes place, years later, in the mind of one of the other pilots. Walking on a beach, watching the waves come in and roll out again, the bubbles rising and bursting and reappearing, he has this realization: "No effort is wasted; nothing dies. All things are transformed and all things live forever. Noble deeds, too, are never lost. Though they may seem fruitless they flower in the depths of time." It has been interesting to tell this modern jataka story from both sides of the traditional jataka pattern. The oral tradition, of course, allows for constant experimentation and recreation. The same teller may relate different versions of a story at different times as his or her own interests and understanding change, as well as to meet the needs of differing audiences.

Digit (pp. 157-160)

"Digit" is also a modern jataka tale, *loosely* based on the now well-known death of Digit the gorilla, so movingly related by the murdered naturalist Dian Fossey in her writings, and dramatically portrayed in the movie, *Gorillas in the Mist*, the film-version of Fossey's life.

This modern jataka first came to mind after reading an account of Digit's death in a *National Geographic* article. Later reflection made me realize that it is much like the jataka of "The Monkey King" (See notes for "The Monkey and the Crocodile."). Modern research indicates that gorillas (as well as chimpanzees and orangutans) are ninety-nine percent genetically identical to humans. There are even theories, based on this, that today's gorillas are the descendents of very early human groups which found their way into a lush and comfortable environment and, over the course of time, evolved to fit their near perfect setting. Relieved from the constant stresses, pressures, and dangers that continuously shaped the rest of mankind, they never developed their intrinsic potential for complex communication and thought. Yet it is there—as evidenced by Koko, the lowland gorilla, who has been taught to communicate in American Sign Language. Interestingly, there is also a Mbuti (Pygmy) legend that the "old man of the forest," the gorilla, was once a lazy man who liked to do nothing but lie around and eat. Gradually he grew a coat of fur and became a gorilla.

Gorillas will, in fact, actually risk and sometimes sacrifice themselves for their families. This has been well-documented by hunters who found that they could only capture young gorillas for zoos by killing many of the adults of the group.

The point of "Digit," "Kogi the Priest," and "Stilson's Leap," as well as, for that matter, all jatakas yet unwritten, is that jataka tales need not be seen simply as tales of long ago. Mahayana teachings emphasize that there are countless Buddhas throughout this endless universe, as well as countless beings aspiring even now at all different stages of the bodhisattva path. Once we accept this vision, we can expect to see jatakas taking place today. The jatakas offer us a potential way of organizing the realities of daily experience. Like all good stories, whether contemporary or traditional, their pretense opens windows into truth. This is part of the mystery of story itself. Fiction is a tool for exploring both what is and what we dream might be. It deals with the mind's interaction with supposedly objective reality. (See note for "The Golden Deer," also note for "Stilson's Leap.")

In "The Monkey King" (not in this collection, but in the Pali *Jataka* as well as the *Jatakamala*), and in the stories of "The Blue Bear," "The Golden Deer" and "The Banyan Deer" (all in this collection), a king learns a valuable lesson by seeing the actions or hearing the words of the wise animal. In stories like "Digit" the observer is no longer a king within the story, but ourselves. Whatever lesson or transformation occurs must now be within us.

Contributions to The Digit Fund, which carries on the efforts of the late Dian Fossey to save gorillas, can be sent to the following address:

> The Digit Fund
> P. O. Box 4557
> Ithaca, NY 14852

Kogi the Priest (pp. 161-169)

An original story which owes much to a traditional Japanese tale—"Kogi the Priest." In this story, a Buddhist priest-painter has a dream in which he becomes a fish. Later it turns out that his dream was true— while in a coma in the human world he really did, for a time, live as a fish. His paintings of fish reportedly became so lifelike, after this experience, that they looked almost as if they might swim away. The story was tran-scribed from the Japanese by Lafcadio Hearn near the turn of the century.

This modern, whaling version of Kogi also owes a debt to Flaubert's *Legend of St. Julian Hospitator*, as well as to a brief anecdote related by poet Gary Snyder in *Earth Household* about a Native American logger in the Pacific Northwest, who found that he could hear the trees screaming as he cut them down. The man gave up log-ging, grew his hair long, and returned to traditional ways.

The story is also a personal homage to the work of two men—the Japanese Buddhist priest-sculptor, Enku, of nineteenth-century Japan, whose simple but dynamic carvings of Buddhas and Bodhisattvas have become trea-sures today, and to Herman Melville, whose masterpiece *Moby Dick* still gives us unsurpassed insight into the hidden life of the sperm whale.

The Naga realm mentioned in this tale appears more fully in the jataka of "The Naga King." There is a Buddhist legend to the effect that, before his complete entrance into Nirvana, the Buddha entrusted his *Prajnaparamita* (Highest Wisdom) teachings to the Nagas. The Nagas were to protect these highest of teach-ings until mankind had evolved spiritually to the point of being able to receive them. Contemporary readers, aware of the last thirty years or so of ongoing scientific research and speculation on the intelligence (and gentle-ness) of whales and dolphins, can only wonder if there might not indeed be something to these Naga legends of old.

Readers of "Kogi," specifically, might find the follow-ing of interest.

> Sperm whale mothers invariably help their young es-cape (Beale, 1839), and 'the mother may be seen as-sisting it to escape by partially supporting it on one of her pectorals' (Scammon, 1874). The rest of the pod either gets directly involved to distract the whalers or stands at close range, as if to encourage and coach those in mortal danger. Males and females alike have

been known to risk their lives to rescue a distressed individual.[29]

> In the far East stranded whales were looked upon as gods. The montagnards of Vietnam believed that a child destined to redeem the world and deliver it from evil would be borne on a fabulous whale. This tradition had deep roots in Indonesia, the Philippines, China, Korea, and Japan, as well as Indochina.[30]

As a Buddhist priest, Kogi makes mention of the first and most fundamental of the Buddhist precepts, which is "Not to kill but to cherish all life." There are ten such precepts upheld in the Japanese Zen Buddhist tradition. The first five of the precepts listed below are upheld by all Buddhists. The ten precepts are:

1) I resolve not to kill but to cherish all life.
2) I resolve not to take what is not given but to respect all things.
3) I resolve not to engage in improper sexuality but to lead a life of purity and self-restraint.
4) I resolve not to lie but to speak the truth.
5) I resolve not to take myself or to cause others to take substances that confuse the mind but to keep the mind clear.
6) I resolve not to speak of the misdeeds of others but to overcome my own shortcomings.
7) I resolve not to praise myself and downgrade others.
8) I resolve not to withhold spiritual or material aid but to give them freely where needed.
9) I resolve not to indulge in anger but to exercise control.
10) I resolve not to revile the Three Treasures (Buddha, Dharma, and Sangha), but to cherish and uphold them.

As mentioned at the end of "Kogi," Manjusri, or Monju (as he is known among the Japanese), is the Bodhisattva of Wisdom. The lion he sits upon is symbolic of the energy and vitality of one's True-Nature. In his hand Manjusri holds a sword capable of cutting through all delusion, all limitation.

> Manjusri represents awakening, that is, the sudden realization of the oneness of all existence and the power rising therefrom.[31]

Samantabhadra, or Fugen, Bodhisattva of Action, appears in the story "Lovely Fugen." Fugen is usually seated on an elephant, an image of the power, sagacity, and dignity of True-Nature.

> When the knowledge acquired through satori is employed for the benefit of mankind, Samantabhadra's compassion is manifesting itself. Accordingly, each of the Bodhisattvas [Manjusri and Samantabhadra] is an arm of the Buddha representing, respectively, Oneness (or Equality) and Manyness.[32]

Notes on *Commentaries*

1. William Theodore de Bary, ed. "Shobogenzo Gyoji," from *The Buddhist Tradition*, p. 369.
2. William Lafleur, tr. *Mirror for the Moon*, p. 47.
3. Quoted by Philip Kapleau. *The Three Pillars of Zen*, p. 157.
4. Joseph Campbell. *The Power of Myth*, p. 71.
5. Renee Grousset. *In the Footsteps of the Buddha*, pp. 218-9.
6. Robert Aitken. *Taking the Path of Zen*, p. 7.
7. de Bary. *Op. Cit.*, p. 370-1.
8. Edward Conze. *Buddhist Scriptures*, p. 20.
9. John Murray. *The Life of Milarepa*, p. 134.
10. Paul Carus. *The Gospel of Buddha*, pp. 221-2.
11. Lama Anagarika Govinda. *Foundations of Tibetan Mysticism*, p. 43.
12. Kapleau. *Op. Cit.*, p. 80.
13. Mark J. Dresden, tr. *The Jatakastava*, 40: 127-30.
14. Rajendralala Mitra. *Nepalese Buddhist Literature*, p. 78.
15. Dresden. *Op. Cit.*, 50: 155-6.
16. Robert Thurman, tr. *The Holy Teaching of Vimalakirti*, pp. 55-6.
17. Burton Watson, tr. *Ryokan: Zen Monk-Poet of Japan*, p. 49.
18. Dresden. *Op. Cit.*, 51: 158.
19. F.L. Woodward. *Some Sayings of the Buddha*, p. 14
20. Mitra. *Op. Cit.*, p. 78.
21. *Ibid.*, p. 201.
22. *Ibid.*, p. 248.
23. Adapted from *Ibid.*, pp. 315-16. Also appears in Eugene Burlingame's *Buddhist Parables*, pp. 313-4.
24. Dresden. *Op. Cit.*, 20: 74-75.
25. *Ibid.*, 26: 93.
26. Kapleau. *Zen: Merging of East and West*, pp. 178-9.
27. Govinda. *Op. Cit.*, p. 232.
28. Antoine de Saint-Exupery. *Flight to Arras*, pp. 104-107.
29. Jacques Cousteau and Yves Paccalet. *Whales*, p. 213.
30. *Ibid.*, p. 247.
31. Kapleau. *The Three Pillars of Zen*, p. 377.
32. *Ibid.*, p. 377.

Bibliography

This bibliography focuses on books I found helpful either for background or as story sources. I have also included a number of books for those who might want to find out more about the Buddhist tradition and for practice.

Life of Buddha and the Jatakas

Beyer, Stephen. *The Buddhist Experience: Sources and Interpretations.* Encino, Calif: Dickenson Publishing Co., 1974.

Burlingame, Eugene, tr. *Buddhist Parables.* New Haven: Yale University Press, 1922.

Carus, Paul. *The Gospel of Buddha.* Chicago: Open Court Publishing, 1915.

Conze, Edward. *Buddhist Scriptures.* New York: Penquin Books, 1973.

Coomaraswamy, Ananda K. *Buddha and the Gospel of Buddhism.* New York: Harper & Row, 1964.

Cowell, E.B., ed. *The Jataka or Stories of the Buddha's Former Births. Translated from the Pali.* London: Pali Text Society, 1895 repr. 1973; distr. by Motilal Banarsidass, Delhi. (3 volumes)

Dayal, Har. *The Bodhisattva Doctrine in Buddhist Sanskrit Literature.* Delhi: Motilal Banarsidass, 1978.

De Silva-Vigier, Anil. *The Life of the Buddha Retold from Ancient Sources with 150 Masterpieces of Asian Art.* London: Phaidon Press, 1955.

Dresden, Mark J., tr. *The Jatakastava or "Praise of the Buddha's Former Births."* Philadelphia: Transactions of the American Philosophical Society: New Series, Vol. 45, Part 5, 1955.

Francis, H.T., and Thomas, E.J., tr. *Jataka Tales.* Bombay: Jaico Publishing House, 1956.

Grousset, Renee. *In the Footsteps of the Buddha.* New York: Grossman Publishers, 1971.

Herold, A. Ferdinand. *The Life of Buddha.* Tokyo: Charles Tuttle Co., 1954.

Johnston, E.H., tr. *Asvaghosha's Buddhacarita or Acts of the Buddha.* Delhi: Motilal Banarasidass, 1978.

Koroche, Peter, tr. *Once the Buddha Was a Monkey. (Aryasura's Jatakamala.)* Foreword by Wendy Doniger. Chicago: The University of Chicago Press, 1989.

Mitchell, Robert Allen. *The Buddha: His Life Retold.* New York: Paragon House, 1989.

Mitra, Rajendralala. *Nepalese Buddhist Literature, (Sanskrit Buddhist Literature of Nepal).* Calcutta: Asiatic Society of Bengal, 1882.

Nhat Hanh, Thich. *Old Path, White Clouds: Walking in the Footsteps of the Buddha.* Berkeley: Parallax Press, 1990.

Pal, Anjali. *Jataka Tales from the Ajanta Murals.* Bombay: IBH Publishing Co., 1968.

Percheron, Maurice. *The Marvelous Life of the Buddha.* New York: St. Martin's Press, 1960.

Poppe, Nicholas, tr. *The Twelve Deeds of the Buddha. A Mongolian Version of the Lalitavistara.* Seattle: University of Washington Press, Studies of Asia, No. 16, 1967.

Pratt, J.B. *The Pilgrimage of Buddhism.* New York: The Macmillan Company, 1928.

Rhys Davids, Caroline A.F., tr. and ed. *Stories of the Buddha. Being Selections from the Jataka.* New York: Dover, 1989.

Rhys Davids, T.W., tr. *Buddhist Birth-Stories. (Jataka Tales).The Story of the Lineage.* London: George Routledge and Sons Ltd; New York: E.P. Dutton and Co., n.d.

Saddhatissa, H. *The Life of the Buddha.* New York: Harper & Row, 1976.

Sangharakshita, Bhikshu. *The Three Jewels. An Introduction to Modern Buddhism.* Garden City: Doubleday and Co., 1970.

Wray, Elizabeth, Carla Rosenfield, Dorothy Bailey, Joe Wray. *Ten Lives of the Buddha, Siamese Temple Paintings and Jataka Tales.* New York: Weatherhill, 1972.

Buddhist Philosophy, Teachings, and Practice

Aitken, Robert. *Taking the Path of Zen.* San Francisco: North Point Press, 1982.

———. *The Mind of Clover.* San Francisco: North Point Press, 1984.

Batchelor, Stephen. *The Faith to Doubt: Glimpses of Buddhist Uncertainty.* Berkeley: Parallax Press, 1990.

Chang, C.C. *The Buddhist Teaching of Totality.* University Park: Pennsylvania State University Press, 1971.

Cleary, Thomas. *The Flower Ornament Scripture: The Avatamsaka Sutra.* (Volume 3). Boston: Shambhala, 1987.

Cook, Francis H. *Hua-yen Buddhism: The Jewel Net of Indra.* University Park: Pennsylvania State University Press, 1977.

de Bary, William Theodore. *The Buddhist Tradition in India, China, and Japan.* New York: The Modern Library, 1969.

Eppsteiner, Fred. *The Path of Compassion, Writings on Socially Engaged Buddhism.* Berkeley: Parallax Press/Buddhist Peace Fellowship, 1988.

Govinda, Lama Anagarika. *Foundations of Tibetan Mysticism.* New York: Samuel Weiser, 1973.

———. *A Living Buddhism for the West.* Boston: Shambhala, 1990.

Hakeda, Yoshito S. *The Awakening of Faith.* New York, Columbia University Press, 1974.

Hurvitz, Leon. *Scripture of the Lotus Blossom of the Fine Dharma (The Lotus Sutra).* New York, Columbia University Press, 1976.

Jivaka, Lobzang. Tr. W.Y. Evans-Wentz. *The Life of Milarepa: Tibet's Great Yogi.* London: John Murray, 1962.

Kapleau, Philip. *The Three Pillars of Zen,* (rev. and expanded ed.) Garden City: Doubleday, 1988.

———. *The Wheel of Life and Death, A Practical and Spiritual Guide.* Garden City: Doubleday, 1989.

———. *Zen: Meeting of East and West.* (rev. ed.) Garden City: Doubleday, 1989.

Kraft, Kenneth, ed. *Zen: Tradition and Transition.* New York: Grove Press, 1988.

Piburn, Sidney, ed. *A Policy of Kindness: An Anthology of Writings By and About The Dalai Lama.* Ithaca, New York: Snow Lion, 1990.

Ross, Nancy Wilson. *Buddhism: A Way of Life and Thought.* New York: Vintage Books, 1981.

Shantideva. Tr. Stephen Batchelor. *A Guide to the Bodhisattva's Way of Life (Bodhicaryavatara).* Dharamsala: The Library of Tibetan Works and Archives, 1979.

Shibayama, Zenkei. *Zen Comments on the Mumonkan.* New York: Harper & Row, 1974.

Soothill, W.E. Wilhelm Schiffer. Pier P. Del Campana. Tr. Bunno Kato, Kojiro Miyaska, Yoshiro Tamura. *The Threefold Lotus Sutra.* New York: Weatherhill/Kosei, 1975.

Suzuki, Shurnyu. *Zen Mind, Beginner's Mind.* New York: Weatherhill, 1973.

Thurman, Robert. *The Holy Teaching of Vimalakirti. A Mahayana Scripture.* University Park, PA: The Pennsylvania State University Press, 1976.

Trevor, M.H. *The Ox and His Herdsman. A Chinese Zen Text.* Tokyo: Hokuseido Press, 1969.

Woodward, F.L. *Some Sayings of the Buddha.* New York: Oxford University Press, 1973.

Yokoi, Yuho, with Victoria, Daizen. *Zen Master Dogen: An Introduction with Selected Writings.* New York: Weatherhill, 1976.

Buddhist Literature, Art, and Travel

Blofeld, John. *The Wheel of Life. The Autobiography of a Western Buddhist.* Boston: Shambhala, 1978.

Blyth, R.H. *Haiku.* Tokyo: Hokuseido Press, 1952. (4 volumes)

David-Neel, Alexandra. *Magic and Mystery In Tibet.* New York: Penguin Books, 1973.

Dotzenko, Grisha F. *Enku, Master Carver.* Tokyo: Kodansha International, 1976.

Govinda, Lama Anagarika. *The Way of the White Clouds. A Buddhist Pilgrim in Tibet.* Boston: Shambhala, 1966.

Harrer, Heinrich. *Seven Years in Tibet.* New York: E.P. Dutton, 1954.

Harvey, Andrew. *A Journey in Ladakh.* Boston: Houghton Mifflin Company, 1983.

Hearn, Lafcadio. *Kwaidan. Stories and Studies of Strange Things.* Rutland, Vermont and Tokyo: Charles Tuttle Company, 1971.

———. *The Buddhist Writings of Lafcadio Hearn.* Intro. by Kenneth Rexroth. Santa Barbara: Ross-Erikson, Inc., 1977.

Ishigami, Zenno, ed. Tr. Richard Gage and Paul McCarthy. *Disciples of the Buddha.* Tokyo: Kosei Publishing Co., 1989

LaFleur, William, tr. *Mirror for the Moon. A Selection of Poems by Saigyo (1118-1190).* New York: New Directions, 1978.

Mathiessen, Peter. *The Snow Leopard.* New York, Bantam, 1980.

Reischauer, Edwin O. *Ennin's Travels in T'ang China.* New York: The Ronald Press, 1955.

———, tr. *Ennin's Diary. The Record of a Pilgrimage to China in Search of the Law.* New York: The Ronald Press, 1955.

Reynolds, Christopher, ed. *An Anthology of Sinhalese Buddhist Literature up to 1815.* London: George Allen and Unwin, 1970.

Snyder, Gary. *Earth Household.* New York: New Directions, 1969.

Stevens, John. *One Robe, One Bowl. The Zen Poetry of Ryokan.* New York: Weatherhill, 1977.

Tanahashi, Kazuaki. *Penetrating Laughter. Hakuin's Zen and Art.* Woodstock: The Overlook Press, 1984.

Tucci, Giuseppi. *To Lhasa and Beyond.* Rome: Instituto Poligrafico Dello Stato, 1956.

Watson, Burton, tr. *Ryokan: Zen-Monk Poet of Japan.* New York: Columbia University Press, 1977.

Zimmer, Heinrich. Ed. Joseph Campbell. *Myth and Symbol in Ancient Indian Art and Civilization.* New York: Harper & Row, 1962.

Earth, Animals, and the Environment

Aisenberg, Nadya, gen. ed. *We Animals.* San Francisco: Sierra Club Books, 1989.

Badiner, Allen Hunt, ed. *Dharma Gaia: A Harvest of Essays in Buddhism and Ecology.* Berkeley: Parallax Press, 1990.

Cousteau, Jacques-Yves and Yves Paccalet. *Whales*. New York: Harry N. Abrams, Inc., 1988.

Fossey, Dian. *Gorillas in the Mist*. Boston: Houghton Mifflin, 1983.

Kapleau, Philip. *To Cherish All Life: A Buddhist Case for Becoming Vegetarian*. New York: Harper & Row, 1982.

Lopez, Barry. *Arctic Dreams. Imagination and Desire in a Northern Landscape*. New York: Bantam, 1987.

——. *Crossing Open Ground*. New York: Vintage Books, 1989.

Lovelock, James E. *Gaia, A New Look at Life on Earth*. New York: Oxford University Press, 1987.

Mowat, Farley. *Woman in the Mists*. New York: Warner Books, 1987.

Thomas, Lewis. *The Lives of A Cell. Notes of a Biology Watcher*. New York: Bantam,1984.

Wylder, Joseph. *Psychic Pets, The Secret World of Animals*. New York: Harper & Row, 1978.

Myth and Story

Ausubal, Nathan, ed. *A Treasury of Jewish Folklore*. New York: Bantam, 1980.

Campbell, Joseph. *Hero With A Thousand Faces*. Princeton: Princeton University Press, 1973.

——. *The Way of the Animal Powers*. New York: Harper & Row, 1988.

—— with Bill Moyers. *The Power of Myth*. New York: Doubleday, 1988.

Colum, Padraic. *Storytelling: New and Old*. New York: Macmillan, 1968.

Erdoes, Richard, and Ortiz, Alfonso, eds. *American Indian Myths and Legends*. New York: Pantheon Books, 1984.

Grimm, Jakob, and Grimm, Wilhelm. *The Complete Grimm's Fairy Tales*. Intro. by Padraic Colum. Commentary by Joseph Campbell. New York: Pantheon Books, 1972

Piggott, Juliet. *Japanese Mythology*. London, Paul Hamelyn, 1969.

Ramsey, Jarold, ed. *Coyote Was Going There: Indian Literature of the Oregon Country*. Seattle: University of Washington ~ ·- 1980.

Van Der Post, Laurens. *The Heart of the Hunter: Customs and Myths of the African Bushmen.* San Diego: Harcourt, Brace, Jovanovich, 1961.

Waters, Frank. *Masked Gods: Navaho and Pueblo Ceremonialism.* New York: Ballantine Books, 1970.

Especially for Children

Khan, Noor Inayat. *Twenty Jataka Tales.* The Hague: East-West Publications Fonds b.v., 1975.

Martin, Rafe. Illustrated by Ed Young. *Foolish Rabbit's Big Mistake.* New York, G.P. Putnam's Sons, 1985.

Dharma Press, of Berkeley, California, has published a series of children's picture books based on the jatakas. These are translated directly from the original texts, edited where necessary to make them more accessible to young readers/listeners. There are about twenty books in the series so far. Among them are:

The Parrot and the Fig Tree, illustrated by Michael Harmon, 1990.

The Rabbit and the Moon, illustrated by Rosalyn White, 1989.

A Precious Life, illustrated by Rosalyn White, 1988.

General

Brickhill, Paul. *Reach for the Sky. The Story of Douglas Bader.* New York: Bantam, 1978.

Capra, Fritjof. *The Tao of Physics.* Boston: Shambhala, 1975.

Dante, Alighieri. Tr. John Ciardi. *The Inferno.* New York: Mentor, 1954.

De Saint Exupery, Antoine. *Flight to Arras.* New York: Harcourt Brace and World, 1942.

Eliade, Mircea. *Shamanism, Archaic Techniques of Ecstasy.* Princeton: Princeton University Press, 1974.

Jablonski, Edward. *Air War.* Garden City: Doubleday, 1971. (2 volumes)

Jung, C.G. *Memories, Dreams, Reflections.* New York: Vintage Books, 1965.

———. *Modern Man in Search of a Soul.* San Diego: Harcourt, Brace, Jovanovich, 1933.

Melville, Herman. Ed. Charles Feidelson, Jr. *Moby Dick, Or The Whale.* New York: Bobbs-Merrill, 1964.

Seed, John, Joanna Macy, Pat Fleming, Arne Naess. *Thinking Like A Mountain, Towards A Council of All Beings.* Philadelphia: New Society Publishers, 1988.

Singer, Isaac Bashevis, and Burgin, Richard. *Conversations with Isaac Bashevis Singer.* New York: Farrar, Strauss, and Giroux, 1986.

Wilde, Oscar. *De Profundis.* New York: Avon Books, 1962.

Zukav, Gary. *Dancing Wu Li Masters.* New York: Bantam, 1980.

Parallax Press publishes books and tapes on Buddhism and related subjects to make them accessible and alive for contemporary readers. It is our hope that doing so will help alleviate suffering and create a more peaceful world.

Some of our recent titles:

Old Path White Clouds: A Biography of the Buddha, by Thich Nhat Hanh

In the Footsteps of Gandhi: Conversations with Spiritual Social Activists, by Catherine Ingram

World as Lover, World as Self, by Joanna Macy

The Path of Compassion: Writings on Socially Engaged Buddhism by the Dalai Lama, Gary Snyder, Maha Ghosananda, Joanna Macy, Rafe Martin and many others

Dharma Gaia: A Harvest of Essays in Buddhism & Ecology, edited by Allan Hunt Badiner

Present Moment Wonderful Moment, by Thich Nhat Hanh

Choose Love: A Jewish Buddhist Human Rights Activist in Central America, by Joe Gorin

Looking for the Faces of God, by Deena Metzger

For a copy of our free catalog, please write to:

Parallax Press
P.O. Box 7355
Berkeley, California 94707